3

MARCH:
ENIGMA

JAN FANCY HULL

A
TIM BROWN
MYSTERY

Cover: Rebekah Wetmore
Editor: Andrew Wetmore

ISBN: 978-1-990187-37-7
First edition September 2022

2475 Perotte Road
Annapolis County, NS
B0S 1A0

moosehousepress.com
info@moosehousepress.com

We live and work in Mi'kma'ki, the ancestral and unceded territory of the Mi'kmaw people. This territory is covered by the "Treaties of Peace and Friendship" which Mi'kmaw and Wolastoqiyik (Maliseet) people first signed with the British Crown in 1725. The treaties did not deal with surrender of lands and resources but in fact recognized Mi'kmaq and Wolastoqiyik (Maliseet) title and established the rules for what was to be an ongoing relationship between nations. We are all Treaty people.

Books by Jan Fancy Hull

Non-fiction

Where's Home?

Short stories

The Church of Little Bo Peep and other stories

Inquire Within

The Tim Brown Mystery Series

January: Code

February: Curious

March: Enigma

April: Sweetland (coming in 2023)

To all who seek family amongst truth, falsehoods, and friends.

This is a work of fiction. The author has created the characters, conversations, interactions, and events; and any resemblance of any character to any real person is coincidental.

Contents

Jan Fancy Hull

March 1, 1999: Waiting for the train

Monday

If months didn't slice each year into a dozen sections, the days would pile up until they toppled over into an unsalvageable jumble.

That was Tim Brown's Thought of the Day as he made the first of several morning coffees while consulting his calendar.

And a month is a really handy way of chopping All Time into manageable chunks.

He flipped back to review what he had done in February, and forward to what he mustn't forget to do in March.

When he'd been working as editor and publisher of *The Times*, South River's weekly newspaper, a week was the most important span of time, and those weeks ran unendingly, relentlessly, like cars on a very long freight train, never a gap or a caboose.

Those weeks had threatened to topple over on him, so he'd taken this sabbatical year away from all that. He hoped to use the time to delve into his community, to bring marvellous issues to light, to accomplish something noteworthy.

How had he done so far?

Well, here it was March already and he was still seeking that marvellous quest. It wasn't his fault that a hypothermic woman had fallen at his feet in February. Of course he had stopped to help her. In January, his Aunt Stella had demanded that he sort out some issues for her. Complying with Stella was always the more expedient response, as resistance was futile or painful.

Speaking of Stella, he wondered how she was feeling this morning. When he and Robert had visited her yesterday, she was a jilted lover suffering from a likely infection, and insult and injury both seemed to be getting the better of her. Showing vulnerability was uncharacteristic of Stella. As the MLA for South River and the Harbours, she preferred to appear iron-clad in the Legislature, though more benevolent to her constituents.

Tim had been concerned about Stella's health, and so was she, though Robert was confident that the ice cream he had left with her, and an antibiotic when she could get a prescription for it, would put her back to rights in jig-time. He wanted to phone her now, but it was still dark out and she might be sleeping. He wouldn't want to disturb her.

Stella didn't share his consideration. It wasn't even seven o'clock when she called.

"Good morning, Aunt Stella," he answered. "You're up early. Everything all right? How're you feeling this morning? Anything I can do for you?"

"Why are you making your voice sound soppy like that, Timothy? Stop it. I'm not an invalid."

"You weren't your usual firecracker self yesterday, if I may be so bold. You had me worried." He finished in a less-solicitous tone of voice. "Are you feeling better, then?"

"I'm up, and I'm not regretting it, thanks to Robert. I'm calling to ask if you know where he got that soup and chili. I'll send Spencer to get more."

"Glad to hear it. *I* brought you the soup and chili on Saturday from the bakery just down the road from you, remember? Robert brought the ice cream yesterday, and those pee-pee test strips. Did you—what did they indicate? Will you need a prescription? Do you have a fever?"

"I prefer not to discuss the nitty-gritty details. I informed my physician of my condition and a remedy will be on its way here as soon as those pharmacists wake up and get to their place of business. They don't seem to realize that people sometimes fall ill on weekends."

"Well, take it easy, Aunt Stella. I'm sure Robert would advise you to do that, too."

"I won't lie in bed when there is important work to be done."

Tim knew that Stella was close to hanging up, which she usually did without warning if she was finished with the call.

"Let me just say this: you usually look like a hot bomb when you go about your important work. If you go out today, based on how not-hot you looked yesterday, you might undo that dynamic image. People may talk, perhaps not in a complimentary way. I strongly advise you to consume all the soup and water you can at home today, and let those antibiotics begin their work. Tell people you've been called away on more important business or whatever you say when you want to be left alone. Take care of yourself, hear me?"

The line was dead now, but Stella would pay attention because he'd mentioned her appearance. She pretended not to notice herself, but it was obvious that she always put a lot of thought and money into how she looked. She made a good first impression when she entered a room, and every time thereafter.

He was a little miffed that she had given Robert the credit for her comforts yesterday. Stella had insisted that he *not* bring Robert to check on her, not wanting him to see her when she was not at her best, but he'd insisted on going. She almost glowed at his attention, in spite of feeling so poorly.

Hey now, he said to himself. *This is nothing, and she'll be fine. Move on.*

Moving on needed a spark. *The disadvantage of chopping life into monthly segments is that one has to get a new train up to speed each month, and it needs a heavy engine.*

He marked regular events in their assigned calendar boxes for the month, like choir practice every Thursday. Coming up this Wednesday was his first-ever massage; that'd be interesting. Skilled workers would finally install the new storm door sometime this month, but the store hadn't confirmed a date yet. His piano would receive a much-needed tuning, date also TBA.

He circled the twenty-first. The calendar had already printed *Spring* in that box. Spring didn't spark the interest of previous years. Sure, he always looked forward to the arrival of spring; who didn't? Like everyone else in the northern latitudes, he was eager for the return of the sun.

But his fortieth birthday also coincided with this Vernal Equinox. He wasn't one to make a fuss over his age, but would he celebrate it? Would he be expected to put on a party? Worse, would someone else feel obliged to put one on for him? That wasn't the project he wanted to think about. It was three weeks away; plenty of time to plan later.

Meanwhile, items like those served as boxcars on the freight train. New events would be the engine that pulled the whole thing along.

~

He drove downtown to his thinking room, on the second floor of the old building that housed *The Times*. He had done some good thinking in this unused room since he'd had it cleaned and painted, and furnished with its one table and one chair. His home was comfortable and familiar, and had some nice features including Gloria, the dominatrix espresso machine, but it lacked people to whom he could say a cheerful and incidental how-de-do. This room had no comforts or distractions, but working nearby were people who, he'd discovered, were sometimes inspiring.

And for what, precisely, would I require inspiration?

As he considered this question, he was gazing through the rippled glass of the old window.

Be patient. Let's not get jumpy.

Whenever he cautioned himself like that, it was usually too late: jumpy had already arrived. Did he simply want to be busy to avoid being seen doing nothing? He was his own boss; he didn't have to justify his time to anyone, not since his mother/former boss had died. She had pushed him to work hard all day and do better tomorrow. He found it difficult to jump off her train, even now.

Her name was Lucia Linda Brown, *née* Johnson. She had nicknamed herself Brownie when she married. She would answer to no other name once she had acquired Ford Brown, the high school football hero, as her husband.

Tim was just thirty when his mother died, not yet fifty years of age. She had smoked cigarettes since high school, so perhaps that accounted for her early demise.

His father died of apparent suicide when Tim was only five years old. He had no memory of that time. What did he actually know about his father?

His mother would repeat a few storylines when pressed, so what she said had become his own memory. "The fool insisted on driving around in that old beat-up brown Ford truck." "Ford Brown did away with himself." "That damn fool left me to raise a family by myself, and I still had to run a business." She didn't invite any conversation on this topic with her little boy, who was the family she complained about raising. *The Times* was the lucrative business she complained about running.

Tim blinked to focus his eyes back in the room. What brought this on? He had come downtown to see if he'd left notes of ideas that would get his train rolling. The room encouraged thought, evidently, but these weren't the kind of thoughts to spark a good project to delve into. Sherlock Holmes, whom he had adopted as his mentor, didn't spend time musing about his parents. Tim might as well go back home and wait for a project to occur to him there, while relaxing in front of the fire with a nice glass of wine. He hoped there was a bit of yesterday's excellent *Fin de février* to start with, before moving on to a mundane *Plonk de Lundi.*

There was a small task on his table: a mailbox he'd bought last week. He wanted it installed at the bottom of the narrow stairs leading up to this eyrie so people could leave things for him there.

He found John, the caretaker, snoozing as usual near the warm furnace in the basement.

"Sorry to wake you, John."

"Huh? Oh, I wasn't asleep. Just listening to the boiler. I thought it was making a funny noise."

"That was you snoring. Listen, I want you to attach this mailbox to the door leading up to my room, as soon as possible, in case there are any letters or parcels for me. Can you do that?"

"Sure, just leave it with me."

"Good. As long as 'leave it with me' means right away." There was no rush, but John usually worked best with a little push.

"Yup. I'll get 'er done, and I'll let the staff know it's here."

"That's not necessary, John. If someone brings an envelope to my door, and it's locked, they'll see the mailbox and figure it out. Just put it up, that's all you have to do."

At home that evening, with the fire burning, wine in a glass, and notes scattered on the coffee-table, Tim was still hoping to find something to delve into that would make a difference in his life.

March 2: New experiences

Tuesday

Tim had mixed feelings about tomorrow's massage experience.

It could be a topic to delve into. He'd never had a massage, didn't really know what it might entail, or where it could lead. That was positive.

But any water-cooler mention of massages always seemed to generate snickers, usually from men.

Do men get massages, or is it only women? Maybe men are supposed to go to a physiotherapist for aches and strains, not to a spa with pan flute tootling and aromatic candles burning? Nothing about that seems scandalous, though.

He did know that the services the NuYu Spa offered would be pure and chaste. He just didn't know *how* it worked, how one entered and partook, so to speak.

This was embarrassing. He needed to consult a man who'd had a massage.

That'd be Robert, but he wasn't due in South River until Thursday, in time for choir practice. They rarely phoned each other between times just to chat. Robert was hugely busy with his students, as Tim had been with the newspaper until he gave himself this year away from all that. Now he had more time, or slower time as he preferred to think of it, but he didn't call Robert just to pass the time.

But this felt important. Tim didn't even know if he should prepare to be naked, and how to prepare if he should.

He called Robert and caught him just out of the shower.

"This is a surprise. Is Stella all right?"

"I'm fine, thanks for asking. Stella's fine, too, or she was expecting to be yesterday morning after she spanked her pharmacist. I haven't called her since. If she's better, she'll bite my head off for asking. If she's dead, we'll find out soon enough. How are you?"

"Yikes! I'm okay, but you sound a bit edgy, Tim. What's up?"

"Sorry. I'm a bit out of sorts for no reason. Well, a reason. The reason I called is that I booked a massage at a little spa in Blockhouse tomorrow."

"Good for you. That'll take your edge off."

"Yeah, well, what I'm calling you about is...you've had massages, right?"

"Certainly. Haven't you?"

"Nope."

"That surprises me. I just assumed you had, somewhere along the way. So what's the question?"

"The question is...what is it like? I mean, what does she do? How should I dress? And undress? And how far?"

"Whaaat?" Robert couldn't hide his amusement. "Oh, you poor bumpkin! You certainly have led a narrow life in so many ways—and I mean that most kindly. Listen: you have nothing to fear. Whoever she is will not want to see any more of your skin than she has to, believe me. You do have to strip to your skivvies, but most of you'll be under a sheet so you won't get chilly. She—did you say she?"

"Yes, she. Melanie."

"Okay. Melanie will uncover whatever part of you she's working on at the time. Then she'll cover that up and go to the next part. She will be discreet. It's not a massage *parlour*, right?"

"Of course not," Tim said, with the vigour of one who had just figured this out a few minutes before.

"Of course not. So, have a shower, wear your good underwear, and enjoy the experience. Tell her where you hurt so she can dig for knots while she makes you feel great all over."

"Okay, that sounds simple. I just—I wondered—do we talk?"

"That's up to her, but she's working, so I doubt it. A little get-to-know-you chat at the beginning, maybe. It's not like going to the hairdresser. They feel they need to talk and cut hair at the same time. They make me nervous, talking with scissors."

"When did you need scissors on your hair?" The hair on Robert's round head was close-cropped.

"Before you."

"Hmm. Can't see it, but I bet you had cute baby curls."

"Okay now, have we addressed your concerns sufficiently? As I mentioned, I just stepped out of the shower, and I am not dressed as fully as you'll be in the spa."

"Nice image. Of course. Yes. Thanks, Rob. Good to talk with you. See you Thursday."

"I enjoyed it too. Gotta run."

~

Tim felt like Robinson Crusoe. That eighteenth-century fictional character, having been shipwrecked on an uninhabited island, successfully reinvented everything he needed. Tim often felt like a castaway. He didn't know how to do so many things—other than run a community newspaper, of course, at which he had been pretty good.

His island wasn't deserted, and the inhabitants weren't cannibals. He might have wished for no observers at all to see him bumble along, but he appreciated company, just as Crusoe did when he found his 'man Friday'. He was grateful for Robert, for his perspectives, his humour, his support. He wouldn't tell anyone about Tim's social innocence.

Was Robert as confident as he seemed to be? Did he have social insecurities? Were there parts of life that he avoided because he had never learned how to "do" them, like riding a bike?

They hadn't ventured down that conversational path in their time together, but Tim thought it would be interesting to go there. He had his own unknowns to contribute to the conversation, and he was developing a curiosity about what other people—successful people, like concert organist and university professor Robert Kirk—knew about things beyond their area of expertise.

These thoughts were leading somewhere. He jotted *Who Knows About What?* in a new notebook labelled MARCH. Perhaps he would open this topic to others, perhaps around a dinner table. He'd have to pick the guests carefully, of course, eliminating anyone who would confess either too many or too few insecurities. Who would that leave, and how would he know?

He'd discuss that with Robert, as he'd be the chef for that dinner.

March 3: Hands on

Wednesday

He needn't have worried about how to dress, undress, or other-wise behave at the spa. Melanie was a professional. She knew what he needed to know, and when and how to tell him. She put him at ease, so when she knocked to re-enter the small room, he was on the table, on his tummy with his face in the donut-pillow, ready for whatever was coming.

She began at the base of his skull, the top of his spine and the shoulder muscles. Tim immediately wondered why he had waited so long in this life to come for such treatment. Her hands were warm, soft, and strong, and they moved precisely how he wanted them to, even though this had never happened to him before.

His skin, muscles, and bones all wanted this so much, this touch from these kind hands. How had his shoulders supported his head before now? How had the rest of his long skeleton hung down and moved him through life?

He thought about when he was young. His mother had even taken him to the doctor because of his constant complaints that his bones hurt. A blood test and an x-ray confirmed the doctor's early diagnosis—that he was experiencing growing pains. Before then, his mother said, she'd always thought 'growing pains' meant bad behaviour.

Melanie checked in with Tim occasionally, inquiring if he was doing okay.

"Mm-*hmm*," he responded, with longer emphasis on the second syllable each time.

She worked her way to his lower spine. He had strained the muscles and ligaments a few weeks before. When her fingers kneaded the injured area, he said a quiet 'Ow' a few times. It surprised him that it still hurt, and that he had verbalized it.

"Sorry," he mumbled into the donut.

"I don't wonder," Melanie responded. "You did a number on yourself there. Hang on: I'm going to hurt you a little, but it won't harm you. I'll free up some of these knots."

The pain wasn't near unbearable, and didn't last. When it was time for him to turn over, under cover of the flannel sheet she held up as a curtain, his back felt freer than it had for a very long time.

The whole experience astounded him. He felt Melanie's hands on his skin, but it seemed as though she was reaching inside him, finding and releasing tension where he hadn't known there was any. He had never felt such—what was it—pleasure? It wasn't sexual, but he struggled to know what it was. Could intimacy be this professional? Or vice versa?

With few exceptions, she maintained contact with him through the whole process, even when she was leaving one side of the table and walking around his long legs to work on the other side. He found her touch comforting. She removed both hands occasionally to briskly rub massage oil between them, and when she touched him again, the oil and her hands were warm and his skin welcomed them.

She worked through her zones, and they spoke very little, or she spoke and he murmured in response. He barely noticed the new age (or ancient, he wasn't sure) music playing somewhere, but he found it exactly right. He was unfamiliar with sandalwood and other aromatics but he inhaled them now as the scent of healing, far more soothing than the antiseptic odours of hospitals and clinics.

Tim also noticed himself in this setting. How unusual for him to remove all his clothing except his boxers, and his socks until she got to his feet, to lie prone on a table, to have a stranger touch him all over. He felt a warm flow of energy from her hands to his body and then to—where? He felt he was vibrating with that energy.

He observed all this seemingly from high up in a corner of the room while his eyes remained closed.

The closest Tim had ever come to such a feeling was sometimes in choir rehearsal, when Robert would ask for the lights to be dimmed. He would lead them in a piece of music, encouraging them to go *into* it. He would have the sensation then of being the singer *and* the music. It was transcendent, and so was this: he became his feelings, yielded to them.

He knew he had been on the table for a long time, and sensed that the session was coming to an end when there was hardly a patch of skin to which she hadn't ministered, with the exception of parts he was grateful she had left private.

He was on his back, the sheet draped over him to keep him warm. She reached under for his right arm, and continued her loving touch right down to his wrist, hand, and fingers.

As she held his hand and expertly manipulated his fingers, an image came to Tim with such an impact that he thought the massage table had collapsed. He jumped, though his eyes remained closed.

Melanie paused, held her grip on his hand and arm for a moment, and then resumed with the left side. A few moments later, she was finished.

"You've been far away, Tim," she said, softly. "Open your eyes and come back to us now."

Melanie placed a tissue in his hand. When he opened his eyes, tears were leaking from their corners, and he dabbed at them.

She helped him sit upright at the edge of the table, wrapped the blanket around him, and rested her hand on his forearm.

"My next client is here now, but I have two rooms, so you just take your time getting dressed. Don't stand up until you feel steady. You've been through a lot here, and I think you'll feel disoriented for a bit."

Tim couldn't speak. He nodded.

Before she opened the door, Melanie said, "After the feeling of being run over by a truck dissipates, I hope you'll feel good, or well, or happy. I'm glad you came and I hope you'll come back. Your back needs more work, but I can fix it. The rest of you needs more work, too, Tim, but you are fearless. We can make you better, together.

Blessings. Bye-bye, now."

He managed a weak smile and nodded again.

The door closed quietly behind her, and Tim immediately missed her presence.

He dressed slowly, feeling like he was in a different body from the one he had walked in with. This one worked remarkably better, he noticed as he bent to put on his shoes.

In the front office, Lisa the receptionist processed his payment and handed him an appointment card.

"Melanie suggests that you come back in about two weeks," she said. "Give us a call. It will be nice to see you here again, Tim."

Tim began driving toward South River, but he pulled over on a wide shoulder, put the gearshift in park, and left the engine running.

What day was it? What planet was he on? What had happened back there? Why had there been tears? What did she mean, he'd been far away? What was the "more work" she said he needed, aside from another massage, and how could she tell?

Tim sat there while exhaust swirled around the car, wondering, and then not thinking at all. He didn't know how long it was before he shifted into gear again, and slowly drove the rest of the way home.

He was reheating leftovers without much interest when the phone rang. It was Robert.

"Just checking in on you. A first massage can be quite a paradigm-shift. How do you feel?"

"Oh, I'm great, thanks" Tim struggled to make his tongue work. "I felt...it was so...she..."

"I see. Did she work on that spot in your back?"

"Yeah, it helped a lot."

"And the rest of you?"

Tears stung Tim's eyes and he struggled to speak normally.

"I—I have some more work to do, she said." He cleared his throat. "She said, uh, she told me I'm fearless."

"Fearless? Wow. It sounds like she found some nerves that don't show up on body charts. That can happen. She must be good, because you don't let just anybody see your interior, you know. Hang in there, Timo. We can talk tomorrow after choir, or sooner if you need to. I bet you smell like you fell into a bucket of incense, don't you? I love that smell. I must book myself an appointment there sometime when I'm down. You take care now."

The massage had been life-altering, Tim was sure, though he couldn't see how or why yet. The phone call from Robert was, too, in a way; it was so rare, but Rob was always on target.

He discarded the image of Robinson Crusoe. Right now, he felt more like a pin in a bowling alley: sometimes he got knocked down, hard, but then the swishing sweeper-thing pushed him into the Gully of Re-set, and the Whatchamacallit From On High picked him up by the hair and stood him on his feet again. It was not a perfect metaphor, but it amused him, and that distracted him from the strikes enough to notice he was hungry after all.

He finished supper, tidied up in the kitchen, turned out the lights and took a book upstairs, a rare thing because he usually quickly fell asleep reading in bed. When he woke around midnight, he turned off the lamp and returned to a deep sleep.

He woke in the wee hours, so he got up to pee. In the bathroom, he found that he had tears in his eyes again. He couldn't recall having a dream that might have brought them on.

Maybe he had an allergy to the essential oils that Melanie had been using. He hoped not. He liked them, and would regret washing them off in his morning shower.

He returned to bed and, after flipping his pillow over to the dry side, fell back to sleep.

March 4: Voices

Thursday

Something woke Tim, something pounding, far away, insistent. *Bum-bum-bum. Bum-bum-bum.*

He wasn't dreaming. There it was again. *Bam-bum.* What was it? Where was it?

Downstairs. Someone was hammering at his front door.

What day is it? Oh Lord, it's Thursday. It's Mrs A!

He grabbed his robe and made a death-defying dash down the stairs to the front door, where his housekeeper, Mrs Aquino, was waving her dusting wand at the high windows, being too short to see through them herself. He quickly unlocked the door.

"Oh, Mrs A, I am so sorry to keep you standing out there. Don't you have your key? You could've let yourself in."

She shook her key-ring at him. "I come in when you not here. Not gonna s'prise a man in bed. You sick?"

"I don't think so. You woke me, though, which is quite a surprise. Can you start work downstairs, please, so I can shower and dress?"

She growled at this, but he didn't stay to argue.

When he came back downstairs, cleaned and dressed, he wrote a cheque for her services, pulled on his jacket and drove down the hill to Main Street, where the light from the Daisy Café spilled out on the damp sidewalk.

He was happy to see his usual booth was available, though it had been occupied. Evelyn, everyone's favourite waitress, quickly came over to remove the plates and cups.

"Hi, hon," she said. "I was beginnin' to worry. Hadn't seen you for a while and you're late today. Workin' hard, are ya?"

"Gosh, no," he replied. "Hardly workin'. I overslept, that's all."

"Good for you. This town would grind to a halt if I did that. What'll it be?"

Tim looked at the empty plates Evelyn was picking up.

"I'll have whatever they had."

~

The Logger's Breakfast Platter was exactly what Tim thought he wanted. He tucked into one of the eggs, one of the pancakes, a sausage, and a bit of the hash browns, plus two mugs of coffee, which didn't taste all that bad if you were drinking it hot to wash down the salty, greasy food. He considered eating more, but put his fork down.

"Discretion is the better part of valour, Evelyn," he said when she came by to offer him yet more coffee. "I'm done, thanks."

"Does anyone know what you're saying, Tim? I swear I don't, half the time."

"Neither do I, half the time. I think it's Shakespeare, but I have no idea what from. Did we have it in school?"

"Beats me. It's always nice to see you, anyway. You take care now."

She placed his chit on the table and removed the platter. "No rush."

He regretted wasting the food, and the money for it, even though it was only a few dollars. His pay continued whether he worked or slept in or took the whole year off, which he was doing.

"You're wasting time."

Who said that? He looked around, but nobody was looking at him. No one in the café could belong to that voice, because it was his late mother's voice. Her voice, speaking Tim's thoughts.

He was wasting time. Here it was, Thursday already, and what had he accomplished this week, this month, this year? The train was barely moving out of the station. If he died today and appeared at the Pearly Gates, he could tell Saint Peter that he'd had a massage yesterday. *Whoop-de-do*. He might just as well ask for directions to the Other Place.

Come on, it's not that bad, is it? Didn't I plan to just delve into things, following my newspaperman's nose, seeing where that led or what insights I might uncover? Gosh, if I'd aimed for insights, I might've found some already, but you can't print insights in a community newspaper and keep subscribers. Who cares what I didn't know before and do know now? What if I'm just the last to find out? That'd be embarrassing. No, delving needs to reveal something that nobody knew before.

He'd been sitting in the booth long enough to feel stiff when he finally stood up, but he was grateful that his back didn't make him want to sit down again. He would certainly book another appointment with Melanie. That wasn't a waste of time.

At the cash counter, Evelyn handed him a take-out container. "Nobody wants to waste all that food, right? I thought you might like to take it home for lunch. You'll be hungry again sometime."

He gave Evelyn a twenty and told her to keep the change. That voice in his head would never have taken leftovers home, nor spent precious time pondering what would please Saint Peter when the time came. She would've just gone to work, and left miserly tips.

He put the container in his car, which he had parked nearby, and walked the few steps to The Times building. He loved the accessibility of this small South Shore town, and was happy to do without some amenities to have it, though he did wish for better coffee.

He greeted the receptionist by the wrong name as usual—an unintentional error but one he seemed unable to overcome. He moved his magnetic white dot on the IN/OUT board to IN, and wandered slowly through the office, saying hello to those who lifted their heads. When he had thoroughly discussed and agreed that March indeed seemed to be coming in like a lamb, and that there were indeed fewer than three weeks until spring, he was ready to be alone with his thoughts again.

Was idle chit-chat always so banal, or was it just that he was yearning for a challenging conversation right now?

Upstairs in the empty room, Tim paced. He reached in the cupboard where he kept the large sheets of manila paper, brought out one, and taped it to the wall. He'd just had a Thought, and

Thoughts like that should be recorded in case they might indicate something.

But he'd forgotten it already. Something about *ACTION*. He wrote that down in red. What about action? Oh, yes, he'd been thinking about those interruptions he'd had in January and February, and felt he'd enjoyed working on them. Was that even worth recording?

He wrote *Enjoyed* below the heading. He replaced the cap on the pungent marker and stepped back to study this revelation. He had spent a lot of time staring at similar sheets, waiting for one item or another to flash its significance to him. He couldn't very well expect this to happen yet with this sheet: it contained only two words. That was hardly a list to work with.

He added *Secret*. That was part of that thought, too. He had enjoyed the action, but he had also kept it a secret—from whom? *From people who might be involved*. He wrote that down. He would've had egg on his face a number of times if he'd just blabbed the first suspicion that came to his mind, since many suspicions and hunches had been erroneous. Perhaps that wasn't being secretive, but discrete. He wrote Discrete beneath People. Discretion was wise, as well as the better part of valour. Nothing unusual about that.

What else did he mean by Secret, though? From whom was his enjoyment of action kept secret?

He tapped the marker from word to word until the sheet was covered in dots. Nothing flashed.

Oh well, this doesn't matter anyway, nothing to delve into here. It was pointless to spend more time on this pursuit of a random thought.

He capped the marker again, turned off the light, and left, carefully locking the door behind him. At the bottom of the stairs, he turned around, quickly climbed the narrow steps, and fished for the key to let himself in again.

"Me!" he said to the empty room.

"Me!" he said to the sheet of paper. "Secret from me. I was enjoying the action in January and February, and I didn't admit it to myself, because I thought it was just distractions. I thought I was sup-posed to be doing something—something intellectual, something deep. All the while, I was figuring stuff out. Well, that's intellectual. And I was doing things. That's action."

Tim wrote *FROM ME!* next to *Secret*.

"And I enjoyed doing those things. I just couldn't admit it to my-self."

He turned the chair around to face the sheet of paper on the wall and sat down. "Why not?" he said to the paper.

A long silence followed this question. He put the marker down. He rotated the chair to look out the wavy window. When he had done that on Monday, his thoughts had been about his late parents, not enjoyable at all. Thoughts about his mother were uncomfort-able because of how she had behaved toward him. He rarely thought of his father at all.

But when he was on the massage table yesterday, when Melanie began massaging his hands, he had a sharp memory of a time when he was a little boy, when his father had sat close beside him somewhere—where was that?—and had squeezed and stroked his hands, and seemed very, very sad.

Tim closed his eyes to reconnect with this scene again. He put his hands together and massaged each one with the other, as Melanie had done yesterday. As his father had done that day.

"I'm so sorry, Timmy."

Nobody was in the room. His father's voice was, though, as clear as if he'd heard it through his ears instead of his memory.

Tim hadn't thought of this scene since it happened, not once in thirty-five years. He hadn't known it was important.

But now he knew. For whatever reason, triggered by whatever catalyst, he remembered this scene with his father, an experience of his own, not filtered through his mother's bitterness. Suddenly, he wanted to know what had happened, why his parents married so young, how and why his father died, and why his mother dis-couraged any mention of his name.

Here was something he could delve into. It wasn't for public consumption, and he might not enjoy doing it, but maybe he would learn things that would permit him to enjoy other aspects of his life more. Perhaps his stress at work, and his continuing stress while away from work, had their roots in the answers to these questions.

What was it Melanie had said yesterday—that he was brave? No. Fearless.

Well, bring on the fearless, Tim. I think we're going to need it.

~

Tim had been disoriented in time and space all day, and was surprised to learn that it was mid-afternoon already, and to realize that he was starving. In his car, he opened the container of leftover breakfast and lifted out a piece of cold bacon, a perfect snack.

He had nothing prepared for supper for him and Robert, so he stopped at the grocery store to pick up a rotisserie chicken and assorted salads, a meal they both referred to as the "refuge of the destitute".

When Robert arrived and saw what was for supper, he said, "What's wrong?"

They both laughed. This was dining low on the hog, but they filled their plates and ate it all.

Tim avoided reviewing his experience at the NuYu Spa before choir practice, in case his eyes might leak again. Robert didn't inquire, as he preferred to avoid any topic that would distract him from the evening's work.

Following choir rehearsal, both were glum. Robert was dismayed at how ragged the choir had sounded, with just a little over a month remaining before Easter. The little afternoon concert he'd announced, which had been gathering bulk with pieces added and instrumentalists, too, was in jeopardy of appearing ill-advised. There'd been a few absences tonight, which hadn't helped. At least Spencer was there to support Tim in the tenor section. Tim had had a brain fade and missed his entry even after Robert repeated the measure to allow him to get it right.

He didn't apologize. While he was always sorry for his errors, he didn't think he had the presence of mind tonight to navigate being chastised for being unable to do what he simply couldn't concentrate on doing. He'd do better next week. They all would.

March 5: Family tree

Friday

Last evening, people were saying that March's lamb had turned into a ragged, dirty, bleating sheep. But this morning's sky was clear and bright long before the actual sunrise, now about a quarter to seven, a full hour earlier than at the start of the year.

Even though it took a cold, cloudless night to achieve this brilliance, nobody complained. Spring was on the way, and cold nights would soon give way to sweet new lambs, gambolling in green meadows.

"Why is it that spring lambs are the only creatures that 'gambol'?" Tim said. Robert looked up blankly. *Of course: he was not in on my thoughts.*

They were fuelling their morning with espressos from a compliant Gloria before Robert left to join the commuters on the highway back to Halifax. Tim was savouring the coffee, the glimmer of daylight, and also his lightened mood.

"Wait – don't answer that." He went to the den and retrieved a dictionary from among several on the shelf. "Our devotional reading this morning is from Merriam-Webster: *To gambol, verb, intransitive: to skip about in play, to frisk, to frolic.* Here endeth the lesson."

Tim closed the heavy book with a snap, releasing a cloud of musty dust. "Yikes. Dust of the ages there. Have we learned anything?"

"Nothing, except you're silly. Glad to see it. You've been mopey, quite un-frisky."

"Gee, thanks, Rob. But it doesn't mention lambs at all. That means that we're all free to frisk, to frolic, to skip about—but be careful of the ice! See you tomorrow."

~

Tim was grateful for his much lighter mood. It wasn't just brought on by his brain releasing some of that drug—what was it called? He couldn't look it up if he didn't know how to spell it. Perhaps the word would come to him later. The point was that he knew what had been bothering him and he was going to devote some of his time to resolving it.

Not only did he have time, he had the methodology, if that wasn't too complex a term to apply to his notebooks and sheets of manila flip-chart paper taped to the walls downtown. He felt empowered—armed, even.

The world outside, especially the business world from which he had escaped for a year, talked of nothing but electronic devices. Palm Pilots were all the rage. He'd seen Elaine Fong, his interim editor, slip a little black device into her purse, and he knew it wasn't a notebook, though it was the same size as the pocket spiral notebooks he liked to use, with a pencil. The closest he wanted to get to automation was mechanical pencils. Eversharps, he called them, though young staff in the office supplies stores always assumed he meant razors.

He rummaged through the drawers in the old desk in the study, and found no fewer than seventeen mechanical pencils of various ages and brands. Four even contained leads.

Where was he going with this?

He needed to put one of those pencils to work in one of those notebooks right away. His mind was wandering—gambolling—and while that was cute when a lamb did it, it was disturbing when a man approaching forty lost his train of thought in the space of five minutes.

He had begun a notebook one Tuesday, which he took out of his backpack now. The only entry was a question: *Who Knows About What?* It was a good question, and he added *Dinner Party topic?* before that thought wandered away.

But he had been thinking of Palm Pilots and that led to Eversharps and…his mother had always called them that, even though that brand hadn't been manufactured in his lifetime. They survived, though, and a few of the seventeen in the desk bore that brand name.

What's my point, dammit?

Then he saw the point, as sharp as those pencil leads. Everything he said, thought, touched, owned, or did, pointed to his late mother, Brownie. When she died, he had felt deep relief that she was gone. Though the prospect had terrified him at first, he now hoped he had changed from timidly and obediently living under her thumb to becoming himself.

Had he?

Just thinking about pencils had launched him back to Brownie Brown. What else did she dominate? How much of what he thought and did was really just him parroting her?

And what about his father? How much of what he knew and thought about Ford Brown was created and edited by and filtered through his mother?

He felt a cloud begin to darken his bright morning outlook.

Stop. This is not a problem—this is my challenge. I can dig into this and get some answers. I know how. Get at it, Tim.

He took coffee and a sandwich of yesterday's mocked but convenient chicken, and drove to his quiet thinking room above the bustle of *The Times*.

~

"Good morning, Raquel, how are you today?"

"Good morning, Mister Brown. It's Rachael, sir. I'm fine, thank you."

Elaine Fong came out of her office, which had been Tim's office until this year. "Hi, Tim. Sorry about last evening. I sang as if I had never read music in my life."

She sang occasionally in the alto section of Saint John's United Church choir, which had rehearsed so badly yesterday.

"Hey, don't apologize to me. I was worse. Robert was discouraged, but he must be used to it by now, poor man. Anyway, I say it's the time of year. Our minds are feeling the urge to get outdoors and, uh, frolic, right? Wait till the time changes and the sun's still up in the evenings. Who'll even want to go to choir then? But we'll get through it."

"Even so, I should have looked over the music at least once before last night, but I had so much—other things pressing. I resolve to do better."

"We're volunteer choristers, Elaine, and we do our best. If the Music Committee will release the funds for section leads, which is already approved, they'll carry us over bumpy times like yesterday. Things going all right here?"

Tim often inquired about the newspaper, but he didn't want any response except what Elaine said now.

"Yes, everything's fine, thanks for asking. Have a great day, Tim."

"Thanks, you too. Oh, by the way, Elaine, what's the name of the drug the brain releases when we're happy? Or that makes us happy?"

"Dopamine?"

~

He locked the door to his room. This project was personal, and prying eyes wouldn't be welcome to peek at his family history as he sketched it and posted it on the walls.

The *ACTION* sheet was still up from yesterday, and he addressed it now to get back in the groove. He'd added *Enjoyed*. Yesterday, that had mystified him. This morning, he thought he was beginning to understand.

"When I'm working on stuff that involves *Action*, my brain releases dopamine, and that makes me happy!"

He checked the door again to make certain that it was locked. Not everyone thought talking to yourself was a good thing.

He added *Dopamine*, mostly as a reminder of the word. He didn't know how it worked, but he was learning to write anything and everything on the sheets. Once they were out of his head, he could review them and cross them off once he had determined their irrelevance.

He started to sit in his old office chair but changed his mind. That wouldn't be Action. He remained on his feet.

He took out two sheets from the cupboard, taped them up, and titled one *MOTHER* and the other *FATHER*. On his mother's page, he began to write her vital statistics:

> *Born: 1940 May 20*
> *Married: 1958 July to Ford Brown*
> *Baby: 1959 March 21 Timothy Johnson*
> *Died: 1991 August?*

He couldn't recall some dates but he'd look them up if it mattered.
He moved to the *FATHER* page.

> *Born: --*
> *Married: 1958 July to ~~Brownie~~ Lucia Linda "Brownie" Johnson*
> *Baby: 1959 March 21 ~~Timothy~~ TJ*
> *Died: 1963 August*

These were simply facts—including his own premature birth. Similar information appeared in his newspaper every week under "Vital Statistics". Born. Married. Children. Died. Everybody does the beginning and the end, and also some bits in the middle one time or more, or not at all.

But Timothy Johnson Brown, in the process of writing down his parents' vital statistics, had just recalled the nickname his father called him: "TJ". Yesterday he thought he remembered hearing him say "Timmy". That was also possible. His mother had never called him anything but Timothy, but his father had called him by a diminutive.

Or so he was remembering. He closed his eyes.

He was home from school. No, from preschool. Or from a babysitter's. Someone was in the kitchen preparing supper, a housekeeper, possibly; his grandparents had moved out or were deceased by then, he wasn't sure. He didn't remember them, anyway. His mother would've been at work at the paper.

His father's old truck rattled into the driveway. Tim heard the truck door slam, and his father's heavy step on the front porch. "Where's my Timmy? Hey, there's TJ!" He lifted him up in a hug. His father was strong.

He opened his eyes and found a tissue to blow his nose.

"You told me I didn't remember him," he said to the sheet called *MOTHER*. "You said I couldn't possibly. When I tried to talk about him, you shut me down. That's not fair. Why would you do that?"

His chest was feeling tight. *Take a break, Tim. Don't hurt yourself. You're looking for some action, remember? And action will give you dopamine to make you happy, right?*

He wasn't so sure about the miracle drug at this moment, but he hoped a walk would be a helpful kind of action on this sunny day.

Striding along the streets of South River wasn't the easiest walk, as he had to keep his eyes on the melting patches of ice and watch for cars where there were no sidewalks, but distraction is distraction, and walking in a hilly town is action. When he returned an hour later to the Johnson Building, he had roses in his cheeks and he was hungry for that sandwich.

He'd had another thought while he was walking, and he took care of it now, adding *Relatives* to both sheets. His only living relative was his aunt. He wrote *Stella Clara, Mother's sister*.

For his father's relatives he wrote *Barbara Ford—cousin??* He thought he might have met her at an event years ago. If she was still in the area, she could have married and changed her name. He wondered why the Brown side of the family had never seemed to be involved with the Johnson side. *Dollars to donuts, Mother would have shut them out.*

He decided not to escalate his interrogation of the two new

sheets on the wall today. He was confident he'd make progress on this project, even as his inner voice reminded him that he had not yet been specific about what he expected that project to accomplish. He would give it more thought tonight, light thought, happy thought, assisted by naturally-occurring dopamine and a bottle of *Vendredi ordinaire.*

~

In the evening, he decided that the list didn't properly tell the whole story, that Ford had married Lucia Linda, aka Brownie, and fathered their baby, TJ, and that baby Timothy was still very much alive.

He needed a better picture of his bare family tree, one that would show everyone as not just statistics, but family. His family.

March 6: Rules

Saturday

Tim had forgotten the rest of Thursday's breakfast leftovers in the car. With genuine regret, he tossed them in the compost bin.

The bread in the cupboard looked suspicious, too. No matter: today was Saturday, errands-day. He'd start at the bakery down-river where he could get a decent coffee and a scone, and purchase fresh bread.

This took him directly past Stella's house. Should he drop in, un-announced, to inquire about her welfare? He chuckled at this: he'd never done it, and she'd might shut the door on his fingers if he tried. He'd phone her later and leave a message. Or not.

She was on his list of people to consult about his *ACTION* project—heck, she was the only one alive—but he'd have to carefully strategize how to approach her to avoid having her shut him down at the outset.

Well, what if she does? I'm a grown man, simply looking for some family background. It's not like I had been adopted and am now seeking secret information about my birth parents, is it?

This question lingered longer than he had expected it to. He sat at an old school desk in the bakery's big window with his cran-berry scone and Americano and pondered. Of course he wasn't ad-opted. He had never heard any rumours about that. His mother didn't strike him as the adopting sort. One would have to have some desire to be a mother if one were to adopt, and she was pretty much lacking in that department if you asked him, and he was the Child In Question.

Pay attention, Tim. Mother would have been seventeen or eight-een. Not a good candidate to be anybody's mother.

He realized he had overlooked his father's role again. Ford must have counted for something in this story. They married right out of high school, by his calculations. They had done what was required to get her pregnant, nothing more nor less than all the other couples in history. Then Ford got a job somewhere and came home after work and hugged his little boy, TJ.

This memory stung his eyes again. He took his fresh bread and left to do his errands.

~

Tim's first attempt at making calzones instead of pizza smelled awfully good when Robert arrived. Their Saturday night meal was almost always Italian, alternating between home-made and delivery. Eating food from their hands while sitting in big recliner chairs in front of any movie at all was a fun break from sitting up and using forks.

Which is why Rob found it odd when Tim suggested they go to the local movie theatre after supper, and indeed Tim was surprised to hear himself say it. "Tonight? Why can't we just sit here and vegetate like we always do? What's playing, some slasher flick?"

"No, you cynic. I happened to notice the posters all over town today, plus a nice big advertisement in my own newspaper. It's *The Cider House Rules*. It looks interesting. It's based on that book by John Irving, so it's a drama, pretty sure no slashing. I thought we might enjoy seeing a good film on the big screen for a change. What say? I'll drive us. I'll have a smidge less wine, but I'll survive. And you can have popcorn. It starts at seven."

"Popcorn? Why didn't you say? Whatever's in the oven smells terrific, though. It'll be hard to leave room for popcorn...maybe just a medium-size bag."

~

After the movie, they cut the leftover calzone into small bites and ate them by hand in the den as though they had been there all evening in front of the electric fireplace.

"I'd forgotten what a difference the big screen makes. Even if it's schlock—like one of your spaghetti westerns—it has a much greater impact, coming at you that big and loud. I do like staying in, but I'm glad we went tonight. Good idea, Tim."

"There was a lot in it, wasn't there? Those rules in the Cider House were hilarious. I tried to jot them down in the dark."

He looked at his scribbles. "Hmm. Help me out here, Rob. First is about smoking, I think? I wrote what looks like 'mo smo'."

"Don't smoke in bed."

"Right. What's this: 'no mac if drink'?"

"No machines. Don't operate the machines if you've been drinking. The cider press in particular."

"You're good! What's next, then?"

"It's all about the roof. Not to go up on the roof to eat lunch or to sleep even if it's hot."

"How do you do that—remember those details? I've been struggling to be a good observer, and I can't remember diddly most of the time. Including my receptionist's name, poor girl."

"I can't help it. If there's a list, a bunch, a handful of anything, I'm mentally recording it without thinking about it. Sometimes I'm at number five or seven before I even realize I'm counting it. Always did."

"I didn't know that. Does it bother you?"

"Not really. It comes in handy. I have to memorize so much music, so I'm grateful that it comes easily. Some of my students and colleagues struggle with it and I feel sorry for them. Mozart could play a piece of music after hearing it once. I may not be that good, but I'm good."

As they prepared for bed, Tim said, "You know, that movie has me wondering about my own lists of rules. We have emergency procedures posted at the office, and it directs people to call me in case of emergency. So when there was a *perceived* emergency recently, the receptionist called me, but on my home phone, even though there was an editor-in-charge right there, and I was also in the building, being part of the emergency!"

"What? Do I know about this?"

"No, I didn't share that little bump. It wasn't a real emergency, but somebody thought it was. They called the police as the list required, and it almost-nearly became a real emergency when they came in acting all policey. Perhaps I should take that list down altogether rather than rewrite it."

"Makes sense. People won't stop to read a list if they smell smoke. They'll get out, which is probably what the list says to do."

"Right. So, is there ever a use for a list of rules? I often wished my mother had left one for me, or even a note, you know, like 'Go your own way,' or 'To thine own self be true.'"

"You do those."

"I try. Mother's list would have been obvious, like the Cider House rules. It seems giving good instruction is more challenging than it appears. I'll delve into that."

March 7: Meaning

Sunday

Church went well, musically speaking. Those who had attended the disappointing rehearsal on Thursday did their best to do better this morning. Those who had been absent did their best to catch up to what they imagined the others had achieved. Pulling together, they recovered nicely, an essential element of performance.

With such concentration on their music, only the most devout of choristers could have said what the sermon had been about. They all recalled the final hymn, though, because the music was painfully dull, and the words were odd, especially the second verse:

Sunbeams scorching all the day, chilly dew-drops nightly shed;
prowling beasts about thy way; stones thy pillow, earth thy bed.

"That sure ruined sunbeams and dew-drops for me!" Jasmine, a young soprano, said. "It makes them sound so sinister." An alto plodded around in the changing room to mock the flat-footed metre of the hymn.

All complaints ceased when they left the choir rooms. Everyone had bad days, as well they knew, and they were prepared to give the minister a free pass in hymn choices once in a while.

Early March was a psychologically uncomfortable time of year anyway. The New Year had long disappeared below the horizon; spring and Easter were close, but were taking far too long to appear. For those who had given up something for Lent, the thrill of self-sacrifice was wearing thin.

"Maybe they should add 'The Season of Disgruntlement' to the church calendar," Tim opined on the short drive home. "They already have the hymns for it."

"I'm not sure if that would help or make it worse," Robert said. "But I am grateful that each day passes on, taking the mood it rode in on. My head is already in the future."

"Mine's in the past."

~

After lunch, Tim suggested they go for a walk, to treat the morning's ennui with dopamine. They drove a short distance to a neighbourhood where they could walk in the middle of the cleared street without risk of ice or traffic. It was a pleasant afternoon, with the weak sun managing to keep the temperature above freezing. They encountered several people, some swinging their arms vigorously, others pushing strollers or being tugged along by their dogs. Everyone sang out greetings about the lovely day, spreading the good feelings around.

Tim said to Robert, "Do you mind if I bring you back from the future to talk about that movie?"

"I don't mind at all. What would you like to discuss? Want me to demonstrate more prodigious feats of memory?"

"Sure, let's hear something!"

"'Good night, you princes of Maine, you kings of New England,'" Robert said in a credible impersonation of Michael Caine.

"That's a great one! I liked that part. There's no telling how much something like that would mean to those boys. Certainly better than telling them to shut up and not cause any trouble every night. Got another?"

"'They outrageous, them rules. We supposed to make our own rules.'"

"Another good line. I was thinking of that list of rules again when I woke this morning. There's a lot to think about in that movie, but I think Irving is pointing out something intriguing by having those rules posted in the Cider House."

"Because nobody there can read them, you mean?"

"Exactly! The people they're posted for never knew what they were about. But, like the fellow said, they were guided by their own rules anyway, every single day. Something about that is bugging me."

"Because?"

"I don't know yet," Tim said. "But I think it has something to do with a project I'm working on. That we know more than we realize."

March 8: Topic

Monday

Tim handed Robert his monogrammed latté with a flourish. He'd been making many lattés to refine that skill, and now enjoyed showing it off.

"Still just my initial—is that all you can do?" Robert teased. "I was expecting something more complex by now, like a slogan, maybe."

"Oh sure, I can do that, no problem, but you'd have to drink your coffee from a trough. You should be grateful I even remember your initial at this ungodly hour."

Robert was soon on the highway back to the university and his bachelor apartment. When he'd been going to work himself, Tim was usually out the door right behind him, though for a much shorter commute. Now, he had the luxury of taking his time over breakfast, savouring the rich coffee he'd learned to extract from Gloria.

He sat at the kitchen island and thought about how much he'd enjoyed the weekend. He picked up a pencil and scribbled his thoughts on the back of a pre-printed grocery list from the supermarket:

A GREAT WEEKEND:
Movie out
Impromptu
Fresh topics
Walking & talking
Dopamine?
Great food

He liked that list. He'd show it to Rob when he returned. He pulled a tack from a business card no longer relevant and stuck the list on the cork board. Then he made one addition, if only for political reasons:

Church

~

He phoned his doctor's office to ask for an appointment.

"Is it urgent, Tim?" the receptionist inquired.

"Nope, not at all. Dr Muhammed asked me to come back periodically, that's all. Not sure what constitutes periodically in my case, but I last saw him sometime in January."

"One moment, please."

While he waited, Tim doodled on another grocery list. He was sketching the scene from Saturday's movie where the doctor drips ether onto a paper mask over his nose and mouth to help him sleep.

"Tim? Sorry to keep you waiting. Are you available next Monday at ten-thirty?"

"Yup. The fifteenth at ten-thirty. Thanks very much. Bye, now."

He looked at his crude drawing of the doctor addicted to ether. *We never know, do we, what people are dealing with behind closed doors. Not a bad way to go, in your sleep, even if it's a drug-induced sleep. Could too much dopamine do that?*

He might want some ether himself to dampen the adrenaline rush after this next call, but putting it off wouldn't accomplish the goal, and he, Timothy Brown, was all about goals today.

"Good morning, this is the office of Stella Johnson, MLA for South River and the Harbours, Edward Williams speaking. How may I assist you?"

"Edward Williams? I don't recognize your name. Are you new there?"

"Yes, sir. I started last Monday. May I assist—"

"Yes. Miz Johnson, please. Tell her it's the Premier. And good luck there, William."

"It's Edward Williams, sir. One moment, please."

Stop tormenting. The poor fellow will have a hard enough time keeping his job without you messing with him.

Edward picked up again. "Miz Johnson says you are not the Premier because he, um, may I tell her who's calling, please?"

"I apologize, Edward, I was just having a little fun. It's Timothy Brown. Just Mister Brown. I'll wait."

He waited a long time on hold, but the line didn't go dead. At last, Stella picked up. "What are you doing? Please do not disrespect my employee."

"Good morning, Aunt Stella. I did apologize for any distress I may have caused your new fellow there. I'll get right to it. I have some questions to ask you and I'd appreciate some time to address them with you. It's not constituency business, and it's not dinner-table conversation, though it may become that. It's something personal I'm working on. I think you could be quite helpful to me."

"What concerning?"

"Family matters."

Stella was silent for a heavy moment. "When?"

He was surprised. She wasn't stonewalling or grilling him. That might come later.

"Anytime that's convenient for you, except Thursday evening or Sunday morning."

"Where?"

"You tell me. You're the one who lives in two places. When will you be at home here? Can I bring you a cappuccino and a muffin?"

"All right. At my home, tomorrow morning, nine sharp."

"Thank you very much. I hope—"

Stella was gone.

Before he lost interest in the telephone, he called the NuYu Spa, and asked Lisa for an appointment with Melanie for the following week.

"How about next Wednesday the seventeenth at three?"

"Thank you, Lisa, that's perfect. I'm looking forward to it."

He marked both important appointments in his pocket calendar.

This month's train was beginning to roll nicely through the countryside.

He hadn't had a chance to ask how much time Stella would give him tomorrow, but if he was taking along coffee and muffins, that'd cover at least half an hour. He'd have a good look at her while he was there. He wasn't brave enough to inquire about her infection, if that's what she'd been suffering from. He couldn't pull off Robert's charmingly intrusive manner.

He was nervous about their conversation, so he took himself for a walk. Despite traffic noise, he was invigorated when he returned. Walking was good medicine. He'd be sure to tell Dr Muhammed.

He didn't want to go downtown today, neither to be amongst people nor to be alone there. He could use the day at home to devise and rehearse topics he would introduce to his aunt. Preparation was essential for any discussion with Stella. His eyes seemed to leak where thoughts of his father were concerned, and he hoped that would settle down. Stella wouldn't tolerate that.

He wrote out the lists of vital statistics he had taped to the walls on Friday.

But what is the topic?

It wasn't about why he liked action, or if action produced dopamine, or why he felt he was keeping secrets from himself. Stella would chop him into little bits if he started out like that. What did he expect her to contribute anyway? She was not the sort who passively followed wherever a conversation might lead, listening without judging, like Robert did.

Aunt Stella, what the topic is...

What the topic was took several walks to get clear in his head. Then he rehearsed aloud so he could hear himself say the words and not be ambushed by them.

He was amazed at how emotional he felt when he said aloud, "Aunt Stella, I want to know about my father."

He said it over and over until bedtime.

March 9: *Sine die*

Maybe Tim would never feel prepared for an encounter with Stella on any topic. Maybe he just didn't want to give her any reason to use her sharp claws on him. They'd been getting along quite well lately. Why mess with that?

After he showered and dressed, he said to the man in the bathroom mirror, "Easy on yourself, now. You're right to feel nervous. It's just the Stella effect."

That was funny. He hadn't put it into words before, but now that he'd said it, he knew "the Stella effect" was a real thing. He'd always been wary around her. She always made him feel that he might put a foot wrong at any moment, and that she wouldn't hesitate to point it out.

He wondered why she was like that. His mother had been the same and worse, but she'd been his mother, and who in the world could ever fathom what motivated their mothers' behaviours? Around *The Times'* water cooler, many complaints were about mothers, but when Mother's Day rolled around, everyone was busy planning sentimental cards and flowers and dinners, with tears in their eyes, though Tim was never sure what kind of tears they were.

On the drive down river, the likely common source of both women's behaviours occurred to him: *their* parents. Stella and Brownie grew to their teens together, ruled by their mother and father, shadowy figures in Tim's memory, long gone when he came along. Maybe they were snarky to their girls, who absorbed their way and grew up using it.

I wonder what I've absorbed, then, and from whom? I don't think

I'm snarky.

Tim considered this a few moments.

But maybe I should be, if that's what Stella responds to.

~

He was slightly late for his rendezvous with Stella due to the lineup at the popular bakery. He rang her doorbell. Twice. *C'mon Stella, it's chilly out here, coffee's getting cold.*

He heard her heels clicking on the foyer tiles and then she opened the door.

"Good morning, Aunt Stella," Tim said, heading directly for the kitchen with his purchases. "Sorry I'm late, lineup at the—"

"Shoes, please," was her greeting in return.

He handed her the coffee tray and bag of muffins and bent to remove his hiking shoes. Her home was a showpiece. *But white carpet between the foyer and the kitchen was a big design flaw*, he thought.

He had intended to greet Stella with a hug, but the moment had passed. He put their Morning Glory muffins on small plates, sliced each open and added a pat of butter, decanted the coffees into mugs, and re-heated everything in the microwave. He set it all on the large island in the kitchen, where Stella was already perched on a stool, watching him attentively. She was almost smiling.

"You move around in the kitchen just like your mother," she said, in response to his raised eyebrows. "She developed that all on her own. It's not a skill I share, to state the obvious. Good to see you inherited that from her. I certainly benefit."

"Thank you for pointing that out, Aunt Stella. As it happens, that's sort of why I asked to see you this morning. Family resemblances. Family matters. You're right, Mother didn't start out doing much of anything in the kitchen. We had housekeepers for that. But she really took to bustling around for her cooking column after I took over as editor. She was hard on herself, though, wasn't she? We usually ate whatever she made unless she sent it home with her assistant. I remember one famous occasion when the first and second tries both went in the garbage can. I don't know what the problem was, but Mother was foul for days. I went out for a burger and took it to the office."

Tim was doing all the talking. Stella was listening, but not joining in. He didn't want her to tell him to get to the point.

"So, to the point of this visit. I've been thinking a lot recently about my family, and I've noticed two things: two, some things are difficult to remember, and one, some things I can't remember because I never knew them. And three, I suppose I should add, a very few are pleasant to remember, like Mother in the kitchen. Without the tantrums."

Stella was nibbling on her muffin, eyes on her plate.

"So, I'm hoping you can help me fill in some blanks."

Stella sipped her coffee.

"Primarily, I want to learn more about my father, more than just my mother's scorn."

Stella put down her coffee mug and pointed her finger at Tim. "You stay away from that. I have no wish to dig up your—that situation. There is nothing to be gained from it. What brings this on? You couldn't be better provided for, with a prominent position at a thriving enterprise that practically runs itself, a solid bank account —my goodness, Timothy, look at yourself! You should wake up grateful every morning. Why dig into things that didn't involve you then and don't now!"

Tim chewed his muffin slowly. He sipped some coffee. His pulse was pounding. Having rehearsed this moment didn't make it any more pleasant. But he had a strategy and he would have to carry it through now or lose forever. He nodded slowly and inhaled deeply.

"So," he exhaled, as though Stella had not spoken at all. "I know my father died when I was five, the summer before I started school. I have very few of my own memories of him, and Mother almost never spoke of him when I was growing up, unless it was to call him a fool, or a damn fool. I know raising me by herself couldn't have been easy. But something triggered a memory of my father recently, and it shook me. It made me want to know more. So I thought I'd start with you. I know you weren't around here much at that time, but I'd love to know whatever you know about him, whether from your own experience or what you might have heard."

Stella slid off the stool and clicked through to the wide expanse of windows at the rear of the house that overlooked the South River as it flowed to the sea. Her arms were folded, her fingers twiddling at both elbows.

Then she turned back toward Tim, still seated in the kitchen, watching her. "You won't like it."

"I'm prepared for that, Aunt Stella. I know he killed himself. Every kid in school made it their mission to share that juicy detail with me. When I tried to tell Mother what I'd heard—been taunted with—she'd shut me down, like it was my fault they said it, and worse that I repeated it to her. Eventually, I learned it was easier to *be* shut down, to forget about it. It didn't have anything to do with me, directly, and nobody or nothing I heard about drove him to do it. Mother didn't seem to have either sorrow or regret. Just dull anger. She was angry about a lot of things, much of which she acted out towards me, sometimes just for coming in the door."

Stella glanced at Tim's stockinged feet and quickly looked away. She appeared to have accepted his re-direction from her outburst. He stood up to get a glass of ice water from the spigot in the fridge door. He had never heard himself speak as he had just done. He had never said those words about those things aloud to anyone in his life.

Stella came back to the kitchen. "I need to consider it, Timothy. I haven't thought about any of that in a long time. I don't want to be rushed into saying things of which I am not certain. Leave it with me."

Tim inhaled to speak, but Stella interrupted him.

"I *will* think about it."

"That's excellent. I'm grateful for that. What I was going to say is I don't want you to edit out gossip from fact. Just point out which is which, when you know it. Sure, I've heard some hurtful gossip, but I've also learned that rumours don't always begin in malice. When people don't have the facts, they just fill in what makes sense to them, right or wrong, especially if they feel they're being kept in the dark. That, in fact, is one value of journalism; we're supposed to find and report only the facts, God help us. Rest assured, though, I'm not going to confront the gossipers: that would only revive the story for them, and that's not my interest at all."

"I think you're imagining that there are gossipers. It's unlikely anyone has thought about your...this issue for many years."

"I wish I could agree, but that's regrettably not the case. In January, I was confronted with, quote, my family's history of mental illness—on both sides, too—unquote. At church. Word is that I've taken leave from *The Times* because I've had a nervous breakdown, the family plague."

"Not that meddling old minister, was it?"

"That's an interesting comment. I didn't think you knew the Reverend Doctor, but I suppose you know everyone. But no, not the minister. Anyway, I want to know what happened in my family, what other people think they know. About my father especially, I want to hear it all. I can handle it."

Stella glanced at the tiny watch on her wrist. "That's all the time I have today, Timothy. I *will* respond. Spencer will be here shortly with the limo. I have meetings in the city and several calls to make along the way. Thank you for breakfast."

"You're welcome. Aren't those muffins great? They cover every category on Canada's Food Guide, I'm sure. Seeds, fruit, coconut, oil —yum! Oh, may I inquire ever so briefly about your health? The last time we were here, you—"

"I'm fine. Tell Robert that, for a musician, he is a very good diagnostician. I'll finish the antibiotics tomorrow, thank goodness. They make me feel awful, which seems counter-productive, but they work. It'll be nice to have a glass of wine again."

They exchanged a few words about the weather's warming trend while Tim pulled on his boots at the door, and then they parted, *sine die*, without having arranged another day.

Tim congratulated himself on broaching his historic conversation. It would likely take masterful manipulation to keep Stella working with him, but he was encouraged that he had begun.

Begun what, Tim? What is your quest here?

He was parked on the ramp leading to the cable ferry that crossed South River. It had pulled away minutes before he'd arrived with a fresh coffee and more muffins to take home, but it'd be back in half an hour and he was in no hurry. He made notes from his conversation with Stella, including *sine die* and *carpe diem*, which he felt he had also done.

What had he "seized the day" to accomplish?

He had stated he wanted to know about his father, which would cover the six years or so of his parents' marriage. He asked Stella to share whatever came to mind without editing. They could sort that out together. He hoped she would play along.

As the ferry smoothly pulled away toward the opposite shore, what he was doing dawned on him. He was delving. *Finally!* He was casting a wide net without prejudging what the catch would be.

Stella was not a delver. Her operating style was surgical, with pre-determined heroes and villains leading to her pre-drawn conclusion. She was the Spanish Inquisition. But he, Tim Brown the Delver, wanted to catch and examine everything, the good, the bad, and the irrelevant. He'd keep the truth and toss back the inedible fiction at the end of the search. He couldn't think of a mission in history that matched his style. Perhaps he was the first.

~

At the Johnson Building on Main Street, Tim went directly to the newspaper's archives corner, where rows of filing cabinets contained decades of local history as it had unfolded in the pages of *The Times*. Gregory Barss, known to everyone as GB, presided over this repository. He had been at the job longer than anyone else at the paper, even Tim, and for many he embodied the beating heart of the enterprise.

"GB, are you in here?"

Tim heard a file drawer rolling shut, and GB's feet shuffling as he rounded a corner.

"Oh, hi, Tim. Always nice to see you. Don't see many familiar faces in here these days. Not so many faces of any kind. What brings you to see us this morning?”

“Vital statistics, GB. Can you fill in the blanks on this random list of names for me?”

Tim passed over the short list:

> Dates of birth, marriage, death for—
> Lucia Linda “Brownie” (Johnson) Brown
> Ford Enright Brown
> Timothy Johnson Brown
> Barbara Brown

GB held the list in both hands to control a tremor Tim hadn’t noticed before.

“Not such a random list, Tim. Misplaced the family Bible, did you?”

“Now see, that’s why I come to you, GB. I would never have thought of looking there, and now I will. Even so, can you get me the vital stats for these? In case I can’t find the Bible, or can’t open it because of the heavy layer of dust on it? My mother’s death won’t be recorded in it anyway, because she’d have been the only one to do it.”

Those who knew GB’s lined face well would recognize the slight squinting of his eyes as a smile. “Time?”

“This isn’t a rush job. I’m researching a little bit of my family history, and I’d like to have all the dates right, that’s all.”

“Must know your own birthday. It’s coming right up.”

“Yeah, but don’t remind me. Just check them all, okay?”

“Call you?”

“No, that’d be too hard, me writing down all those dates. Just write the info on this paper and keep it here. I’ll check back with you. I’m in and out.”

“Good, Tim. Fresh edition tomorrow, usually busy for a few days getting that filed.”

“I understand. Now tell me, how’s your dear wife?”

“Poorly, Tim, thanks for asking. Always tell her when you ask. Makes her smile. Not much else does.”

"Is she—do you have home care for her?"

"Oh, yes. She's failing, though. Help comes in twice a week now."

Not for the first time, Tim wished GB and his wife were a branch of his own family tree, though nothing was keeping him from caring about them or offering assistance.

Being related always includes obligations sooner or later. Whether you act on them or not.

He went to his room to retrieve the coffee flask he'd left there last week. The new mailbox was hanging on the door, and there was a pink message note in it, the kind receptionists used the world over.

According to the note, the newspaper's accountant had called him yesterday. Tim prayed it wasn't urgent. Surely he'd have called again if it were. What would be urgent? He was certain that the business was going along smoothly. If it were not, he would've expected Elaine to sound the first alarm, and she hadn't.

"Nothing to worry about, Tim," he told the rear-view mirror as he drove away. "What is worrying is your nervous reaction at the first hint of trouble at work. You went to a lot of effort to put a fail-safe plan in place, and people are being paid good money to see that it works, so cool your jets."

He practised deep breathing. It made him feel light-headed, but it did help quell the panicky feeling. Did deep breathing also produce dopamine? He'd have lots of questions for Dr Muhammed about that. Meanwhile, before he returned that pink-slip phone message or got into anything else that would fill his gut with heebie-jeebies, he decided to go for a walk.

He drove up Main Street, inland along the river, and parked past the big high school. Traffic was light, which was good, because snowbanks forced him to walk on the pavement.

It was nice to walk, though, with the light breeze in the big pines and the river tumbling noisily over boulders far below. The river was all fresh water here, draining from far inland. Below town it was mixed with salt ocean water, down to where it became ocean below the ferry, where he'd just been.

At home, the feeling of well-being continued as he returned the call to the accounting firm.

"One moment please, Mister Brown. I'll put you through."

He chuckled at being "put through" a telephone wire by the matronly receptionist. Business language was often not good English, though it used English words. Everyone inside the moat understood what was meant, and outsiders pretended to catch on until they did, too.

"Tim! Were you away? I left a message for you a couple days ago!"

Hazen Awalt, of Awalt & Zinck Accounting, known as "A to Zed", had been the newspaper's accountant for a very long time.

"Hi, Hazen. You know I'm not in the office this year, which is why I made the custodial arrangements with you and the others that I did. So what's up? Oh, before you answer that, let me give you my cellular telephone number. You can easily reach me on it, if I happen to be where there's a signal."

"Tim, can you come to my office? Now? I'll get your phone number then. Come right over and Margaret will let me know when you arrive."

"I can, Hazen, but why? Please tell me there's no trouble."

"I'll be waiting for you."

A forty-five minute walk with all the good feelings it generated couldn't compete with the dread Tim now felt.

He drove to A to Zed's offices, in a new building in the industrial park, in an area that had been excavated and left looking like a gravel pit. But the board room that Margaret escorted him into had expensive furniture and nice lighting, and the blinds were pulled at the windows, hiding the ugliness outside.

"I'll tell Mister Awalt you're here," Margaret said. Tim almost asked her if she'd be 'putting him through', but he checked himself. *Being silly is a sign of nerves, or aggression.*

A pitcher of water was on the table and he poured himself a glass. The walk had made him thirsty.

The accountant came in and closed the door. "Good day, Tim, how's it going?" He reached across the burnished wood table to shake Tim's hand. "Feeling any better?"

Tim would have asked his accountant to explain that question except his concern about the business' finances overrode his annoyance at the suggestion that he had not been well. "I'm fine, Hazen. What's up, please?"

"Well, as you know, we're not due for our first quarterly review until after the end of March, which would put us sometime into April—"

"I know when April is, Hazen. Can you please come to the point?"

"Yes, and April, as you also know, is a very busy month in the accounting world, with the filing of personal income taxes being required by our friends at Revenue Canada, or Canada Revenue Agency as they call themselves now."

Tim was building steam. "Hazen, I was worrying that you'd called me in because there's something wrong financially at *The Times*. Can you please just put my mind at rest that that's not the case, or tell me what it is, if it is? Please?"

Hazen Awalt's operating system had been forever set on slow, as had his father's before him. In fact, he had always seemed older than his father, even back when he started as a junior accountant. A growing hearing problem made it worse, as he seemed unaware of the intake of a client's breath indicating that they wanted him to pause in his ponderous sentences so they could jump in without being rude. His clients joked that A to Zed's slogan should be "If We Ever Get There".

"Something wrong? I hadn't heard that, Tim. How so?"

"Sorry I interrupted, Hazen. Carry on. Why did you request that I come over right now?"

"Well. We were hoping you would agree to move your scheduled Q One Review ahead to May."

"To May. Why?"

"It's good news, really, for Awalt & Zinck, and for our clients by extension. We have recently acquired a large client which, we discovered a bit after the fact, traditionally facilitates their employees' income tax returns. As you may know, personal tax returns are a loss leader for a firm like ours, but they can lead to more valuable work. Hence, short term loss, but leading to—"

"I know what a loss leader is, Hazen. You're asking me if I will postpone a very important accounting review, which we planned and discussed several times last year, to sometime in May, so you can service a new client, do I have that right?"

"We appreciate that very much, Tim, yes, thank you."

"And meanwhile, if anything has gone awry in my business, instead of finding and dealing with it immediately after three months, as we planned in great detail, you want to defer it to sometime in the fifth month, do I have that right?"

"Tim, everything looks good. I don't think you have anything to be concerned about."

"You've seen reports? Can you make that statement with confidence?"

"Well, I've requested my staff to alert me, and nothing has come to my attention. It's all standard stuff."

"Is it? Compared to what? I'm not there, that's not standard. When I *was* there, I spent many hours going over the reports line by line, year over year."

"Yes, you did. You're one of our most thorough clients, Tim. Never a penny missing."

"Well, I didn't intend to be sloppy now, when I'm farther away from operations than I've been since I was fourteen years old. It's a huge risk for me, Hazen. Did you forget that there's a new editor on staff, approving expenditures, hiring staff? Did you notice major renovations last month? Did you notice any changes in revenue, up or down? Did you forget that we're paying your firm extra for extra attention?"

"If you have concerns, have you addressed them with your interim editor? A Miss Fong, I believe?"

"I know her name, Hazen, thanks, and I'm not going to ask her what *she* thinks about our financial position. We set up our quarterly reviews with *you*, and I've been trusting that we would conduct them *as planned*."

Tim spoke a little more loudly, so Hazen could hear, and because he felt like shouting.

"As a matter of fact, I've given very little thought to finances so far this year, believing that you and the rest of the oversight panel would keep the ship afloat, and alert me if—*if*—something looked suspicious. Which is why I called you in a panic when I found your message, which you left with the newspaper receptionist, of all people. Sure makes me wonder if you *are* paying attention. By the way, here's my card with my phone numbers on it: one is my home phone, the other is mobile. Now, Hazen, if you don't have adequate personnel to do the personal tax returns for a new account that you've committed to do, then you have some choices: raid the tax kiosks in the shopping malls, or farm the work out to one of your many competitors, or work harder and faster yourself—or be prepared to lose my business!"

Hazen held up both hands. "Tim, please. You're overreacting. I meant no disrespect to you or your firm. I was hoping for a favour, but I see that you're unable to alter our arrangements, and I have no problem with that. We can certainly handle all the work that comes our way, including yours, and we will continue to give it our best attention. Thank you for coming in, Tim. Please accept our continued best wishes for your health. It takes time, sometimes."

Tim wasn't interested in learning what Hazen thought "it" was. He knew the reference to his health was a reminder that some people thought he'd taken this sabbatical due to a nervous breakdown.

He said, "See you on or before the middle of May," and left without a handshake.

While Hazen was genuinely suffering hearing loss, his secretary, Margaret, had no such difficulty, though she gave no sign of having heard any of Tim's stressed talk. As he passed her desk in the lobby, she said, "Oh, Mister Brown, do you mind if I check my contact information for you?"

He gave her a card with his two phone numbers on it, thanked her for her attention to detail, and left.

~

What time was it? Tim's head was pounding, his mouth was dry, his stomach was growling. He hadn't had anything to eat since the coffee and muffin at Stella's first thing this morning, and the glass of water in A to Zed's boardroom. *He'd better not charge me for that.*

Drizzle or sleet was beginning to fall, not good for driving or walking. Given the mood he was in, an accident could put him over the emotional edge. So he drove home, opened a can of thick pea soup, and lit a fire. As the soup and fire warmed and calmed him, he felt more like making notes on what he had accomplished earlier in the day.

If not accomplished, at least addressed.

When it came to facing dragons, he mused, there were two strategies. He had ignored Stella's tirade this morning, and she had simply capitulated. She often escalated when he attempted to defend himself. When he didn't, she had nothing to fight against, so she relaxed.

Hazen's opening request had been weak and insulting, and Tim had quickly breathed fire himself. Would he have deferred his appointment if Hazen had simply said he had to do it and that was that, without adding excuses about another client? Possibly. Nobody likes to be told that another client is more important than they are. Good for A to Zed, but that meant nothing to Tim. Why should he be inconvenienced? Hazen didn't even offer to reduce his fee.

Tim poured himself a glass of *Mardi fâché*, and pressed a speed-dial number.

"Good afternoon, this is Elaine Fong, Editor at *The Times*. How may I help you?"

"It's me. How're things at the coal-face? Oops, it's Wednesday, my copy is still on my front porch. Should I rush out to see it?"

"Hi Tim. It's the usual excellence here. You can rush out *when* the paper is delivered, which will be tomorrow morning, since today is still Tuesday, thank goodness."

"Oops, again. I knew that. Just checking up on you. Listen, I won't keep you, I just want to put a bee in your bonnet. You have an uncanny way of finding resources when we need them, as you did with that painting contractor last month. So, I was just wondering, should we be reviewing our accounting firm, do you think? No rush, no urgency. Just a thought."

"Tim, I can see right through you on this. You've taken a year away from the grind, and you often said that you didn't care for finance, though I must say you did it very well. So you're not just casually mentioning that we should search the market for this service. Is there a problem? If it's urgent, I'll get on it right away."

"You're scary, Elaine. Your x-ray vision is noted. I bet you can see me over the phone. Where am I right now?"

"Sitting by the fire with a glass of wine, though that doesn't take super powers. I can hear the fire crackling, and the sound of your nose in a balloon glass is unmistakable."

"Am I that predictable? Don't answer that. And no, nothing urgent, but I do raise the topic because of an incident today. We've been with our firm, A to Zed, since forever. In fact, I wouldn't be surprised if we were their first account, and vice-versa. But I have the feeling that they're taking us for granted, and I don't find that acceptable from any professional who is performing critical services for me, for premium fees. So I just want to check around. As a new account, we'd get scrutiny, attention, respect, tickets to ball games, that sort of thing."

"You go to ball games?"

"I might if they came with a plane ticket to Boston or Montreal. Never mind. Just keep your ears on, okay? Something interesting might show up. If nothing does, in a couple months maybe we'll ask A to Zed to do a forensic audit for us to see if they can find a lost penny."

"That'll cost you a pretty penny, but I get your point. Not urgent. Preventative, perhaps? Complacency is bad, I do know that. I've seen it in many of the papers I've worked for. Some were too far gone to rescue, but they defended their poor methods—like giving free ad space to their best customers, which makes zero sense—right to the end. I'll let you know what I find, or don't find. Have a good evening, Tim."

He was so grateful for Elaine Fong. When he'd been searching for an interim editor for this year, no other candidate had impressed him as she had, and she was proving her worth. She loved the small town newspaper business. He wished he could keep her on even when he did return to work.

He'd thought enough about work of all kinds for one day. The crackling fire in the grate and the rattle of sleet on the windows were soothing sounds through the evening, and he accomplished nothing more in his delving.

March 10: Ebenezer

Wednesday

Waiting is passive. There's no dopamine in that.

Tim made a latté and tried a new design in the foam, unsuccessfully, but the effort was drinkable anyway. He browsed the newspapers—*The Times*, and *The Daily* from the city—to see what entertainment was coming up.

It'd be so great if South River had a professional live theatre. But we could never support it.

Maybe there were theatrical plays on DVD. Why not? He would go to the movie store this morning and find out. A bit of Shakespeare would be a pleasant change from the action films or westerns he and Robert had been playing recently, mostly with the sound turned down so they could talk while the stagecoaches rattled into Dry Gulch and out of Dodge.

He pushed aside the papers and made a *To Do* list for the day. He was expecting the damaged front storm door to be replaced, and where was it? He was also waiting for a Sherlock Holmes book he had ordered from a bookstore; was it in yet?

~

He phoned the building supplies store first, because he knew they opened early.

"When did you order the door? I don't see it."

"Weeks ago. Coming from Montreal, but still, it was supposed to be here by now."

"Oh, wait, here you are. I think it's here, hang on."

Tim noticed his nerves tingling. *Maybe I do have a mental illness, and well-earned, if so.*

"Sorry to keep you waiting, Tim. Yup, your door's been here for a while, but the shipper forgot to include a threshold, and your current one will need to be changed to fit this door, so we had to wait for it. We didn't want the installer to get there and not be able to complete the job, right?"

"Right. Thanks for checking, I appreciate that." Tim was mollified. "So, is it ready now?"

"Yes, it is. It had been moved the list of calls for me to make today, that's why I couldn't find it when you called. How about this Friday morning at eight?"

While he was still in the mood to make calls, he phoned the blind piano tuner, who had put him off until March to reduce risk of stumbling over ice and snow. Alphonse Dufour advised him he was scheduled for Wednesday afternoon, two weeks from today, "weather permitting".

"Oh, surely the snow will be gone by then," Tim said. "It'll be spring. Fingers crossed."

"I hope you're right, but I'll confirm the day before. Crossed fingers don't help me if there's ice."

Two appointments made, that was something; the train was rolling. He didn't phone the bookstore because it was Wednesday and they wouldn't be open mid-week this time of year. He'd try on Saturday.

~

At the video store, the clerk was puzzled when he inquired about plays on DVD. "Games? We have lots over there." He pointed.

"No, not games. Theatrical plays. On stage. In theatres. With actors."

How does one explain what a play is? He'd never considered having to do that, and his brain was struggling to find words to describe it.

"Can you name one?"

Tim glanced around the store. "Is there a hidden camera? A *play.*

With actors. Talking. On a stage. Like Shakespeare? If you don't have any, no name will help us. Okay, how about *Julius Caesar*?"

"Can you spell that?"

The clerk looked it up on the computer at the counter, then pointed to the back of the store. "It might be back there. It says we have one copy."

Tim hadn't especially wanted *Julius Caesar*, but he didn't want to keep playing charades with this kid either. He went in the direction of the clerk's finger, and looked at the plastic cases in the back corner.

"Bottom shelf, it says," the clerk called to him.

He wasn't able to read the titles while standing, and bending over required him to read upside down, so he was on hands and knees when he found it: *Julius Caesar*, a movie made in the seventies, starring Charlton Heston. A movie of a play was as close as he was going to get in South River today.

He picked it up, stood up, brushed the dust from the knees of his pants, and proceeded to check it out.

"It's not due back for two weeks," the clerk snickered.

"When was it last rented out?"

"Um, sometime last year."

"Good. I'll return it sometime this year."

~

While eggs boiled for lunch, he read the sleeve of the DVD. Big name actors were in it. Like anything Hollywood produced, it'd be bigger and better than anything William Shakespeare had ever envisioned. He thought it might be fun.

In fact, it might be a whole lot more fun than a dry, black-and-white recitation of the bard's story. Yes, it could be, given the right setting.

Tim's head was filling with details of that setting and a whole lot more. Now he really did have something to make notes about. This'd be good—if Robert supported his crazy idea. Maybe not so crazy, but better as a plan than a surprise.

He called the newspaper front office.

"Good afternoon, *The Times*. This is Rachael. How may I direct your call?"

"Hello, Rachael," he said, happy that he got her name right. "You may direct my call to you, ha-ha. I noticed that you had put a phone message in my mailbox the other day."

"Yes, Mister Brown. John told me the mailbox was there and that I should leave messages for you in it now."

"John who? Our caretaker? What would he—listen, the reason I'm calling is that the mailbox is *not* the place for telephone messages. If someone calls you looking for me, please give them my two phone numbers, okay? I'm not in regularly, as you know, and we shouldn't let a message gather dust, right?"

"Okay, Mister Brown, you're right. I'll tell John."

"It's not really any of John's business, though, is it? I asked him to put the mailbox up. He did. That ends his involvement in the project. If anyone gives you instructions about what to do with my messages, it should be me. So: phone calls for me, give them my numbers. Simple. Okay?"

"Okay, Mister Brown. My phone's ringing."

"Thanks, Raquel. Bye-bye."

He often got his receptionist's name wrong. Sometimes he minded doing it.

~

GB had suggested he research the family Bible. *Now, where would it be?*

This question amused him. When one inherits an old house that has been in the family for generations, one inherits its contents, too, and given all its nooks and crannies, not all contents may be brought to light or attention. They might remain unnoticed even if they are visible, especially if the seeker grew up in the house him-self.

Tim had replaced some items of furniture as they became threadbare, but with only one person sitting on anything most days, items faded or became out of style faster than they wore out. Mrs Aquino's aggressive cleaning kept dust at bay, at least as high as she could reach, which wasn't at the very top of the ornate bookshelves, where he found the Bible.

He carried it to the coffee-table in the parlour, but that wasn't the right position for reading, so he took it back to the kitchen island. He sat on a stool so he could hover over the pages of the heavy book.

Nobody had turned the pages in this volume very often, that was evident. Many were stuck together, likely ever since the Bible had left the print shop.

Inside the front cover was an inscription, written in ink, in a flowery script:

> *Presented to Ebenezer Johnson on*
> *Easter Sunday 20th April 1930*
> *upon the occasion of the consecration of*
> *Saint John's United Church,*
> *from a grateful congregation.*
> *~ 1 Samuel 7:12*

He was curious about the verse from the First Book of Samuel. It took a bit of flipping back and forth, and some sneezing from the dust, but he came to it eventually:

> Then Samuel took a stone, and set it between Mizpeh and Shen, and called the name of it Eben-ezer, saying, Hitherto hath the LORD helped us.

"Well played," Tim said aloud. "Somebody knew their scripture."

He thought the record he was looking for would be between the Old and New Testaments. The stuck pages crackled as he flipped past books with names totally unfamiliar to him, in spite of his constant attendance at church: Habakkuk, Haggai, Malachi.

Then there it was: *Family Register of Ebenezer Johnson—*

He quickly closed the book, though he left his finger in to mark the place. He didn't want to read it. Not yet. He had glimpsed hand-written entries beginning with his grandmother's name, which he couldn't recall. There'd be a page of Births, Marriages, and Deaths. He'd see how up-to-date the entries were, who was in and who was missing. But not yet.

A dark red ribbon was at the binding, a bookmark. He pulled it out, placed it where his finger was and closed the book.

What was the holdup? These weren't family secrets. All of this information was available in public, if you knew where to look in the cemetery. He hadn't gone there to do his research. It mightn't be easy to walk around. There might be leftover snowdrifts. The ground might be soft.

It was time for another walk, and it might as well be in the vicinity of the cemetery. He made no promises to go in, but he put a notebook and pencil in his jacket pocket, just in case.

The "Gates of Heaven" were locked. A small sign asked visitors not to enter if the gates were closed, "for safety reasons". What those reasons might be weren't pleasant to contemplate. He chose to keep walking on the street, avoiding research that included a risk of falling into a collapsed grave.

March 11: Secret message

Thursday

Tim made his wake-up espresso while half-humming, half-singing a song based on John Donne's famous poem, though slightly altered this morning.

> No day is an island, No day stands alone.
> Each day's joy is joy to me, each day's grief is my own...
> you gotta walk that lonesome valley...yes you do, yes you do...

He was still entertaining himself when Mrs Aquino arrived with her armload of cleaning tools. He held the door for her and sang with renewed vigour, earning an eye-roll from his audience of one.

Still feeling the lightness, he headed to his regular booth at the Daisy Café. When Evelyn breezed over to pour coffee and take his order, he looked around at the multiple vacant seats.

"Did I miss the memo, Evelyn? The place seems empty this morning."

"I guess you did, hon," she said. "Big prayer breakfast up at the hotel. I thought you might've gone there."

"Oh boy, I missed a prayer breakfast? Fifty men lined up at steam tables for soggy toast and scrambled eggs. All the church leaders taking their turn praying into the microphone while your breakfast gets cold and nobody can talk. Hmm. Too bad I didn't know about it. I guess I'll just have to stay here and have you bring my hot breakfast to me in peace."

Evelyn slapped him gently on the shoulder with the laminated menu. "I'll bring breakfast to you anytime. Ann-eee-time!"

Tim had a happy puzzle to work on today, and he wanted to solve it by the time choir practice was over this evening. It was unrelated to the heavier matter of his family tree, and Robert would need to approve it. But the fun part required a random person with specific attributes, and that person had not occurred to him yet. He had few friends and fewer relatives to choose from. It had always been that way, but he hadn't noticed it so much when twelve hours of every day had been devoted to The Job.

His notebook page was still blank when Evelyn brought the bill and cleared away his plate.

"Doin' your homework, hon? Doesn't look like you got much done, there. Something I can help you with? I'm not much of a Shakespeare, but I'm pretty good with numbers."

Though the sky was overcast outside, the breeze of her laughter seemed to blow the clouds away and brighten the small café. She was consistently cheerful. He envied that.

"Not today, Evelyn, thanks. But I'll definitely keep your math skills in mind."

Tim wrote a name on the blank notebook page, then erased it, traced over it, and drew a line through it. *That's enough.* He tucked the notebook in his pocket and went to his white room next door, just in case an Idea or some other distraction was lurking there.

None was.

He drove home, taking the longest route possible without actually going somewhere else. He hoped, in vain, to spare himself the spectacle of seeing all the doors and many windows propped open as Mrs A aired out the house, the furnace blowing heat at the same time.

He didn't think she was even aware that he had come back. She kept the vacuum cleaner running almost constantly unless she was moving the cord from one outlet to another. Its whirring masked any sound he might make.

He brewed half a pot in the twelve-cup, poured it into the thermos, put that in his backpack with a piece of bread and cheese, and left again, this time with the big Bible under his arm. Mrs A had not detected his presence. Burglars could have stolen the Bible.

What if they had? It hadn't moved from that top shelf in a decade, and if someone had stolen it before he looked for it yesterday, he'd never have known.

~

No one had noticed him in the office earlier when he'd wandered through, aimless and empty-handed. This time, the place seemed to light up.

"Hey, Mister Brown, studying up for Easter?"

"You don't see that every day, someone carrying a Bible."

"Doing your Sunday School homework?"

"Gonna preach a sermon?"

All this from simply carrying the large book tucked under his elbow. Tim was surprised at how recognizable the Good Book was, and yet how unusual it seemed to be that he was carrying one around. *Maybe I'll do it more often, just for kicks. Or maybe not.*

~

He wanted to keep his equilibrium today and avoid sliding down any dark paths that might appear without warning. It was Stella's warning about exploring his family history that made him extra wary, more than he would have been on his own.

"You won't like it," she'd said.

Well, putting it off won't change anything. Dates are just facts. Let's have a look.

He pulled at the free end of the red ribbon to return to the *Family Register.*

"Good morning, Ebenezer," he greeted his grandfather. He read his grandmother's name, trying to recall if he'd ever heard it spoken. "Poor thing." That was the only way she'd been referred to, in his memory. *Your grandmother, poor thing.*

He gathered she had suffered from some mental or emotional illness, and had been admitted to a facility for treatment, from which she had never returned. It was her ghost that was rumoured to be visible in the attic windows of the Johnson Mansion, the house Tim had inherited and where he lived.

Bertha. Her name was Bertha. *Maybe what sent her around the bend was that no one had ever called her by name. Maybe that was too much tenderness for Ebenezer.*

Grandfather had spread his largesse all over the church he had built, and publicized it in his newspaper, but he had kept his wife from her dreams. Perhaps she was haunting the attic, still hoping to hear her name spoken.

At least I can say it now when speaking of her, for whatever good that might do.

Then he turned the parchment page.

Under *Births*, two baby girls: Lucia Linda and, not two years later, Stella Clara.

Seeing those names written close together there in what he supposed was his grandmother's—Bertha's—ornate handwriting, he recalled what little he'd heard about her. Bertha fancied herself to be descended from Spanish royalty, and did her best to decorate the house in what she considered Spanish style. Tim hadn't seen any of it, as the family took it all down after she—Bertha—had been taken away. What a shock it must have been to her to live out her final days in some austere ward decorated in institutional green.

They couldn't take away her little girls' names, though: "Beautiful Lucia" and "Bright Star". But even there, she wasn't able to keep her grip entirely. Lucia wholeheartedly embraced her married surname and stuck a nickname on top, forever burying "Lu-chee-ya", or "Lucy", and Johnson, beneath "Brownie" Brown.

Stella had retained her given name, though not likely because of respect for her parents. She wasn't the nickname sort, and nobody seems to have dared to hang one on her.

What might they have called her on the playground, if any of her playmates had been so bold? Shorty?

He laughed out loud. *She'd kill me if I ever called her that.* He'd been called "Beanpole" many times, but that nickname implied some kind of over-achievement, however unwelcome it was to an adolescent. "Shorty" would imply a deficiency in stature that Stella barely overcame by wearing shoes with killer heels, and only after she was an adult.

Tim turned the remaining pages of the Family Register, but they were blank. He peered closely, in case old ink had faded, but there was no evidence that anybody had ever written on the thin paper. The baby girls lived on, forever young in this Record.

This Bible was Johnson territory. Tim knew that Ford and Brownie married immediately after they graduated from high school. That can't have been popular with their parents on either side. Tim had never had the impression that they'd been inseparable sweethearts, judging by the way his mother spoke of him, on the rare occasion that she did. If they'd started out hot, they had cooled rapidly. There was no framed wedding photograph in the house, though who could judge why or why not, after a suicide?

He wondered if there was a Brown Family Bible somewhere. One was expected to be found in all "better" homes, earlier in the century, anyway. The definition of "better homes" had changed a lot from his grandparents' time. Ebenezer and Bertha wouldn't know what to think of these modern times.

I suppose I'll be considered old-fashioned soon, too, if I'm not already.

This hadn't gone badly. Perhaps Stella had exaggerated her warning that he wouldn't like whatever he might find. Did she think he was expecting clear lines of history and civility, and would be devastated if such was not the case? He would turn forty in exactly ten days: he was old enough to handle whatever skeletons were in the closets, in his old house or elsewhere.

But he closed the Bible. Time was up for the day.

Besides, he had something else on his mind. He'd make a nice pre-choir supper, and a tasty snack to go with a good port afterwards, to accompany the crazy idea he wanted to put to Robert.

As he bent down to pick up his backpack, he leaned on the Bible, and noticed a tiny gap in the thousand-page book. More sticking pages, he assumed. He flipped the book open to smooth them out, and there was a little envelope, the size that might have contained personal notes when people wrote them on flowered notepaper.

He picked it up. Nothing was written on it. It was sealed.

He held it up to the light, first at the window, then with the overhead light bulb behind it. There was something inside, possibly one folded sheet of paper. He couldn't see any handwriting through the envelope.

He sat down again.

What to do? Would he, should he open it?

Yesterday you were afraid to read the Family Register. Now you're frightened of a little envelope. What's wrong with you?

He thought about this for a few moments.

"But I did read the Register today, didn't I? I wouldn't say I'm frightened. I'd say I'm, um, being prudent. Aunt Stella said I wouldn't like it, whatever 'it' is. She is a drama queen, but she knows about some things. So, I'm proceeding with caution. I have choir practice tonight, and I want to plan something fun with Robert. This is not the time to go rushing in where angels fear to tread, where bodies may be buried. I'll do it tomorrow."

He replaced the envelope in the Book of Proverbs, where he'd discovered it. He wondered if the placement was deliberate, if there was a subliminal message in the verses on the page. A quick scan showed that there were advice and admonitions enough to cover multiple life situations. He'd read that later, too. Maybe.

~

Robert was down in the dumps when he arrived from the city. He declined Tim's offer of just a little wine to soothe his jangled nerves. He wouldn't break his iron-clad rule about not drinking at all before any choir or organ event. And that made him even more morose. The blazing fire and pre-dinner Earl Grey tea helped, but not a lot.

"I don't want to poke into your professional business, Rob, but really, I do. What's got you so down?"

"I guess I can tell you. You'll find out anyway. The Music Committee has put off funding the section leads until April."

"What? Why?"

"Oh, who knows. It's that Cheryl Yukyuk, wielding her tiny authority again. Over-exercising it if you ask me."

"Cheryl's a tough one, I agree. Passive-aggressive. What's she done?"

"Postponed their meeting. The one at which I was going to get funds approved to pay our section leads. She's convinced the church Board to put it off until April or May, when they will have all the financial statements ready. Even though we know they have the money now, and if they don't, they certainly will after the Easter concert we're putting on. Ticket sales alone will pay for the extra singers for months. And the choir will sing so much better with leads."

"Indeed we will," Tim said.

"Don't you see? She's doing this deliberately to sabotage our Easter concert. Without the extra singers, I don't think we can do it. I was anticipating the budget approval, and I pledged what surplus cash we have to the instrumentalist. We simply *must* have the trumpet in the 'Hallelujah Chorus'!"

Robert usually kept his troubles to himself. He focused on planning and preparation, and did his utmost to make things happen as he envisioned them. If, rarely, some unforeseen obstacle popped up, he wasn't well-equipped to negotiate, and responded emotionally instead.

But a little bell was ting-tingling in Tim's head. A tiny accounting bell. A little bell with A to Zed engraved on it. Hazen Awalt attended Saint John's United Church, and sat on its Official Board. He wasn't the treasurer, but his firm audited the church's annual financial report.

Cheryl Hawryluk's husband, Marty, was the treasurer.

"Rob, I know who tossed the stick in your spokes. It stinks, but it wasn't done to trip you up. I believe it was done as a favour to, ah, someone else, and the choir's consequences were unintended and unforeseen. Also not thought out."

"Really? How do you know?"

"Do you have to ask? This is a small town. Everybody knows everybody. Everyone's hand is in someone else's pocket, whether they know it or not. You're an outsider, so they'll take you in or leave you out, according to the situation. But I can see the thread in your story and the hand that's pulling it. I think I can make it right with one phone call, and I won't even have to raise my voice. Will you let me try that?"

"*Let* you? Sure. When?"

"Give me a day or two. What's today, Thursday? I'll do my best tomorrow. Monday at the latest."

"Will there be trouble? God, I dislike that woman. 'You aren't authorized to do that, blah blah blah.'"

"Easy, pardner. I agree one hundred percent, but you want this to go your way, so we must suck it up, buttercup. Cheryl can be *almost* nice when she thinks she's done something herself, even though everyone around her must pave the way."

"Better you than me. Thanks so much, Tim. Her phone message knocked me back."

"Never fear, Tim is here. I think we can win, and Cheryl won't know she's lost, nor to whom. Now sit, eat, settle yourself. Your celestial choir awaits."

Practice went well. Robert was back to equilibrium, ready to tip over to happy if only the choir would give him what he asked them to do. Tonight, they really tried, and that was enough. It was a volunteer choir, after all. Morale rarely improved by increasing the whippings.

After choir, they relaxed in the den, enjoying the snacks Tim had prepared. True to form, Robert had moved on from the budget issue. Tim's promise to look into it was as good as resolving it.

"By the way, Rob, I have something to share with you."

Tim went to the corkboard in the kitchen and retrieved the list he'd made on Monday morning. "Here, have a look at this."

A GREAT WEEKEND:

> Movie out
> Impromptu
> Fresh topics
> Walking & talking
> Dopamine?
> Great food
> Church

"Interesting list, Tim. I thought about the weekend, too. I love everything we do, don't get me wrong. The routine is comforting. I know, when I get on the highway to come here, exactly what I'm heading toward, and I like it all. Love it all."

He pointed at the list. "I didn't want to go out to the movie, but it was really interesting. Doing that was impromptu, and that's good, as long as there's not too much of it. 'Fresh topics' means that we discussed the movie, I guess? Instead of things like Cheryl Yuckity-yuk?"

"Easy now."

"Sorry. And I liked going for a little walk. We can do more of that, now that winter is finally leaving us. What else did you list? Dopamine?"

"I have an appointment with Doctor Muhammed on Monday to ask him about it. I think activity makes me feel better. I've been for several walks this week. I like it."

"Good. Now what's this about great food? That's not unusual, is it?"

"No, aren't we lucky? We always manage to make a great Sunday dinner, especially, though I do say that my calzones were *molto bene*, ha-ha."

"No argument here. Will you make them again? Pretty please?"

"I will grant your plea. Some day."

"Great! You end the list with church. Really? Church is part of a great weekend? I'd love a weekend without it."

"I meant choir. Church is where we sing, and I don't mind it. Though I hope we don't have to be dragged through that "Forty days and forty niiiights" again. Ever."

"You're just complaining because you had to sing a *d* with the altos a few times. It's good for you."

"Nope. The altos hated it, too. It's a dirge, and not in a good way. Anyway, it was good to take note of those good things."

Tim opened the bag from the video store. "So here's what I had in mind for our entertainment this weekend. Have you seen it?"

He handed Robert the DVD of the *Julius Caesar* movie.

"Can't say that I have. Must I?"

"Yes, you must. Here's what I was thinking. It has all these famous actors in it whom we may know, starting with Charlton Heston, hubba hubba."

"Really?"

"No. Too full of himself, and wooden as a stick, as I recall. But the robes and leather skirts would be fun. Now, I propose that we use ol' Julius as the entertainment for Sunday dinner, with food during breaks, like we did with the madrigals and such last month. Are you with me so far?"

"I may be. Are you thinking of inviting guests?"

"Yes, but the hitch is that our only television and player are in this very den, where it's nice and cosy for watching, and I don't really want to drag it all to the dining room. So, instead of multiple guests around the dinner table, I suggest we squeeze in just one guest, someone who has a sense of humour and won't be offended if we poke fun at the great man."

"Heston?"

"I meant Caesar, or Shakespeare, but whoever. We want someone who can laugh."

"It sounds risky. Do you have someone in mind? I know you do. Who is it?"

Tim shook his head.

"I can't believe I'm saying this, but my only nominee is Evelyn, the waitress at the Daisy Café."

"Have I met her?"

"Unlikely. I don't think you've ever been in the Daisy, but I've been eating breakfast or lunch there forever. I go there every Thursday morning to get away from Mrs A. Evelyn and I were in school together. If our stars had aligned differently, we might have been an item. But they didn't and we aren't. She is an incorrigible flirt, and she brightens my day. She's been slinging eggs and sausages and bad coffee for decades, and I confess I've never thought of her as anything other than the waitress I look forward to seeing each week. But she's a nice person, and I'd like to give her a chance —no, to give *me* a chance to get to know her better. I think she'd fit right in. I like her."

"Then fit her in, Timo. There's always a risk when you invite someone new into your den, but I'm sure we won't offend her. We invited Helen and Elaine last month, and that worked out really well. It's just a meal."

"Speaking of which..."

"Sure, I'll plan it. Are there any meals in the movie?"

"Gosh, I don't know. A bun fight, maybe?"

"Never mind. I do know that the Romans reclined to eat, and used their fingers. Sitting up straight and eating our dinner with weapons is a late development. Olive oil, meat and fish, cheese, bread, whatever, I'll figure something out. We're not going for historical accuracy, I hope?"

"No, we're not. Not if Heston is on the screen. We're going for fun. Hey—let's wear costumes! I'll tell Evelyn the answer to the what-to-wear question is a toga—or a robe for the lady, wouldn't it be? That'll set the mood—which might bomb, but I don't think so."

"You can be in charge of costumes. I'll check with an English classics prof. He should have some ideas."

"English classics? Not Italian?"

"It's a Shakespeare play, isn't it? Everyone's idea of authentic historical speech is to do it with a British accent. Not Italian. I bet Heston won't say, 'Friens-a, lenn-a me you ears-a.' I'll pick up the food on my way here Saturday afternoon, or phone you to get stuff at the local stores. Okay?"

"Okay! Thanks, Rob, this'll be a hoot! I can feel the dopamine already!"

March 12: Portals

Friday

Tim's confidence in Sunday's Shakespeare shenanigans was shaky. Misjudging someone's sense of humour could backfire, and he didn't want to jeopardize the status quo with Evelyn. He liked seeing her at the Daisy. If his invitation turned out to be a disaster, he might have to switch to another diner and that was unthinkable. He'd mull it over.

But today was New Door Day! The store had promised the installer would arrive at eight o'clock to remove the old and install the new and better aluminum storm door. This wasn't just some fragile wood frame with bug screening, though some versions of that style did have curb appeal. The current door had lost its curb appeal when it had received a big dent in the flimsy lower panel.

The installer arrived at five minutes to eight, and got right to work. Removing the door wasn't as easy as Tim had imagined. The frame was screwed and cemented to the opening. Tim didn't stay to watch him—it was chilly with the doors wide open for the second morning in a row—but he heard the struggle.

The man called out, "You're not planning to use this old door for anything, are ya?"

"No, I'm not, but you're going to take it back to the shop, right? One of the guys there wants it for his hunting cabin, I think? Donnie? Donnie somebody."

"Oh, okay. He's got access to parts there if he needs 'em, then. Can't help bending this part. She's glued down solid."

Tim took refuge in the den and closed the door. Donnie would get the old door, or what was left of it, for free, and he wasn't going to get into a quality debate about it.

He turned his attention to Robert's quandary with the Music Committee's meeting, postponed until after Easter. Poor Robert, aiming high. All he wanted was a little support. Or a lot, sometimes, but he always gave more than he asked for.

Tim was certain that he could persuade the tight cast of characters looking after the church's treasury to loosen the purse-strings so Robert could hire the section leads. Easter was supposed to be filled with rejoicing, and this would guarantee a joyful noise.

He sat with his fingers steepled, as Sherlock Holmes did in the book's illustrations, tapping the tips together as he rehearsed what he would do. He would need to be strong but fair, and each person who played a part must feel as though they had done the most good. It if were up to him, he would simply approve the request, and chastise the others for using church positions as their own little fiefdoms. But it was not up to him and that would not work.

He finished making a list of the arguments he would present, and went out to the kitchen to get the phone. He detoured to the foyer to check on the job. The old storm door was lying partly on the brown lawn, partly on a burlap-wrapped rhododendron. The installer and his truck were gone.

Tim peered through the small windows in the main door. Across the street, a lineup of vehicles inched around the drive-thru lane of the donut shop. The installer's truck was there.

"Good for you, buddy," he said, steaming up the glass in the door. Tim had fuelled his workdays with rivers of coffee and mountains of sugar donuts, but he had never idled in a lineup while the pay-clock was ticking. Maybe he would, in future. It seemed sort of independent.

He phoned the office of Awalt & Zinck Accounting. Margaret put him through.

"Good morning, Tim. Hazen here. Good to hear from you again."

"Hazen. I might have been a little less, um, understanding of your situation than I could've been the other day. I was quite concerned, really. As you know, I'm relying on people like yourself to look after my affairs while I'm taking my sabbatical, and I felt like I was being overlooked a bit, maybe, right?"

"Tim, you know Awalt and Zinck would never let our clients down. Your account—*The Times*—is one of our largest and oldest accounts, and—"

"Those were my exact thoughts too, Hazen. But then it came to my attention that you are making a similar request of other clients, such as our church, and I know you wouldn't risk that account too if you really, absolutely, didn't need to. You wouldn't want to bring on a new account if it meant that you'd lose two old, very loyal ones. Not only would that cost you, but there'd be talk, and you and I both know what harm can be done by gossip."

He could hear Hazen breathing deeply at his end of the line.

"So, the way I see it, Hazen, you're trying to cope with a staffing crunch, maybe just a short-term one, but it occurs at a time when everyone's looking to A to Zed for everything from aye to zee, ha-ha. We all need the services you provide, above and beyond what we pay our bookkeepers to prepare the accounts for you to review."

Hazen was trying valiantly to cut in, but Tim gave him no space.

"So, we all want you to succeed. A rising tide lifts all boats, as my grandfather Ebenezer used to say."

Tim had no idea what his grandfather might have said about this, but Ebenezer wasn't able to intervene on his own behalf just now.

"And we all know the damage a too-low tide can do, too, right? Anyway, here's what I'm suggesting you do, as your friend. I don't know what you call it in accounting-speak, but can you produce a projection for me, comparing year-to-date with previous years, adjusting for known changes, calendarizing how things should look if trends continue, that sort of thing? Just for my eyes only? I'm not asking you to predict the future. We couldn't hold you to that, but you can show trends, surely. Maybe you have a computer program that can do that at the touch of a button. It would be unofficial, of course. You can bring it up to date for our meeting with the other trustees, on May seventh if that works for you. I'll just tell the other trustees that I requested the date change for personal reasons. I don't want to stand in your way, Hazen, and if I didn't say it the other day, I do now: congratulations on snagging a big one!"

Hazen found his voice. "Tim, I—I think we can do as you request. An unofficial projection would give you what you want to see, until May seventh? Here, let me write down that date. Can you ask your bookkeeper to get January and February figures over to me right away? I really appreciate this, Tim."

"Oh, no problem, Hazen, glad to help."

Tim paused long enough that it seemed he was done. "Oh, by the way, Hazen, about the church account."

He thought he could hear a quiet moan from the accountant, but perhaps he was just saying "Hmm?"

"The choir has been very frugal in our expenditures in the last year, borrowing music in lieu of purchases where possible, things like that. We have long planned to engage four strong choristers who could carry each section during absences or when we find a piece especially challenging. Ha-ha, I often do, and I'm very often the only tenor, also. But I'm no lead singer. Anyway, we've had many conversations about this. We were expecting the funds to be released soon, perhaps a little in advance of the official financial report, but especially in time for Easter. Again, the funds are there. So, I was wondering if you could see any solution to our dilemma?"

"I'd like to help, Tim, but I'm not the treasurer. That would be too close for comfort, you know. Unethical."

"Goodness, we wouldn't ask anything unethical. You know Cheryl Hawryluk, right?"

"Yes. I know Cheryl."

"Cheryl has decided she must put *all* new expenditures on hold until after the whole process is approved, which has now been delayed because of *your* current situation, I believe, your new opportunity. Even though it was approved in principle several times. So, I was wondering if you could intervene."

"I don't see how."

"I do. Cheryl approaches everything she does as though she's doing a personal favour for someone, not as her duty as a trustee. So here's what you do: you call her and admit you're squeezed. Say it's because your firm was asked to 'help out' another company, not because you bit off a business so big that we all have to help you chew. She'll like the helping out story. Then ask her if she could do you a big personal favour by letting some pre-approved items go through now because you'd feel badly if they're held up. Tell her that you will personally guarantee them, but she'll get all the credit. Furthermore, I'll guarantee that the choir director will thank her publicly at the Easter Sunday concert, for her moment of glory. Whaddya say, Hazen? Can you do this for me?"

"It's quite unusual, Tim."

"Mm-hmm."

"Cheryl's husband is the church treasurer."

"Yes, I know. Let her deal with him. If you go to Marty first she'll never agree. She wants to be special, so let her be. She'll tell him that you said it was okay. We just need the go-ahead."

Hazen let out a long sigh.

"You drive a hard bargain, Tim."

"Mm-hmm."

"All right, I'll do it."

"Thank you, Hazen. The choir and our director will be most grateful to you, as am I for your continued careful oversight of my own business. By the way, I'll reserve two tickets for the Easter Sunday concert for you."

"Oh, that's very kind of you but you don't have to do that, Tim."

"It's no problem, Hazen. You can pay for them at the door. I look forward to seeing you and Mrs Awalt in the audience."

He hung up. It was Tim's turn to let out a deep breath. He'd done it! He'd crossed the threshold from pushover client who always did what was always done, and he'd finessed both situations with some brilliant *quid pro quo* negotiating—with no bloodshed. Sure, he'd had to give up a little of what he wanted, but he hoped it wouldn't matter in the long run. And since A to Zed hadn't offered to compensate him for his inconvenience—or risk—he was free to leverage something that mattered a lot to Robert, and to him by extension.

This was a red-letter day. When he returned to work next year, he hoped he'd take this kind of negotiating skill back with him.

He heard a squeaking noise at the front door, and went to investigate. The installer was cleaning the windows of the new storm door. The old door was on the truck, the wrapped rhodo none the worse for having propped it up temporarily.

"All done, sir. If you'd just sign here, I'll be on my way. Oh, and here's the keys."

"It has keys?"

"Sure. This is a nice door you got. Here, I'll show you. This window pulls down, see, not up like your old one did. And it pulls the screen down as it comes. So if you want the window open to let in a little fresh air, you can open it a couple notches at the top, and lock the door in case you're out in the back yard or gone for a coffee. And the screen won't etch the glass. It's a first-class door. In doors, you do get what you pay for."

Tim waved the man on his way, then glanced at his watch. Almost noon. Perfect timing to tackle the next item on today's action list. So far, so very good.

The lunch crowd hadn't arrived yet at the Daisy Café, and the little round table in the front window was still available. The last time he sat there, he'd faced the front entrance to his own office building. This time, he thought he'd look downriver, to see something new or nothing at all, he didn't mind.

Evelyn came to his table. Was she ever not at work? "Is your clock broke, Tim? Breakfast's over now."

"Hi, Evelyn. No, I know. It's not my regular day to be here, either, but I fancied a bowl of soup for lunch. Got some?"

"Comin' right up, hon. Crackers or biscuit?"

"Crackers, please. And tea, black, no sugar."

"I know that part."

He enjoyed the chunky soup and the people-watching. The soup was filling. He'd take a short walk to settle it down, and to calm his nerves as his next encounter approached.

He paid the bill and asked Evelyn, "I was wondering, could you give me a couple minutes when the lunch crowd disperses? I'm going for a walk now. How about I come back in half an hour?"

"You want to talk to me? Am I in trouble?"

"You know you're not."

"What about, then?"

"I'll tell you when I come back."

Evelyn glanced at the big clock above the kitchen's service window. "Give me an hour, Tim, if you can. A full booth just put in their order and I'll need to look after them. By that time, I'll be happy to sit down and have a cuppa with you."

"Only if you let me buy."

~

Should he? Should he not? Tim dithered about inviting Evelyn to his Caesar party with every step. He was on Main Street, and every route was uphill from there. He wasn't in the mood to challenge hills just now, with a bowl of soup literally under his belt. Instead, he walked across the "old bridge" and crossed back again at the "new bridge". Still plenty of time, so he walked the loop again.

As he walked, the topic changed from whether he really wanted to be friends with Evelyn—he did—to why he didn't have any friends to speak of.

Have I set the bar too high? What do I want friends for, anyway?

The answer to the second question came right away. *Because I'm bored with just me.*

Was that it? Bored? Perhaps it was deeper than just wanting to be entertained. Perhaps a fellow wanted companionship, light company.

That could be a slippery slope. He had Robert, and would do nothing to interfere with their relationship. He often wished for more time together. What if they were together every day? In his heart of hearts, Tim didn't think that would work well. They were like oil and water—no, more like oil and vinegar, very nice together in the right proportion.

Still fifteen minutes before it was time to see Evelyn. Tim entered *The Times* building and went up to his room, thinking he might as well take the old Bible home in case Stella called to discuss the question he had posed to her.

No. What good would the Bible do? Stella wouldn't be talking about Ebenezer and Bertha, he was sure of that, and there wasn't any time to do it this weekend anyway. If she called, he could ask her about the envelope, still tucked between the gilt-edged pages, though he thought it was preferable to show it to her rather than describe it over the phone.

Her reaction to seeing it might be a clue to something. He was willing to bet she knew something about it. Or what was in it.

If it contained dirt on her, though, wouldn't she have destroyed it long ago? Yes, but only if she knew about it. She was unlikely to come across it while reading the Bible.

He left the room empty-handed.

When he entered the Daisy, a family of six was just pulling on their coats. Mom, dad, two children, two grandparents. *Such a lovely cliché. My family could share a restaurant table with another family and still leave seats to spare.*

Evelyn waved to Tim and indicated a booth. "Take the side facing the back, please, Tim, so I can keep an eye on the house. We're open 'til three, but it's just the tea and pie crowd now."

She brought tea and pie for them and slid into the booth. "Not often I get to sit in my own joint, and with my favourite customer, too. This is a real treat."

"I bet you say that to all the guys," Tim said, instantly regretting it.

"I guess I do, but I don't mean it," she replied, looking directly at him. "I know I tease you a lot, Tim, but it's just my way of telling you that I see you and I like you. I wish we—I wish there was a way we could be better friends. I think we'd have fun."

Boom! There it was, his pitch, already made for him. He noticed that Evelyn looked different sitting across the table from him: more sensible, more lovely, frankly. She had lowered her waitress persona and was just herself sitting there, stirring sugar into her tea, spooning the whipped cream aside from the top of her pie.

"So, what'd you want to see me about, Tim?" She looked tired, too. The Daisy opened at seven every morning, six days a week, and she was on deck from when the door was unlocked until it closed again at three. *How did she do it?*

"Evelyn, this may sound weird, but you just said what I came to say. That I like you and I—I want us to be friends. You know what I mean by friends—"

She reached across and laid her hand on Tim's arm. "Honey, I knew that before you did. It's all good. I don't need a lover, thank you very much. I may, again, one day a long time from now, but not now. But we're not talking lovers. We're talking friends, right?"

Evelyn's voice sounded different, too. She was speaking in a conversational tone, not the stage-voice she used when she was on her feet, making every booth and table in the place feel as though she was there just for them.

"Right. I've never really had close friends, you know. I know lots of nice people, in church and employees at the paper, but both of those situations come with baggage. And at the end of a work week, I didn't want more to do with people. I wanted to crawl under the covers and not talk at all."

"I hear ya, Tim. Me, too."

"And, as you know, I've taken this year off, lucky me, to see if I can, uh, do things differently. Or better, at least. So I have more free time these days, and I'm noticing that I do miss spending time with people." He leaned in. "Just not certain people, sorry."

Evelyn erupted in the wild laughter she was famous for. "Oh, Tim, we are so much alike." She reduced her volume again, but her smile remained. "So, what should we do? I'm not an intellectual to your standard, I'm sure, but I can be good company. Go for a drive, maybe? My old car isn't much. What do you drive?"

"Mine's nothing much, either. Gar Greene is urging me to buy a new truck that would cost more than some homes around here, but I don't see the point. Anyway, yes, a drive sounds wonderful. But first, I do have a suggestion, and I hope it's something you're game for. You mentioned Shakespeare earlier. Well, here's the link."

Tim explained the theatrical movie idea, with wine and food. And optional togas. Evelyn's eyes opened wider with each detail.

"Tim, I have literally no idea what you're talking about. I've never been to such a party, but I'm game to give it a go. I'd like to meet Robert, too. I've only seen him in church, the one time I went. What can I bring? Nothing from here."

"Oh, I dunno, how about some grapes? Not many, they're so expensive this time of year. Yeah, some grapes and something to dip them in. We'll have lots to eat. Robert's in charge of the menu."

Tim polished off his pie in seconds. They stood, hugged, and parted, both happy.

~

As he sniffed the cork from a fresh bottle of *Vendredi rouge,* Tim thought something fundamental had shifted today. The new door looked very nice as he pulled in the driveway. He had resolved a complex tangle of business that could have made a lot of people unhappy. Best of all, he'd found a new friend, standing in the well-worn shoes of an old friend.

Whatever Stella would bring to his family history, he felt strengthened for the challenge. He might not like what he learned, but Melanie had said he was fearless, and tonight he was beginning to believe her.

Robert phoned late in the evening, exultant that he had received the go-ahead directly from Cheryl. He'd be a bit late arriving tomorrow as he wanted to deliver music to the new singers first.

Also, he would bring all the bits for Sunday's Roman feast if Tim would get fresh shellfish.

March 13: Narrowing

Saturday

Tim again practised the new insignia for Robert's latté foam, and impressed himself with how well it came out. He'd serve it tomorrow or Monday, whenever his only customer requested that frothy drink.

He didn't have a lot to occupy himself with today, since Robert was bringing Sunday dinner ingredients. Tonight would be Italian —not Roman—but this week it would be delivered.

He phoned the bookstore in Lunenburg to confirm that his Sherlock book was finally in, and then the seafood shop to reserve something fresh from the cold Atlantic.

In Lunenburg, Tim parked on the historic waterfront. Ships were tied up at the wharves, still wearing their winter coverings. A cold wind blew across the harbour and brought tears to his eyes, but he was here to walk and that meant runny eyes and nose anyway.

He made a great loop, which included the inevitable steep streets of the town, and when he returned to the car, he was carrying a hardcover copy of *The Adventures of Sherlock Holmes*, and fresh oysters and mussels. He was puffing just a little, but very happy that he had taken the opportunity to exercise on the empty sidewalks.

Tim had passed a coffee-shop on the route, but didn't want to go in with the shellfish. It was just a few degrees above freezing outside, no warmer than his fridge would be, so he put the oysters in the trunk and drove back uphill to the café for a large cappuccino and a ferociously delicious sticky bun. He brought Sherlock to the tiny table, but the new hardcover book didn't flop open easily the way his family Bible did. Different binding methods, of course.

So he took out his notebook and entitled a list *What's in That Envelope?*

A piece of paper.

That's all he could say for sure. *But why would anyone put a blank piece of notepaper in an envelope, seal it, and preserve it—or hide it —in the Bible?*

They wouldn't. They would write something on it.

Perhaps it contained the latitude and longitude coordinates to where the family fortune was located. *If that's the case, it should lead to The Times building.* The fortune for at least three generations of his family had been produced there. He didn't expect there was more.

Maybe it was a confession, ridiculous as that seemed, but this wasn't the time to eliminate the ridiculous. If he was delving, as he defined it, then all things must be considered.

All right, then, what would the confession be about, and from whom? He wasn't aware of any crime that his forebears might have suffered or committed, other than doing business the way it used to be done.

What about a suicide note from my father?

As soon as he thought it—and added it to the list, faithfully—he discarded the notion. He couldn't recall seeing a sample of his father's handwriting, but that little envelope didn't come from a man, in his opinion. If it had, what was there room to write on the little paper inside? "Brownie made me do it" or "Goodbye, cruel world"? *No.* Ford had already said, "I'm sorry, Timmy."

His grandmother, Bertha, was the only person who had made entries in the Bible, so maybe the envelope was hers. That'd be interesting. Tim knew she hadn't been well, so if this was a note about her suffering it wouldn't be new news, just details. He would read it, out of respect, if so.

The thing was, it was there for a reason, that seemed certain. Someone had folded a note and sealed it in the envelope to keep it, not to discard it in the trash.

If the person meant to hide the envelope, from whom were they hiding it?

Was there someone who should *not* learn what was in the envelope?

Stella and Brownie had been children in what was now Tim's house, but Stella had run away to a convent as soon as she graduated from school, which struck at her father's pride. Ebenezer had disowned her. Maybe that was why she reacted badly to Tim's interest in exploring family matters. It must have been a tumultuous time in the Johnson home.

The note wouldn't be about that. It wasn't "I hate Father."

Grandmother Bertha was likely in the asylum by then, and Grandfather Ebenezer was unlikely to write a note of contrition about it and leave it in the Bible for some future Johnson to discover. His will was the place for that, and his message had been clear: all for Lucia Linda, nothing for Stella Clara.

Tim drummed his fingers on the cover of the Sherlock Holmes anthology. What would Sherlock do with this challenge? Would he hold it up to the candle-flame? Tim had done that, substituting window-light and an electric light bulb. Would the great detective know the source of the paper, perhaps some shop on the banks of the Thames? Quite likely. Tim couldn't match him there, but there was no monogram on the envelope nor shadow of a pansy on the paper inside, so he was confident that there weren't any such clues to overlook.

He wrote the names of the people most likely to have any direct or indirect involvement with the envelope: *Ebenezer, Bertha, Stella, Mother, Timothy*.

Then he made his first decision to narrow the choices: ~~*Ebenezer, Bertha, Stella*~~.

Dollars to donuts, Brownie had hidden the envelope in the Bible. This would have been back when she was capable of getting up on a stepladder to reach it, so that'd be twenty years ago or more.

Brownie'd be confident that Stella would never flip through that or any Bible. Her convent days were far behind her, and she didn't appear to acknowledge any faith or creed except when it suited her earthly ambitions. So Brownie hadn't hidden the envelope *from* or *for* Stella.

Tim's cup was empty. He knew the busy little café needed his table, so he gathered up his things and left, convinced that Brownie had left the envelope for her son.

~

Robert arrived late and happy after giving his new singers their scores for a quick review before tomorrow morning. He was floating several inches off the ground. Tim crossed his mental fingers that nothing would burst this balloon before the Easter Sunday concert.

They ate their loaded pizza in the kitchen so that Robert could infuse and marinate the odd assortment of food he had assembled to accompany tomorrow's movie. Several times he asked Tim, "Does she like artichokes?" or "Is she okay eating raw oysters, d'you think?"

Tim's response each time was the same.

"Beats me. You do you, and Evelyn will like it or eat cheese. She's easy."

He knew so little about Evelyn. He'd known her for years, had seen her happy and sad, as she had seen him, and he knew they had a kind of comrades-in-arms trust in each other. Everything else, like things Robert was asking about now, were just details. They'd learn as they went along.

Tim knew Evelyn would be wondering the same about them and this hokey movie-dinner idea. But she'd love Robert. They'd be fine.

March 14: Caesar

Sunday

Robert was delighted at the stylish heart Tim had drawn in the steamed milk. "Simple, yet effective. Message received. Thanks, Timo."

The choir room was the scene of happy confusion as choristers made accommodations and found gowns for the new singers. They all filed into the choir loft when Robert pushed the buzzer, and sang hymns and the anthem with conviction for the appreciative congregation.

Tim saw Cheryl Hawryluk in her regular pew. She was beaming. Hazen would have called her and begged her indulgence, so she would believe these new voices were there by her power. Her husband, Marty, was expressionless. Who knew what the dynamics were between them? Cheryl had been given an opportunity to win, and she had evidently run with it. Tim wasn't going to ask. He liked being the Invisible Hand in this matter.

~

The scene at home after church was less sublime, as Tim and Robert prepared for their afternoon's entertainment. It still felt risky to Tim, but what the heck?

Sometimes you just need to go with your heart.

"I was just thinking, Rob."

They were taking a break after shifting the recliner chairs in the den to make space for a big armchair they had moved in from the parlour.

"About redecorating, or new furniture?"

"No, definitely neither. I was just thinking that it's easier to entertain people for serious reasons. Even when we had Helen and Elaine here to sing canons and rounds, we didn't question if they'd enjoy it. But humour is a different animal altogether, isn't it? That saying is backwards, you know, 'Laugh, and the world laughs with you'. It should be 'Cry, and the world cries with you; laugh, and you might offend someone.'"

"You might have a point there. Let's sit and cry together for a bit. That armchair is a beast. Whew!"

Tim brought out spare bed sheets—one floral, one striped—for their togas. He rummaged in a closet and found some plastic vines of ivy which they fashioned into laurels for their heads. He had extras in case Evelyn decided not to bring her own costume.

Evelyn was punctual. She hugged Tim as soon as she entered the foyer. That was a first, and it felt right.

"Welcome, Evelyn. Here, let me take your coat."

She handed her coat to Tim, revealing a gold lamé gown, with a plunging neckline and a tasselled gold rope tied at her waist. As she bent over to pull off her boots and slip on gold sandals, she said, "I was hoping the cops wouldn't stop me on the way. I would've had to say I'd dressed up early for Hallowe'en. How do I look?"

She stood in a golden glow. Robert came from the kitchen at this moment, and was—for a moment—speechless.

"Robert, this is my friend Evelyn Whynot. Evelyn, this is my partner, Robert Kirk."

Robert found his voice. He reached out and took Evelyn's hand, bowed deeply, and said, "Welcome, my lady. Thou dost honour us with thy radiant presence this day."

Then he straightened up—a head shorter than Evelyn—and exclaimed, "Wow!"

"I understand 'wow'. I don't speaketh that other language so much. Nice to meeteth you, Robert."

"The feeling is mutual, Evelyn, and the wow wasn't just for the gown. Come in, come in! Timothy, attend thee to thine guest. Hast thou lighted the torches? Sit ye in their warmth whilst I fetch a flagon of wine!"

"I heard 'wine'," Evelyn laughed.

Tim showed her to the parlour, where the fire was indeed blazing. He and Robert quickly wrapped themselves in the sheets and tied them at their shoulders. When they each had a glass of wine, Robert raised his glass.

"Friend! Romans! Beautiful country-woman! Lend me your ears. Let's drink, dammit!"

They laughed, raised their glasses, and sipped.

"This is a new taste, Rob," Tim said. "What is it?"

"Mead. Fermented honey, sort of." He made a face. "Too sweet for my taste. How about you, Evelyn?"

"Listen, I'm just a passenger on this bus. It's all new, and I'm having a blast already. I do have a bit of a sweet tooth, so this tastes good to me."

Robert presented a plate of dates stuffed with cream cheese and nuts. "These will go nicely with mead. We'll sugar up to start and go downhill from here."

Downhill they went, sliding into puns, jokes, and small talk as Robert began to learn about this new person with whom he appeared to be quite fascinated. Everything they did or said, every odd bit of food and wine served, brought out laughter, sometimes because it worked, sometimes because it didn't. But the mood was set. Fun was the name of the game, and each played with skill.

Then Tim announced that it was showtime, and invited them to move to the "theatre", which was the little den, stuffed with large, cosy chairs.

"Holy, this is nice," Evelyn said. "I might as well stop saying that, but your house is so big, Tim, it's wonderful to have so many different rooms. And two fireplaces!"

"One is real, and this one, not so much. But thanks, I get by, ha-ha. Here's a shawl in case your gold lamé is a little skimpy for your, uh, shoulders."

"Thanks, Tim. These aren't my shoulders, by the way. I know you know that much."

Robert collapsed into his chair, paralyzed with laughter. "Oh, honey, I need to take you back to the city with me."

"Careful with that 'honey', Rob. Evelyn has formidable skills. I'm not sure you can beat her at the teasing game!"

Tim pushed 'play' and the film began. It was supposed to be an authentic portrayal of the Shakespearean play, *Julius Caesar*, and perhaps the script was, but the actors were as inauthentic as could be, with the possible exception of John Gielgud. All who were not born in Britain wandered in and out of their British accents. Everyone spoke of "Cees-ah". It seemed like the cast of *The Godfather* were trying on Shakespearean costumes.

The first ten minutes were rowdy, and that was just the viewers in the den. They mocked the speech, compared togas and gowns, and Tim was busy with the remote, pausing, rewinding, and resuming. He set the remote on a small table in front of Evelyn between times.

Around ten minutes in, all three spectators dove for the remote amid shrieks of laughter: Charlton Heston and other male figures had appeared, inexplicably naked except for large g-strings, and seeming very uncomfortable.

They tussled over the remote until Evelyn gained possession of it. She hit the Pause, Rewind, and Play buttons, until the questionable scene appeared on screen again.

"Pause! Pause! Pause!"

They stared, and agreed: this was puzzling and gross.

"Good God," Robert said. "Some things, once seen, cannot be unseen. If this keeps up we'll all need therapy."

"That right there is the picture of my love-life," Evelyn said. "I fall for the hunk, but then I ask 'Why-hy-hy?'"

"They are very well-oiled, though," Tim said. "Perhaps they've just been out back playing gladiator?"

"No, it's so they can get away easily, like greased pigs," Evelyn said. "But that's just my experience. This is fun! Let's move on!"

She pushed Play again, and soon they were hearing the shivery voice warning Caesar to 'bewah the Ides of March".

"That's tomorrow, by the way," Tim said.

"What is?"

"The Ides of March. The fifteenth."

"What's it mean?"

"It's mid-month, the day when debts were to be paid. Every month had an ides. But in this particular March, Caesar was going to have to pay more than money on the fifteenth, big-time."

"You're some smart, Tim. I always knew that."

"Smart enough to look it up in one of these big, musty books. But nice of you to say."

"Hey—pause!" Robert got up from his chair. "They're drinking wine. Anyone here need a top-up?"

They enjoyed Robert's food and beverage pairings, talking over the movie, sometimes pausing it. They agreed that it was an awful production, and that Caesar might have died from boredom if they hadn't seen him stabbed multiple times before he carefully laid himself down on a ledge to die.

By unanimous agreement, they fast-forwarded through some scenes, though they all sat up when a shimmering apparition appeared on horseback, and for reasons unknown to them, shared an oily massage with Charlton Heston.

"Ooo, Richard Chamberlain," Robert said. "What do you suppose his role is?"

"Exactly what you see there," Tim said. "To keep you in the theatre until the end. Eye candy."

"It's working, but only just. Let it finish with the sound off. Their silly talking irks me. They wouldn't know iambic pentameter if they tripped over it."

The food and company were far more interesting than the movie, and they agreed that Shakespeare should sue for the travesty. But still, they had fun.

Evelyn had switched to sparkling water, and accepted a decaf coffee to go with the small cakes Robert had brought from a bakery in the city. "These aren't authentically Roman," he said, "but neither was that movie."

"I really was looking for an actual theatre production," Tim said, "but this is South River. Anyway, I think we did okay, don't you? Robert's roasted artichokes were delicious, and we were favoured with Queen Evelyn's company. How good is that?"

"Queen Evelyn of South River." Robert bowed low.

"Stop it now. I'm just that Dame Evelyn of Whynott. I must leaveth now because Monday morning comes early at the Daisy Café. Guys, thank you so much for inviting me to share this, um, spectacle. I had a blast. I'm really happy to get to know you better, Tim, and to meet you, Robert. I hope we'll do it again, and I hope we won't need to wear bed-sheets, or this silly thing." She swished the skirts of her gown.

"Oh, are you sure? You can wear it anytime. They're gorgeous—I mean the *gown* is gorgeous!"

"C'mere, honey." Evelyn pulled Robert to her bosom. "There. That's all you get. They're on display only because there's no way I can hide 'em."

She and Tim hugged, more chastely but also with feeling.

"More, please," she said to Tim.

"You betcha," he replied. "Drive carefully."

The men cleared away the debris of their faux Roman feast, still with their togas tied to their shoulders. It was not quite bedtime, so after they dragged the armchair back to the parlour, they sat in the den to decompress.

"You liked her," Tim said.

"I love Evelyn! Where have you been hiding her? She is so genuine. And she is beautiful. A different hairdo and she'd be a knockout. I wonder what kind of clothes she wears. Not that dress, I guess?"

"Ha ha, no. She wears a waitress uniform, but it looks pretty much the same as that gown with those—you know—in it."

"I bet she gets a lot of tips, then. How did you two meet, again?"

"We were in school together. She never left South River, that I can recall anyway. Our workplaces are side by side. I've been her customer for twenty-five years. She's a big flirt, but as she told me, she knew before I did that I'd never be her boyfriend."

"I just love her," Robert said. "I meet lots of women who are smart and/or beautiful. None of them has anything over Evelyn. She's the genuine article. I hope she'll be back again."

"I hope you'll both cometh back again," Tim said with a laugh. "I promise not to pick a schlock movie next time."

March 15: Ides

Monday

The weekend had absorbed Tim's attention. Far better than feeling directionless. He added to the list from last weekend:

A GREAT WEEKEND:

Movie out	*Movie in*
Impromptu	*Not as planned*
Fresh topics	*Certainly were*
Walking & talking	*Talking*
Dopamine?	*Evelyn?*
Great food	*Ditto*
Church	*Choir*

All in all, the weekend had been great.

Now it was time for more serious pursuits. He had left his queries with GB and Stella last week, and neither had turned up anything for him yet. He'd visit the office this morning to make it easy for GB, and he needed to poke Stella. A poked Stella was not a pleasant creature, but he didn't want to sit on his hands waiting, either. He wanted to hear something about his father.

He knew, from recent experience, that sometimes random bits of information could lead to good thoughts, insights, clarity, conclusions. He'd proven that. He'd followed GB's suggestion to look in the family Bible for vital statistics, and that had led to the envelope.

The envelope. What a tidy little mystery that was. Tim was intrigued by it, but he had also been unwilling to open it. He wasn't sure why, but he thought it might be contravening the Rules of

Delving if he did. Besides, he valued the challenge of trying to learn the contents by the very process of delving.

As he was trying to practice it, delving involved assembling all circumstances and accounting for them all until one conclusion was left standing. If he opened the envelope at this stage, he might find himself at a conclusion, and not be motivated to investigate everything else. He might know a *Who* or a *What*, but not the *Why*.

It most likely contained a message from his mother to him. If so, what could she possibly want to tell him in this way? Brownie had never hesitated to speak frankly to him about other people, and he'd often wished she wouldn't, especially when he was a boy.

"Well, this isn't very cheery for a Monday morning, Tim," he said aloud.

He brewed coffee, selected morsels from yesterday's feast, and drove downtown to see what information he could shake loose.

~

"GB, how's things this morning?"

"Catching up, Tim. Was AWOL for two days last week. Sorry. Told Miss Fong to dock my pay."

"She won't do that, GB. Were you ill? Are you okay?"

"Missus Barss took a turn. Called the ambulance. Spent too long in emergency, but got her looked at. She...she...can't go on."

He pulled out a wooden chair and sat down hard.

"GB, do they say she's seriously ill? Is that it?"

The old man nodded, but kept his head down so Tim wouldn't see his tears.

Tim squatted beside him. "Listen to me, my dear friend. If there's anything I can do, please tell me. I don't want to interfere in your private life, but are you—do you need money? What do you need?"

"No, not money. More time, though. Would be good to spend a little more time. Before she goes."

Tim's heart was breaking. He had walked right into a tragedy, and he felt both sorrow and regret. Could he have helped GB and his wife before now? He knew they kept their lives private, but shouldn't he have pushed a little, to make certain that the best help was available?

What kind of help was best when the one you love, as GB loved his wife, was dying? If a cure wasn't on the table, then surely comfort and respect could be?

"I'm going to take you home, GB. Just sit here for a moment."

Tim knocked on Elaine Fong's door, and didn't wait for her to beckon him in.

"What's up, Tim?"

"It's GB. His wife's ill—terminally, I think—and he needs to go home to be with her."

"Of course. I'm so sorry. How can I help?"

"Not sure. Just letting you know. Has anyone been working there with him?"

"Not exactly *with* him. You know how he protects his empire of clippings. But I did assign our new hire to job-shadow him. He's observing, looking over his shoulder. GB has actually begun to explain his system a bit. It's not that hard to follow, really. But many of us don't use it. Do you?"

"I do. That's why I came in to see GB this morning. I'd asked him for some vital stats."

"Did he do it?"

"Not sure. He said he'd been off last week."

"Right. What's happening now? Did you say you're taking him home?"

"Yeah. I want to assess the situation with his wife. He mightn't be back until...a while. Gosh, it makes me so sad. He's been like family—like a kindly old uncle to me. God knows I don't have an excess of family."

"I'm sorry, Tim. This must be hard. Listen, why not give me your vitals request? I can give it to Harold to see what he can find for you."

"Who's Harold?"

"The new hire. Nice guy. He's shadowing the bookkeeper too, and both nerdy tasks seem to suit him. Give him a try?"

"All right, but I want it kept confidential, meaning that the information shouldn't be left lying around, for sure not in my mailbox, all right? Maybe Harold could leave it with you and I'll get it later? It's just—it's personal, that's all."

"Not a problem. Write it down, and go see to your—your uncle, with my best wishes."

Tim re-wrote the list of names, slid it across the desk to Elaine, and returned to the open office. He saw the familiar red head of a reporter in a cubicle, and leaned over.

"Hi, James."

"Oh, hi, Mister Brown. How's tricks? Got another good story for me?"

Tim had involved James Olsen in helping him investigate a matter in February, and they'd both enjoyed their collaboration.

"No, but I do have a favour to ask. GB needs to go home because his wife is quite ill, and I want to drive him so I can see what's going on there. I don't think he'll be coming back to work for a while, so I was wondering if you would mind following us in his car?"

"Sure...but...how about you drive his car and I follow you in my Jeep?"

"Of course. How thoughtless of me to suggest you'd drive a twelve-year-old Chevelle. Thanks, James. Meet you at the front door in a few minutes."

Tim watched GB fumble with his coat buttons. He knelt to help him pull on his winter boots.

"Soon time to change these winter tires, GB," he joked.

"Not yet, Tim. Still could snow."

"I hope not. Let the snow melt. I'm eager to see the mud."

They walked to GB's old car, which was very low to the ground, especially for Tim's long legs. He drove them carefully to GB's small home on a side road just outside of town, with James' bright orange Jeep following.

Inside the Barss home, two thoughts collided in Tim's head. One, that it was good to have a small, one-level home when you needed it; and two, they sure needed it now.

Mrs Barss—her husband had always referred to her as Missus Barss, so Tim had followed suit—was reclining in an ancient vinyl recliner chair beneath a pile of blankets and comforters, near an oil stove that was putting out as many BTUs as a smelter. The ceilings were low, and the air smelled of hot pee.

Never mind that, Tim, just look around. Observe.

GB had gone directly to his wife's side when they entered. "Not to worry, my dear. It's Tim, from the paper. He wanted to visit you."

He leaned close to hear her whisper. "I don't look my best today. Does he want tea?"

"She says would you like some tea, Tim?"

GB turned toward the deep enamel sink, which was full of unwashed dishes.

"Hello, Mrs Barss. You're very kind, but don't bother with tea for me today. Make some for yourselves if you like. I don't mean to pry, but may I ask what the schedule of home care workers is? How often do they come in, now?"

"Twice a week, but sometimes they don't come. We manage."

GB sat on the sofa, and Tim sank down beside him. The air was several degrees cooler at that level. The heat was making his head pound.

"How did you make out at the hospital? You had to go to emergency, I think you said?"

"Yes, Missus Barss was finding it hard to breathe. It's better now. She got one of those..."

"An inhaler?"

"That's it."

"Does it help?"

"Think so. Doesn't it help you some, Missus?"

GB spoke the latter part of this sentence a little louder, leaning in to his wife. She lifted up her left hand, which held the inhaler. Without prompting, she inhaled as well as she could, and then exhaled while pressing the top of the pressurized container, blowing the medicine into the room.

"Not sure what it's supposed to do," her husband said.

Don't panic, Tim. Observe. Assess.

"GB, who's your family doctor?"

"Used to be your mother's friend, Doctor Parkin, until she passed away. He left the area, then."

"That was ten years ago or more."

"Mmm-hmm."

"Who now?"

"Didn't need anyone. Just didn't think of it then. Things changed, but the local docs aren't taking anyone just now."

Tim glanced at his watch, remembering he had an appointment with his own doctor in twenty minutes. "I have to run back to town right now, folks, but you stay here and rest, both of you. I'll be back as soon as I can find you some proper attention, okay?"

"Whatever you can do to help Missus Barss will be good."

GB was beginning to heave himself up from the sofa.

"Stay where you are, GB. Bye-bye, Mrs Barss. I'll be back."

Mrs Barss waved her inhaler and responded with a rattling four-syllable "By-he by-he."

James' sport vehicle was reverberating with music from an impressive sound system. Tim climbed up into the passenger seat, strapped himself in, and asked James to drop him off at the Medical Centre. It wasn't far from the office, so he'd just walk back when his appointment was over.

"Want me to turn it down?" James pointed to the player in the dashboard.

"No. Thanks. Leave it up. I like it. Who's singing?"

"Do you need to ask? It's Cher. 'Do You Believe in Love?'"

"What?"

"That's the song."

"Oh."

Cher sounded as though she was right in the back seat, under the rag-top.

Tim arrived on time, and the receptionist waved him right into Doctor Muhammed's office.

"Good morning, Tim. How are you doing? How's the year off working out? Last time you were here, I think you were falling asleep reading a boring book. Has that improved?"

"Gee, I'd forgotten about that already. Yes, thanks, all better. I drink enough coffee to keep my heart beating, and I have enough challenging interests to keep me motivated most days. Some days."

"Good. Remember, I offered to make coffee for you sometime that will awaken all your senses. What brings you in today?"

"Well, I had a simple question in mind when I made the appointment, didn't intend to take up more than a few minutes of your time, but—"

"And your simple question is?"

"About dopamine. I know our brains produce it, to keep us from becoming depressed, I think? I've been going for walks lately, now that the snow banks are melting, and that activity seems to make me...would you call it happy? Is that dopamine?"

"It could very well be dopamine. Or endorphins."

"Is there a pill form?"

"For what?"

"For...I dunno. It just feels good to feel good, and when I wasn't active—I mean physically active—I guess I didn't have the same outlook."

"Do you mean you felt sad, or depressed?"

"Maybe. Sometimes. A little bit?"

"If that's a question, Tim, I cannot answer it for you. I hope you aren't asking for a drug that insulates you from the normal range of feelings, happy to sad. But note I said 'range'. Some days we're up, some days we're down. This is normal and I would not want you to miss out on life by taking a pill. So, keep living, and caring. And walking."

"I will. Now, just this morning, I discovered that an elderly couple, who are very dear to my heart, are both in serious medical distress, I think. And they haven't had a family physician for a decade, I just learned. That embarrasses me, but you don't know what people don't tell you, right? So, she has something wrong with her lungs, finds it hard to breathe or speak. The hospital emergency gave her an inhaler which I'm certain she's not using correctly. And he's acquired a tremor."

Tim made his hands shake in imitation of GB.

"I just came from their home. They say they have some kind of home care twice a week, but I doubt that. I think she needs to be in the hospital and be assessed for a nursing home. Her husband works for me, but he's long past retirement age. I just kept him on because I…I love to have him around. He's like family. The work isn't physically taxing. But I took him home this morning because he didn't look well, and she's worse."

"Do you have power of attorney for them?"

"Me? No."

"Do they have any children? Relations?"

"None that I know of."

"Can you bring them in here to see me?"

"Oh, gosh, that's very kind but I don't think I can. She looks very feeble to me."

"Okay, Tim. I'll follow up with the ER. I'll speak to whoever saw her and try to get an assessment. We'll take it from there. Will I consider you the next of kin?"

"I'd be honoured," Tim said, and his throat suddenly ached. "Here's my card. I'll be at either of these numbers. Thank you so much, doctor."

"Thank you for advocating for them, Tim. It sounds like they both need help. Why are citizens in this blessed country living without medical care? I assure you I do not know the answer to that. Not a good answer."

Tim left the doctor's office. After searching the parking lot for his car, he remembered it wasn't there. He walked the short distance downhill and across the bridge.

Once he was back inside the Johnson Building, Elaine Fong beckoned him into her office. She handed him a sheet of paper, which contained the names of his forebears, their dates of birth, death, and any marriages.

"Already? Thanks! Your Harold is fast. What are these numbers and letters?"

"He gave you the cabinet, drawer, and file number if you want to look up what we have on file for these people. He's good at it, and likes it. Our staff might access the resource if the service is faster, frankly."

"He just might inherit that empire. If GB wants to come in and cut the newspapers up, I'd insist that he be made welcome to do that. But he and I and you would all like to see the archives used."

"If? How's he doing?"

"Oh boy, not good, I think." Tim shook his head. "His wife is very bad and he's stressed trying to look after her. I have a physician looking into their care."

"Whatever we can do, just say the word, Tim. A number of staff came by already to ask about him."

Tim's eyes filled. "Look at me," he sniffed, wiping his eyes. "They'll be fine, I'm sure."

There was a bright yellow envelope in his mailbox, despite his instructions that nothing be put in there unless he had requested it. He was sitting at his table, preparing to open the envelope, when his cell phone rang.

"It's me, Rachael, Mister Brown. I know you didn't want me to put anything in your mailbox, but the lady insisted that you'd want it. Sorry."

"That's fine, Rachael. Thank you."

It was a flowery thank-you card from Evelyn.

> Dear Tim and Bobby:
> I was awake half the night, thinking about our lovely evening. Such silly fun! The kind you can have with friends. I hope there's more.
> Sincerely,
> Your Friend Ev.

He'd be sure to show the card to "Bobby". Last evening's fun seemed long ago now, pushed away by the cares of today.

Today is the Ides of March. Are there debts I should pay?

GB had given him constancy, for which he was indebted. He'd been slow, but steady, thorough, reliable. There had never been a word of care expressed between them, except when Tim would ask about Mrs Barss, and GB would say how much that meant to her and to him.

That wasn't much. He could escalate that. He could do meaningful things for GB and his Missus. He could express his feelings, tell him he cared.

He hoped Stella wouldn't call today. He was too distracted to be able to engage in the usual fencing-match with her. If she thrust her sword, he might not parry; maybe he'd lose a limb, or an opportunity to come back to the topic later.

He looked at the pages Elaine had given him, printed on company letterhead.

> REPORT FROM *THE TIMES'* ARCHIVES
> REQUESTED BY: Mr. Tim Brown
> DATE: 15 Mar 1999
> RESEARCHED BY: Harold
> COMPLETED 15 Mar 1999

That was impressive, though it was an un-approved use of company letterhead.

Couldn't he just add company info to the print-out?

Stop it, Tim, don't squelch initiative. If GB had produced this report on embossed linen-weave stationery, you wouldn't have said boo about it.

True, but that was GB. This new guy has to earn his privileges.

Yes, Mother.

That was not a good line of thinking. Brownie's was not a management style he wanted to emulate.

What was in this impressive-looking report?

> Lucia Linda Brown neé Johnson:
>   b 1940 May 20
>   m 1958 July 17 to Brown, Ford
>   d 1991 August 21

Ford Enright Brown
    b 1940 January 25
    m 1958 July 17 to Johnson, Lucia Linda
    d 1963 August 1
Timothy Johnson Brown
    b 1959 March 21
    m 0 result
    d 0 result

Tim observed wryly that Harold had not been found either dead or married. Why had he wanted this information, anyway? He knew it already, didn't he? But the point of this investigation, this quest, this delving, was to verify what he did know, to fill in the blanks in a very blank family history, using facts, not his mother's melodramatic expressions of her "needs".

His cell phone rang again. It was Doctor Muhammed.

"Tim, I spoke with the internist at the hospital who treated Mrs Barss on Saturday. He feels she should be admitted, but her husband had objected strenuously. He claimed he could take care of her. What do you think?"

"Oh, that stubborn old man. No, he's not capable. He needs attention himself, in my unqualified opinion. Their place looks, uh, unkempt. I don't know what the home care people are doing for them, but possibly they're not being paid for enough hours to do housekeeping. I panicked when I saw the mess they're living in."

"All right. We'll send an ambulance. She'll be admitted today. Can you be at their home, to let them know what's happening?"

"Yes, I can. I'll go now."

"Very well. The ambulance should be there within an hour or so. Oh, and don't take any food, not for her, not even water. I know it sounds unkind, but we don't want to hamper any procedures."

"Okay, glad you mentioned it. And what about her husband?"

"You can take him to see her tomorrow. Not tonight. Let's make an appointment now for me to see him. I'll put you through to the front desk, all right?"

"Yes, put me through. Thank you so much, doctor."

The earliest appointment available was ten days away. Doctor Muhammed was very busy.

It's very kind of him to take them on.

He drove to the Barss home. It seemed to have sunk just a little closer to the ground since he'd left there this morning. So much heaviness was in there. He tapped on the porch door and let himself in.

"Hi GB, hope I'm not disturbing. May I come in?"

"Sure, Tim. Just made some tea and soup. Want some?"

"Thanks, but I just had lunch, GB. Did Mrs Barss have some?"

She was in the big chair, eyes closed. Tim couldn't tell if the pile of blankets had been re-arranged, didn't know if she'd been up to the bathroom, didn't want to ask.

"She didn't want anything. That's not good, is it, Tim?"

"No, it isn't. So, here's my news," Tim said, sitting once again on the old sofa. "My doctor has agreed to take you both on as patients. He's very good. He phoned the hospital and spoke with the docs who saw Mrs Barss on the weekend. They'd like to have her come back in and stay awhile. They can look after her personal care while they have a look at her medical needs, okay? An ambulance is on its way now."

"I told them I could look after her!"

Tim was surprised by GB's outburst, but he understood it. "I know, GB. You want to do that more than anything. You're a kind man, and your kindness toward Mrs Barss is wonderful to see. But now, the kindest thing you can do is let the experts fix her up, right? Sometimes what a person needs is more than a little puffer thingy."

"What if they keep her?" The old man was weeping without shame. "She—she's everything. Has been since school. She was the girl. No kids, didn't matter. Always together."

Tim reached over and put his arm around his old friend's shoulders. They sat like that for a long time, until there was a rumbling of a diesel motor in the lane.

"'Scuse me, GB, I'll go see if they need me to move my car."

When he stepped outside, the air felt as though winter had returned with a vengeance, compared with the furnace-hot interior of the little house. The ambulance manoeuvred close to the doorstep, then Tim led the crew inside. They filled the little front room.

"Hi, Mrs Barss," the attendant said. "We're going to take you to the hospital now, okay?"

Missus Barss' thin blue eyelids barely fluttered. The attendant clipped a device to one of her fingertips, and they worked quickly when they read the numbers on the monitor.

Someone asked GB for his wife's health card, and since they'd just used it on the weekend, he knew where it was.

Tim stayed solidly next to GB as the attendants carried his bride out to the back of the ambulance. They gave her an oxygen mask and connected her to a heart monitor. Then the crew closed doors and wasted no time pulling out of the yard. When the vehicle was out on the road, Tim heard the siren wailing. It *was* an emergency.

"Will we go see her now?"

"No, GB, not now. The doctor asked me to tell you not to go in tonight. They'll need to hook her up and fix her up tonight, and we'd only be in their way. She won't know you're not there, I'm pretty sure. I wouldn't be surprised if they give her something to make her drowsy. They always seem to be doing that in hospitals. Must be needed. Anyway, I'll come get you around one o'clock tomorrow and we'll check in on her then; that's when visiting hours start. Right now, why don't I just tackle these dishes and tidy up a bit for you?"

"Can't have you doing that, Tim, that's too much. Pick away at it. Gets done. You're too kind."

"Are you sure? I don't mind at all."

"Can't let you. Gives us something to do."

"Okay, but don't work too hard at it. Oh, and speaking of work, don't give us a thought, GB. Let's get through this patch, okay? You'll be welcome back at the office whenever you want to come back. No rush."

Against GB's wishes, Tim ran the hot water while he rinsed and scraped the dishes and pots. He found detergent, and filled the sink with soapy water. He wiped the counter top and laid a clean towel on it.

"There, let them soak a bit, then just set the clean dishes on the towel. Mother nature can dry them overnight."

In a flash, more likely, in this heat.

GB looked defeated, despondent. Tim didn't know what else to do. "Do you have something here for your supper?"

He looked in the fridge, but wasn't confident of anything there being edible. In the cupboard were cans of beans and stew. He brought out one of each and held them up. "Any preference?"

GB shook his head slowly, so Tim decided supper would be stew. He located the can opener and a bowl, but couldn't find a clean saucepan so he scrubbed one that was soaking in the sink.

"There. All ready for supper. Now, GB, I know you're sad, and there's no way around it. But please do eat your supper, then go to bed, and I'll come get you at one o'clock tomorrow. Okay?"

"You're a good man, Tim. Always liked being around. Your mother was tough, but she cared, was good to us. Didn't want to re-tire. Just Missus and you, all we have."

He burst into tears.

"Hey now, hey now. You still have me, GB. You've always been like my uncle, and I would miss you a lot if I didn't see you, at the office, or here. I'll see you tomorrow."

If anything could be harder, Tim didn't know what it would be. Arguments with Stella always called for strength, but this—this needed tenderness, and reassurance, and caring. Who is prepared for that? He certainly wasn't. Not that he didn't have those qualities, but all at once like this was tough, for a dear old friend.

He had described GB in that way to Elaine, and it felt every bit true. He knew it always had been.

~

Tim drove home, his head spinning. One thought began to float to the top. Once home, he called Elaine Fong to update her about GB and Mrs Barss.

"Yes, very sad. But Elaine, between you and me, they're living in squalid conditions. I mean, the house is so cluttered everywhere, and the kitchen counter—yikes! I wouldn't be surprised if they have rodents. I know not everyone is a great housekeeper, but this seems to be more than just dusting. It makes me wonder: do we pay GB a living wage? It sure doesn't look like we do."

"Just hang on a sec, Tim. I'll bring that up on the computer."

He could hear her keyboard clickety-clack.

"Ah, here it is, Barss, Gregory. Hmm. Not management level, but good clerical, I'd say. Fits in our range. At the provincial average."

"How do you know this?"

"Because I'm interested, and I checked. What we pay our staff is important. We do okay."

"So, GB wouldn't be living in squalor simply based on his salary from us?"

"I wouldn't say. But there's no way of knowing what employees spend their income on."

"Not on his house, nor car, nor housekeeping, that's for sure. Poor old guy. I think he's been slipping for some time, just didn't want us to know. And I've been mostly absent for the past two and a half months, so I wasn't paying attention. Now it may be too late for both of them. But, if he didn't spend his wages on buckets of wine, as I do, then he must be sitting on a nice bank account."

"That's beyond my reach. How'd you like Harold's report, by the way?"

"Excellent. I forgot about it, the day has gone so sideways. It's great, very professional. Printed on our letterhead, too." There, he'd said it.

"Oh, that won't go on. He made up that format on the spot, and printed it on letterhead just for you. No, indeed; the reports will come out on regular printer paper. But it's got me thinking, Tim: it's a service we can sell to outside entities, I think. Unless you object, we'll pursue it. Not going to spend a lot of time on it, but something may come of it. A nice little revenue stream, potentially."

~

Tim hadn't had a Monday like this since he'd begun this sabbatical year. No day had been like this one. He was grateful for leftovers which he put in the oven, though a can of stew might have satisfied him tonight.

He poured a glass of wine from one of several bottles Robert had opened yesterday in a valiant attempt at pairings, and put some easy jazz in the CD player. He couldn't possibly follow a movie or television program tonight.

He just sat and thought about what GB had said about him. And about his mother: tough but good to the Barsses. Caring.

You just never know about people.

March 16: Uncle

Tuesday

Tim was puzzling about family, those two daughters of Bertha and Ebenezer in particular. Stella and Brownie were both stern, judgmental, and quick to give him a verbal smack intended to sting. And yet, people outside their family seemed to think of them as kind and caring.

Sure, people can be two-faced, but neither woman seemed duplicitous. Both characteristics could be true, though he had felt more of the stings than the balm.

He wondered what GB meant, that Brownie had been good to them. She provided a big turkey at Christmas to everyone on the payroll. Had she done more? If so, he was unaware. Had he left anyone in the lurch after her passing? Did they think he was a Scrooge? He'd try to get more details from GB today, or later, if he was too preoccupied with his wife's condition. It'd be crass to ask him to itemize Brownie's largesse, but he'd look for a way to work it into the conversation.

Tim was sincere about thinking of GB as his uncle. He had not been a very attentive nephew. He'd do better. It looked like GB would be a widower very soon, and the old man would need his company more than ever. Maybe it was time for him to retire. Tim was relieved that Doctor Muhammed was going to take him on as a patient. He'd fix him up.

GB could come to the office and sit in a corner in his file cabinet fortress as long as he liked, and Tim would drop by for little hellos whenever he was in, maybe take him for drives sometimes, and breakfasts at the Daisy Café.

Tim liked thinking of this. He was filling in some gaps in his life.

It felt healthy to have family and friends to care about. His circle was expanding.

It was noon, time to take GB to the hospital. Tim picked up his cell phone, which he had plugged in to charge, but had forgotten to turn on this morning. He did so now, and saw there was a message. He pressed the buttons. It was from Stella.

"Timothy, if you are still determined that we discuss topics better left alone, I will have time available a week from today, the morning of Tuesday the twenty-third. At your house. Please confirm."

Next week? What's wrong with now? Does she have to break the Great Seal on some vault in order to talk to me about my father, whom I can barely remember and whom she quite possibly had never met?

She'd given him a date, so he'd have to accept it. Right now, he had a date with his uncle.

~

He rapped loudly on the porch door and stepped inside.

"Hi, uncle, it's me, Tim," he called out, grinning. Might as well be upbeat and cheer the old man up after his lonely night alone. He didn't hear a response, so he knocked again, opened the inner door and went inside the house.

GB was on the sofa in the front room where he had been yesterday, leaning slightly forward, head down, hands in his lap. He looked sad. Tim's first thought was that he might have received a bad-news call from the hospital. Or maybe he was just asleep.

"Having a snooze, uncle? It's time to go and visit your wife at the hospital. Ready?"

GB didn't move.

Tim glanced around the room. The house was cold. The stove was not pumping out excessive heat. The tin of stew was still on the kitchen counter, unopened. The dishes were still in the sink, but the soap bubbles had evaporated.

"What's..."

Oh, no.

He crouched in front of the old man.

"Hey, GB," he said softly, and touched the cold hands.

He sat on the sofa next to GB and put his arm around his shoulders as he had done yesterday. "Couldn't stay any longer, hey, uncle? You looked after her as well and as long as you could. She'll be all right now. They'll take care of her, don't you worry. You can rest now."

Tim rocked them both gently, lowered his head, and wept.

~

Later, he found the phone book, looked up the number for the funeral home, and called them to come for GB. He assured them the death was due to natural causes, probably happened over twelve hours ago, no ambulance required. He said he thought the body would be cremated, but he'd have to confirm that and get back to them. The deceased's wife was in the hospital, unable to act, and he hadn't looked for the will yet. Yes, he would come over later this afternoon to complete arrangements.

While he waited for the hearse, Tim searched for a desk or cabinet where their wills might be. GB would have kept their personal records as meticulously as he'd done for *The Times*, Tim was certain.

He opened the door to their tiny bedroom. An odd display on the wall at the foot of their bed attracted his attention. He stepped into the room and flipped on the overhead light.

The whole wall was covered in layers of letters and photographs. Stepping closer, Tim saw immediately what they were: Missions for Kids, Children for Christ, and several other organizations that collected monthly subscriptions from donors to support the education of children in third-world countries.

The letters were addressed to "Dear Grammy and Grampy," in children's handwriting, thanking them for their money and telling them how well they were doing in school because of their support. These children might substitute for a real family, but how much money had these operations taken from the Barsses over the years? A lot, judging by the layers of photos and letters.

Tim wondered if this is what his mother had "helped out" with. Had she given them money for these scams—that's how he thought of them—or had she even sponsored some on her own behalf? If he looked through all these letters, would he find some addressed to "Dear Mother Brownie"? He didn't dare look.

He'd been yearning for family. He was working hard to connect with his own family, and here was a whole mural of family caring, shared by people he cared about, but it was not for him. It was for unknown children far, far away. They could have the money, but he envied the affection, the interest. It was so unfair.

Without thinking, he punched the wall of letters, hard.

"Ow! Oh, shit!"

He was very lucky. His right fist had gone through the thin wallboard into the gap between studs. He slowly withdrew his hand and waggled his fingers. His knuckles were scraped and bleeding slightly but nothing seemed to be broken. His hand pulsed with pain.

"Serves you right. Settle down! These are harmless people. They meant well. They didn't do this to cut you out. They probably hid all this from you because they thought you'd disapprove—and you do, so get over yourself. This is not your business. Smarten up!"

He was chastened now, and grateful that nobody had witnessed his outburst. He rearranged some of the letters on the wall to cover the hole. His knuckles had begun to swell and were throbbing.

He returned to his search. There was a tiny closet behind a curtain. Hesitantly, he pushed the curtain aside.

"Bingo!"

A file box, similar to ones they used at *The Times,* was on the top shelf, labelled *IMPORTANT PAPERS* in GB's familiar handwriting. He took it out to the front room and sat again on the sofa, placing the box between him and GB.

"I'm just going to check in here, Uncle, to make sure I have your will. I won't read it. I'll give it to the lawyer to do that. We just need to know if you made any, uh, final arrangements."

He unwound the string that held the lid closed and looked inside. He knew what he was looking for, and when he saw the folded blue document, he pulled it out just far enough to read the title. Satisfied that he had what he needed, he dropped it back in the box and wound the string around the buttons again.

He heard tapping on the porch door: the funeral home people were there. He hadn't heard the hearse come in the driveway. The vehicle ran so quietly, not at all like the ambulance's rumbling diesel and sirens. The attendants spoke and worked quietly.

Tim kissed GB's head and then turned away as they carried his remains through the narrow doors to the hearse. He didn't want to see any awkwardness. He was not disrespecting his old friend. He was protecting himself from memories he'd rather not have.

After the hearse drove away, Tim stood in the middle of the little kitchen. He didn't know what he was supposed to do here. Who would clean up and deal with the house? Mrs Barss couldn't live here by herself. She'd have to go to a nursing home if she could even leave the hospital, which had seemed doubtful yesterday. Who made those decisions?

He phoned his lawyer and explained the situation. A law firm Tim had never heard of, perhaps now defunct, had drawn up the will. His lawyer instructed him to bring the documents over right away.

He phoned the hospital to inquire about Constance Barss, and learned that she'd been admitted to Intensive Care.

"Can you connect me to that floor, please?"

While he waited, he wondered if things could get worse for the Barss couple, and if worse would be better.

"Hello, may I speak with the Head Nurse, please."

"This is she. Nurse Smith. How may I help?"

"I'm Timothy Brown. I sent my, uh, friend Constance Barss to the hospital by ambulance yesterday. I'm calling to inform you that Gregory Barss, her husband, has passed away, suddenly, unexpectedly, today. If Mrs Barss regains consciousness and asks about him, will you tell her? I think she'd be very worried if there wasn't a message from him."

"I'm so sorry, Mister Brown. What an awful time for them. I'll notify the staff. Thank you for letting us know."

Tim looked in the bathroom for a bandage for his hand, not because it was bleeding—it wasn't—but because he didn't want to have to explain the injury in the next appointments. Finding only a box of band-aids, he applied several to cover the worst of the abrasions.

He closed the house and porch doors tightly, making sure they weren't locked, since he didn't know where a key might be. Perhaps one was in GB's pocket.

He called Elaine Fong's direct line on his way to the law office.

"Hi Tim. What's the verdict?"

"A bit of a plot twist, I'm afraid. Mrs Barss is in intensive care."

"Oh, dear."

"Yes, but...GB is...he died."

"What? How? When?"

"Natural causes, it seems. Could have happened right after I left there yesterday. The term "passed away" seems right for GB. He was sitting right where I'd left him. No sign of a struggle or distress of any kind."

"Oh, Tim, I'm so sorry. I know you were very fond of him."

"Thanks."

"Staff cared about him, too. How do you want to convey this message to them? Do you want to do it?"

"Oh, I...I hadn't thought about that. I'm on my way to see the lawyer just now."

"I'm sorry to be pushy, but we are a weekly and today's the deadline. Do you want his obituary in this week's issue?"

"His funeral will likely be Friday or Saturday. So I guess the answer's yes. Can it?"

"Of course it can. So, do you feel up to making the announcement to the staff? After you see the lawyer?"

"I—I can't do it, Elaine. Can you, please? I just came from their place and I'm—"

"I understand completely. I'll tell them. It's about GB, but it's about your loss, too. I'll get Harold to work on the Obit. I hope GB kept his own file. It'd be just like the barber's kids going without haircuts for the supplier of Obituary info to leave himself out."

"Wouldn't it? He was so self-effacing. D'you know I never heard him use a personal pronoun until yesterday when the ambulance came for Mrs? He was quite distressed."

"I noticed that, too. Odd. He was a lovely man, though. You were very good to him, Tim. I know you'll miss him."

Tim lost his breath at this, managing to gasp "Gotta go" before disconnecting.

He took the file box and was ushered directly in to see his lawyer. The secretary offered beverages and he accepted a glass of water.

"As I expected," the lawyer said. "They left everything to each other, so nothing happens until the second spouse dies, unless–"

"Good." Tim interrupted. "Just tell me, can we hold the funeral this Friday, and does the will state whether the body must be buried or cremated, open casket, graveyard plot, any of that?"

"Hmm. No, I don't see any reference to that. Let me check in here."

He took the other documents from the file and laid them out on the desk.

"I don't see anything like a pre-paid funeral home contract here, or membership in a memorial society. Were you expecting anything like that?"

"Yesterday I might have said I'd be surprised if they had made such arrangements, but you never really know about people, do you? They spent a...they supported one international charity a lot and were unlikely to save money aside for themselves. So, can I tell the funeral home to go ahead with cremation? And do I have the authority to make these choices? Mrs Barss is in a coma in the ICU, so she can't, but I don't have any official standing.".

"We'll take care of that for you, Tim. We'll call the funeral home right away, while you're driving over. You should go there now. Sorry for your troubles."

They were expecting him at the funeral home. The staff were experienced in dealing with the dead, and made it as easy as they could for him. They said there was no rush, but he told them he wanted the obituary in tomorrow's paper and the deadline was right now. He made selections from their list of services. He wanted things to be simple, in keeping with the deceased's lifestyle, and respectful, in keeping with how his colleagues felt about him. They understood.

He signed the contract, though the marks he made with his awkward left hand bore no resemblance to his long-established signature.

He called Elaine. "Add this to GB's obit, please: survived by Constance, his wife of over fifty years. Gosh, I hope that's still true when the paper comes out tomorrow. And also say he was the longest-serving employee of *The Times*, and will be sincerely missed by management and staff and all who knew him. The funeral will be Friday at ten, reception following, all welcome. Say the body has been cremated. Interment at a later date."

"Got it."

"Did you find a photo of him?"

"Luckily, Harold found him in a group photo when the paper received an award for something a couple years back. We can crop it. He looks good. He's smiling."

"I'm so glad. Print it big. I'll be home if you need anything else from me."

~

Tim's right hand was swollen and hurting like heck, especially when he flexed his fingers, which was hard not to do. He peeled the bandages off, carefully washed the scrapes, and examined what he had done to himself. He decided against applying ointment, fearing it would sting more than the soap and water had done, which was a lot. He found some gauze and loosely wrapped his hand with it, put some ice cubes in a towel, and held that to his injury.

He rummaged in the freezer for something to eat one-handed for supper. Visions of GB's kitchen stuck with him. It was shocking to see the conditions they lived in. What did the home care workers think about it? Who would they have reported it to?

While supper heated, Tim took stock of all that had transpired today. He'd begun with such high hopes. He'd been looking forward to a happy day, the beginning of a happy future with his uncle. Instead, he'd faced loss and sorrow—and uncharacteristic anger, he admitted—and funeral tasks, none of which he'd seen coming.

He had done his best today. It helped that he could say that.

He felt sorry for himself, missing something he'd only just realized he wanted so much.

He'd been frustrated because Stella couldn't see him until next Tuesday. Now he was glad of the delay. Death and funerals weren't tasks you could put off until you had the time.

Maybe Stella would tell him something good about his father, so he could miss him, too.

His hand ached less when he held it across his chest. He ate supper left-handed, finding the fork as foreign in his left hand as the pen had been.

The rent-a-minister at the funeral home would have attempted a eulogy, but Tim wouldn't allow it. He'd be proud to bid farewell himself to the uncle he never had.

Better rehearse it, Tim, or you'll be blubbering at the funeral, and it's not about you.

He spent the evening talking aloud about GB, organizing his thoughts. He was sorry that he knew so little to say.

He'd start with that, an apology of sorts.

March 17: When the saints

Wednesday

"Hi, Aunt Stella. I'm calling to confirm our date next Tuesday morning, as you asked. You can let me know the precise time later, if you wish."

"Do you have a cold? Are you ill?"

"No."

"Then why do you sound like that?"

"Maybe because our longest-serving employee died yesterday. I'm sad."

"My condolences. What name?"

"Gregory Barss. GB. He worked in—"

"GB died? Oh, I'm sorry to hear that. Lovely man."

"You knew him? How?"

"As you say, he was a long-serving employee, dating back to when I was actually serving my child-labour time there. Later, when I was campaigning as MLA, I made certain to visit everyone I knew in the riding, and thus became re-acquainted with GB and his wife—oh, what's her name?"

"Constance. Connie. Known to all as Missus Barss."

"Yes. How's she doing?"

"Not good. She's in Intensive Care. Here's the thing: I went to pick him up yesterday morning to visit her in the hospital, and he was just sitting there on the sofa, dead. He wasn't supposed to do that."

Tim's throat constricted, and he struggled to compose himself. Stella didn't intervene. "Sorry. *Ahem.* Thankfully, I don't think she's aware of what's happened. She's very ill, obviously. He exhausted himself trying to care for her while still coming to work. He said they had home care workers coming in, but I'm beginning to doubt they were from any agency, because the place was a shambles."

"Oh dear. When's the funeral?"

"Friday at ten. There'll be a reception after."

"The funeral home will look after anything you need and some things you don't. Say yes to it all. A long-service employee of *The Times* must have a good send-off. People will be watching. You don't have to do the running around yourself. Get your lawyer on it, too. You just concentrate on giving a good eulogy."

"I've done all that, thanks. And I was practising my speech last night."

"Good. If you need my help, call my cell."

"Thanks, Aunt Stella. I'm out of my element here."

"We always are, Timothy, unless we have the dubious benefit of a prolonged illness to warn us it's coming. Will there be anything else just now?"

"Just that I'm looking forward to our conversation next Tuesday. Thanks for that."

"Don't get your hopes up. I have something to show you that might be of interest. I know you were fond of GB, Timothy. I'm sorry for your loss. Take care, now."

Tim tried to say thank you, but he could only whisper it. Yes, he was feeling emotional, and condolences from his aunt felt extra poignant this morning.

He asked Gloria for a double espresso to shock him into a more businesslike frame of mind. He retrieved his own newspaper from the porch, and was pleased to see the treatment his staff had given GB's obituary.

Shaving and dressing took a long time, wrong-handed, but by the time he left for his massage appointment in Blockhouse, he was less fragile, and ready for some comfort.

"Welcome back, Tim," said Lisa, the receptionist at the NuYu Spa. "We've been looking forward to seeing you again."

If this was a learned speech, it was just fine. It sounded sincere when Lisa said it. She directed him to the room where Melanie would meet him shortly "to address any issues you may have".

He undressed more confidently than he had the first time, and sat waiting on the edge of the table, wrapped in the sheet she would drape over him as she worked her way around his frame.

"Hello again, Tim. Lovely to see you today. How are you feeling?"

This woman didn't ask that question like she was talking about the weather. She cared about his response, and sat down to wait for it. He couldn't get away with a "Fine, thanks" response.

"Thanks for asking, Melanie. I'm in some turmoil today. My—a dear old friend died unexpectedly yesterday—or maybe it was Monday night, but I discovered him yesterday when I went to take him to see his wife in the hospital. She's also very ill. I was prepared for her to go, which would be a mercy for her, likely, but I wasn't expecting him to just slip away like that. Maybe he decided to go on ahead of her, maybe wait for her on the other side." He paused. "I don't believe that, but I'd like to."

Tim looked at his bruised hand in his lap. "Oh, and something angered me, and I punched a hole in a wall, can you believe that? So my right hand—you can't massage it today, okay?"

Melanie kept her eyes on Tim's face, still listening.

"Last time, you unlocked some memories. I think you noticed. They weren't bad memories, but they triggered a bunch of emotions. I've been addressing them, but it's slow going. They're on hold for a bit now while I deal with this other…"

Tim's chin trembled. "Here I go again. You'll think I'm the guy who weeps every time he comes here."

Melanie took a deep breath. She stood in front of Tim, and took both his wrists in her hands. "Breathe with me," she said, and led him through several deep, calming breaths, in and out.

"I told you before that you were fearless," she said. "That wasn't just words. I can feel your strength, and your vulnerability, which many people are afraid of. You went deeply into yourself last time, and I'm not surprised that you encountered many thoughts. You may not understand all of them yet, but this is a safe space for them. Believe me when I say that you have the strength for them. Now, if you're ready, lie down with your face in the donut, and let me see what you've done to your body since last time."

As she rubbed her oiled hands together to warm them, Melanie said, "Use this time to feel whatever you feel. If your head is quiet, accept it. If your head is busy, ask it to give you these moments. The world will wait for you. It's just an hour."

The hour felt long and luxurious, and over too soon.

"Okay, Tim, you can come back to us, now."

"Oh, must I? That felt so good..."

"Well, that's all the arms and legs you brought in with you today, so my work is done. If you bring in more another time, we'll negotiate. I think you were more settled today?"

"Yes, settled is a good word. My back is much better, my shoulders—all of me feels great. And my hand will heal. It's a reminder that a bad temper carries its own punishment."

"Do you have a bad temper?"

"Not that I ever saw evidence of. This was a first, and since I don't want a broken right hand, I hope it will be my last."

"It happened for a reason, though. You are encountering emotions that are trying to surface. That's beyond my training to explore."

She selected a business card from a small box on a side table, and placed it on his folded clothes. "If you'd like to talk things through, I highly recommend this fellow. I'd be happy to see you again, too, but don't overload yourself with therapists. You'll learn what kind of help you need. It's not being selfish. You know what they say in the airplanes: put your own oxygen mask on first, otherwise you can't help anyone else."

As with his first visit, he felt a tide of energy leave the room with her, but he felt he'd kept some of his own this time, too.

~

Sidewalk signs outside every restaurant, diner, and pub proclaimed that their Irish stew or green beer was the best, and the Catholic church hall had a line-up for stew. Tim would accept the odd beer if it was required of him in a social setting, but green beer was asking too much.

Instead, he visited the restaurant that made the best fish and chips around, ordering two pieces of fish, which was a huge serving, and extra fries, extra tartar sauce, and extra coleslaw. He hadn't eaten much in days, and he was suddenly ravenous. This would certainly fill one hole in his middle.

At home, he turned on the oven to crisp up the fries. The light was flashing on his home phone. Before checking for messages, he dug around in the back of the wine cupboard for something to match the day. He found a bottle from the Sainte-Famille vineyard, bought sometime last summer when he and Robert had taken a rare road trip. It seemed apropos.

The message was from Robert. As he was listening to it, Robert called again and Tim answered.

"Hi, Rob. What's up? I was just listening to—"

"I got Stella's message about your friend that died. I'm so sorry, Tim. Why didn't you call me?"

"Stella called you? Well, he was, you know, he…" Tim began to weep. "I've known him since I was a kid. He's just always been there, Rob, a sweet, gentle man. He's an old man now, way beyond retirement age, but he seemed to like coming to work so I just kept him on. The job wasn't taxing, and he was slowing down a lot recently, but he…I…sorry."

"It's okay. Stella told me you'd be more upset than you'd let on. When did it happen?"

"Yesterday. I was taking him to see his wife in the hospital—oh God, Rob, I forgot to check on her. Let me hang up to see if the other messages are from the hospital, please? I'll call you right back."

The other messages were all from Robert. He erased them and called him back.

"Sorry. No messages from the hospital, so it looks like there'll just be one urn at the funeral. Thank God. I can't tell you what a shemozzle I've been in with the arrangements. They had—they have—no family, so I'm trying to take care of things. I told him he was the uncle I never had. I hoped we'd spend some time together, and I'd be his nephew. Too late."

"You must be so disappointed."

Tim blew his nose. "Yes, I am. I'm crushed. I finally realized on Monday what he meant to me and—*poof*—Tuesday, he's gone. That's cruel, Rob."

"What were you doing this afternoon? Are you okay? I mean, it's okay to be teary, but are things getting done? Are you stressed?"

"I was at the spa for a massage, and I sure did appreciate that. It's only an hour and some, but time in that room is measured in light-years, it seems. I just got home. I picked up a huge order of fish and chips for supper, and I dug out that bottle of Sainte-Famille we bought last year. I'm starving and I plan to eat it all."

"Why the Sainte-Famille?"

"Because today is Saint Patrick's Day, so that's the saint. And GB was my pretend uncle, so that's the *famille*. If it weren't for you and Stella, I'd have no family at all, so I'm happy to add GB, even if it's posthumously, now."

"That's the spirit. I'll welcome him, too. I hope the wine's drinkable."

"When is wine not drinkable?"

"Of course. The funeral is Friday?"

"Yes, at ten. I'm giving the eulogy, so I've been practising it. I can't write anything down because I, uh, bumped my right hand the wrong way and, wow, is it sore. Still can't hold a pen. Or a fork. So I'll wing it. I'm talking through it so I won't break down. People mightn't understand."

"You don't have to apologize for caring for someone. Tell the people whatever you want to say about your uncle, and let them see how you feel. That's what funerals are for. I think you'll be fine."

Tim took a deep breath. "Melanie, my massage therapist, has been getting me to breathe deeply. It helps."

"Good. Now, today's that annoying Irish saint's day, as you said, so I taught this song to a music class today. Are you ready for a little humour?"

"If it's coming from you, sure."

"Okay, here goes: 'Let's not have a sniffle, let's have a bloody good cry. And always remember the longer you live, the sooner you'll bloody well die.'"

"Ha-ha, it's true. Is there more?"

"Yes there is, but it's quite irreverent, not appropriate for your delicate situation this evening."

"You should teach it to the choir. We could sing it at funerals. It'd be very popular."

"And I'd be looking for a new church position. Speaking of work, I'm just waiting to hear from a grad student about taking my classes on Friday morning, maybe all day. So when I come down tomorrow for rehearsal, I'm hoping to stay over."

"Really? But why? That's a lot of—"

"To attend the funeral of my uncle-in-law, that's why. For you, Timo. Don't argue. I'll do it if I can. See you tomorrow, anyway. Don't stress, now. Enjoy your fish. Big hugs."

Tim poured a generous glass of the wine, chilled it with an ice cube, and waited for the fries in the oven to achieve the perfect degree of crispness. He pondered. Stella had alerted Robert? That was very nice of her. Robert would come to the funeral? Tim would be extra nervous, but comforted to have him there. Robert would cut through his mental clutter if need be, and keep him focused on what he needed to do.

He laid the fire, one-handedly. The crackling wood and heat were comforting. The fire-burning season would come to an end soon, judging by the level of firewood left in the woodpile outside, if not by the weather. He'd miss the fire, but spring did offer other attractions.

The fries were dark brown at the tips, just the way he liked them. He filled a plate with them, one piece of the battered fish, and sides, and took it to the parlour. The day was darkening, but he didn't turn on the lights. There was enough light from the fire, and he didn't need to see to write. He slid to the floor between the sofa and the coffee-table, and ate supper with his fingers.

He thought about calling Stella to thank her for calling Robert, but he wasn't certain what they'd talk about after he said that, so he didn't. He thought about calling the hospital to ask about Constance Barss, but he didn't do that, either. He did get up to reload his plate and wine glass, and returned to the floor, close to the fire. When his thoughts strayed toward regrets, he steered them back to fond memories of GB, for his eulogy.

It wasn't that the old man—or the young man that he once was— said or did anything especially memorable, but he was always there. Always there. That's high praise, when you think of it. He was steady, dependable, reliable.

He wasn't demonstrative, not big on showing affection, but you knew how he felt about you, and when I say 'you' I mean everyone on our staff.

He didn't laugh out loud much, but his eyes twinkled.

He studiously avoided any reference to himself, for unknown reasons, deflecting to "we" if he was forced, but you were never sure who the "we" was referring to. Sometimes it was The Times, *and sometimes his family, which, as far as I know, was just himself and Constance, whom he always referred to as Missus Barss. His love for her was an unbroken bond.*

When they took her to the hospital because she was too ill for him to care for her any longer, I think he didn't know how to live without her.

I know this isn't theologically correct, just my fiction, but to me it seemed like he knew she wouldn't return home, so he decided to go where he'd be ready and waiting to take care of her when she, too, passed over.

He thought he might have to edit that a bit for the funeral. It was fanciful, and also difficult to say without tearing up, as he was doing now.

He thought about Robert's phone call. He was such a kind and perceptive man, quiet and supportive as needed, and then singing a saucy Irish song to pull him up. Tim remembered a bit of it, and sang, through tears "...always remember, the longer you live, the sooner you bloody well die."

He thought of his father. He didn't live long, but died soon anyway. Stella had something to tell him about it. That was good of her.

Tim drank toast to the memory of the recently discovered and dearly departed—his grandfather Ebenezer, grandmother Bertha, father Ford, mother Brownie, and uncle GB. They were the sainted family he would celebrate tonight.

March 18: Sign language

Thursday

The woman stood at the foot of Tim's bed. She wore a white gown, and her raven hair fell about her shoulders. Had she spoken, or shaken the bed to wake him? He didn't know. She didn't speak. She didn't seem to be disturbed or threatening, so he simply lay still, and they regarded each other for a few moments.

Then, keeping eye contact with him, she slowly raised her right arm and pointed upward. He blinked his eyes, and she was gone.

~

Tim awoke from a restful sleep, and was brushing his teeth when he remembered the night visitor. He stopped mid-brush and frowned at his reflection, then checked behind himself in the mirror. He turned toward the hallway connecting the bathroom and his bedroom. He walked to the top of the stairs and switched on the light to better see the door leading to the attic.

There was an old-fashioned sliding bolt in the door. It was closed.

Drooling toothpaste, he returned to the basin to finish his morning tasks.

"Who was that last night, Gloria? Did you see anyone down here? I know that wasn't you." The powerful espresso-maker had a mind of her own, a personality deserving of a name, but she had never wandered the house by night or day.

He was mystified. The apparition wasn't real, of course. It was a dream, generated by the fish and chips and wine, on top of all the recent turmoil. He was grateful it hadn't been a nightmare.

What was she pointing at, though? The attic? What would be in the attic? Bones?

"Oh, no you don't. Stop it. Whoever that wandering lady is, or was, she would have been properly buried. There's never been a rumour that any relative had 'disappeared'. Her body is not buried in the back yard. There are no bones in a trunk in the attic. Settle down."

To settle, he drank a double espresso before Mrs A arrived. He reminded his housekeeper that the new front door had a key, so she could open the windows if she felt she must, and lock the door, just to be safe.

"Nobody come," she said.

"Well, yes, in fact, I did, last week. I came in and made coffee and left again and you didn't know I was here. I didn't steal anything,, but somebody could have. I'm not comfortable thinking that you're unprotected when you're working here. So close the doors and open the screens if you must, okay?"

"What you say," she said, dismissively. "See you."

~

Thursday was his regular day for breakfast at the Daisy Café, but he debated whether to go in. He hadn't seen or heard from Evelyn since Sunday, and so much had happened since then. He felt oddly shy. Were they friends now? Had he understood it correctly?

"Stop it," he said to his rear-view mirror. "You second-guess yourself every time you find something that's good for you."

The car ahead of him stopped to turn left. He saw it just in time. *Too close!*

"Pay attention to the road, ya doofus," he muttered to himself. "But what you say is interesting, Tim, about second-guessing. Must make a note of that—when it's prudent to do so."

In the Daisy, he seated himself in his usual booth. Evelyn hollered across the room to him, as usual "Be right with ya, Tim, with a cuppa your favourite brew."

He smiled and waved as he lamely jotted down his most recent insight with his left hand: ~~You~~ *I second-guess anything that's good.*

He doodled a coffee-cup and saucer, with steam rising from the cup. The curls of steam were words: *hot, weak, bitter*. He heard Evelyn approaching, so he quickly closed the notebook. She might ask why he didn't write *delicious* on the drawing.

She brought coffee and a toasted English muffin and slid into the booth. "This is just for starters. I wanted to tell you I saw the obituary in the paper last night, and people have been pointing it out to me this morning. Nice old fella, Mr Barss. How're you doing?"

Tears again stung Tim's eyes.

"Oops," Evelyn said. "Didn't mean to turn on the waterworks. But we're friends, Tim, and friends share hard times as well as schlock movies."

Tim smiled. "Thanks for the card, Evelyn. That was nice of you. We'll do more."

"Sure. You shoulda called me when it happened, Tim. I have broad shoulders—real ones—and I can help, even if it's only to listen."

He cleared his throat. "Thanks, that means a lot. I'll do better. I guess I'm still learning how to be friends. And family."

"Me too. I was hoping you wouldn't say 'why didn't *you* call *me*?'"

"To you? Heck, I'd never do that. Anyway, I've been busy with GB's affairs, and my head's been full of thoughts and memories. I accidentally hurt my hand, too, see, and I couldn't write the eulogy, so I've been trying to memorize it."

"Hey, Ev!" someone called from a few booths down.

"Hay is for horses!" she shot back without turning. "Be right there, hon."

She started to slide out of the booth. "What can I getcha, Tim? You need to keep up your strength. The platter?"

"Gosh, no, I'd never finish all that. I over-ate last night. How about a poached egg on this muffin, and more of that strange hot drink?"

"You got it." She pressed on Tim's shoulder as she went to serve her other customers. There was warmth in her touch, and it reminded him of Melanie. He knew some very fine people.

He doodled more drawings and notes, left-handed. When Evelyn returned with a fresh English muffin and a poached egg on top, he noticed that the muffin under the egg had been cut into four sections, and the upper half had been buttered and spread with jam.

"You'll spoil me," he said.

"Been waiting to do that all my life," she replied. "Glad you're letting me, now."

When he went to the cash register to pay, Evelyn said, "No charge."

"You needn't do that. Here." He paid enough for the breakfast and a large tip, as usual.

"You needn't do that. Here." She pushed the money back across the counter.

They looked at each other and burst out laughing.

"You're very kind, Evelyn. I accept your gift—today only. Next time, back to normal, okay? It'll be too hard to keep track of whose turn it is to be generous. Deal?"

"Deal. Thanks for comin' in. Can I give you a hug?"

"I'd like that, but not today, okay? I don't want to lose it in here, and it seems like kindness brings on the tears. Thanks, though."

"Okay, soldier, carry on. See you soon."

He wondered where he should go next. Not home: Mrs A would be in full flight, and a person might be wounded if he got in her way.

The office was a logical place. He hadn't been in there since Monday, when he'd taken GB home. He'd have to face the staff sometime, so it might as well be now.

"Good morning, Mister Brown. It's good to see you," Rachael at the reception desk said.

"Good morning, Mister Brown. It's good to see you," said everyone he encountered as he walked through the office to the back stairs. Somebody had obviously schooled the staff in how to greet a grieving man.

It worked. He was able to return their greetings with a smile, and stay in control of himself, though his chest tightened when he passed GB's file cabinet empire. The overhead lights had been turned off in that corner, and a flip chart stood at the entrance:

In fond remembrance
of our friend and colleague,
GB
(Gregory Barss)
"We'll look you up."

Tim stopped to admire it. Then he walked to Ed Garamond's cubicle and leaned in. "Beautiful memorial poster, Ed."

"Thanks, Boss. I liked having the old guy around. No matter what kind of turmoil we were in out here, he never changed. He was like the steer at a bullfight."

"Oh, do you say? I hadn't thought of him that way, but he *was* calming."

"Calming, yeah, that's what I meant. Oh, and James came up with the tagline there."

"James did? It's clever. I don't see James in here now, but I'll congratulate him on that flash of literary brilliance."

There were several coloured envelopes in his mailbox, undoubtedly sympathy cards from staff. He put them on the table in his room but didn't open them. *I'm not afraid of sealed envelopes,* he told himself. *But there's a time to open and a time to keep closed.*

His cell phone rang.

"Hi Tim, it's Elaine. I saw you come in. May I come upstairs for a moment?"

"Sure."

He closed the door to his room and took a rag to dust the chairs in his visitors' room across the hall.

"Have a seat, Elaine, such as it is. How's biz? Nice obit for GB, thanks for that."

"Biz is good, Tim. Yes, everyone pitched in to research the obituary. James came up with the line on the poster."

"Ed told me. It's great."

"James seems to admire you a lot. I thought you'd want to know. Ever since you worked together on that story last month, he's always quoting you. You're full of wisdom."

"That's news. He did need a little kick up the stairs, so I'm glad to hear he's working out."

"Yes. So, may I ask—"

"I'm okay, Elaine, but I'm vulnerable to sympathy, so—"

"I get it. We'll keep it businesslike."

"Thanks. You'll be coming to the funeral tomorrow?"

"Yes, of course."

"Would you like to speak, at all? He was your employee, too."

"No, not I. But this is what I wanted to tell you: some of the staff have known GB and his wife for many years, and they've been sharing their memories here. If you're comfortable with that sort of thing, you might ask the audience—or whatever you call the mourners at a funeral—if anyone would like to say a few words. Or at the reception. There'll be one?"

"Yes, a reception. Just in time for lunch. Come hungry. That's a great suggestion, to ask the staff to speak. I've known GB for so long, yet I know so little about him."

He cleared his throat. "I'll try to keep it together tomorrow."

"You'll do fine. What happened to your hand? That bruise is ugly."

"Ah, yes, that. It is ugly, isn't it? I wanted to punish some unseen people, I guess, but since I'll never find them, I did it to myself. No broken bones."

"There's a story there, but I don't have time to hear it today. Got another edition of our relentless newspaper to generate. Another time? You're looking well, though, and that's good."

Back across the hall, Tim sat in his rolling chair and let the waves in the window-pane lead him to random thoughts, beginning with the staff wanting to express their own feelings of loss. He was impressed with their respect for GB, and the humorous tagline on the poster indicated their collegiality.

They're a good bunch.

And Evelyn, she was right in there like a dirty shirt, but still tentative, as he had been, careful not to put a foot wrong in the new territory of their friendship. He liked their caution; it meant their relationship was important. They would take care with each other and they would mean something to each other.

He remembered his night-visitor. *Who the heck was she supposed to be? Why was she pointing upward?*

His first thought was that she was pointing to the attic in his old house. He'd gone up there a few times as a child, but it was dusty and foreboding, and as far as he could recall, his mother had discarded all vestiges of ancestry, including any trunk large enough to contain bones. He wasn't motivated to go up there on the recommendation of a spectre he'd only dreamed up.

Or perhaps she was pointing farther up. Not to the attic, but to Heaven, the place where his own imagination persisted in telling him that GB had gone to wait for his wife.

"Well, I can't interpret apparition sign language," he said aloud. "I don't know who you are, madam, so we'll just have to go our separate ways. Especially you."

Thinking of GB and his wife reminded Tim that he hadn't yet gone to see Mrs Barss, so he locked his room and left the office building.

~

Mrs Barss was still in the ICU. They let Tim enter her room, but just briefly as he wasn't really next of kin. That person was in an urn at the funeral home.

Her skin was translucent, her pale eyelids even bluer than when he'd last seen them on Monday. *Was it only four days ago? Time flies when you're not having any fun at all.*

"Hi, Mrs Barss," Tim said from the foot of her bed. She was hooked up to monitors and tubes and he didn't want to bump any. "It's me, Tim. I'm sorry to find you here. GB was hoping to look after you forever—and I think he will. I know he will. He's gone on ahead to get ready for you. Everything's being taken care of at home. I hope you're not in pain."

There wasn't a flicker of recognition from the frail woman. Her breaths were almost imperceptible. Tim went to the nursing station.

"Any details I can share? I'll be speaking at her husband's funeral tomorrow and people will ask."

"Her condition is very precarious, Mr Brown. She appears to have suffered a series of strokes. Her attending physician has determined No Code, meaning she will not be resuscitated if she goes into cardiac arrest."

"I agree one hundred percent. She's ready to move on. She has business elsewhere."

The nurse smiled. "Many of our patients do. Our challenge is to sort out which to fight for and which to let go."

"May I ask your name—oh, I see it's on your tag. Susan, may I ask what your shift hours are?"

"I work twelve hours. Seven to seven. I'll keep an eye on her for you."

"I know you will. My phone numbers are here if you need me. Call anytime."

~

It was time to get ready for supper and choir. Tim had debated whether to skip choir tonight, just to avoid another barrage of sympathy, but Robert wouldn't take kindly to that, not with Easter and their concert just over two weeks away. The choir members were his community, and he'd be rude if he didn't allow them the opportunity to express their condolences.

Or maybe they wouldn't even make the connection between him and GB. He rarely talked about work in the choir loft. He was there to sing, to escape from work.

Robert arrived and they sat for tea. He was concerned about the weather, and glad to be off Highway 103 for the night. Precipitation was forecast and the temperature was dropping. There would be freezing rain, maybe even snow.

"Oh, do you think so? Tim said, peering out the window. "It's almost spring and gambolling weather. Let's be done with talk of snow, shall we?"

"*Que sera, sera*," Robert replied. "I just hope it doesn't start until the choristers get home tonight."

"Your cares are boundless, aren't they, Rob? I know I appreciate it."

Robert had been successful in finding instructors to cover his classes for Friday, so he had an extended weekend in South River. He went upstairs to make some calls.

"All arranged," he said when he came back down.

"What is?"

"I'm playing for the funeral tomorrow."

"What? You? What about their usual organist?"

"I told them you would pay her anyway. But I will play."

"Sure, but are you sure you want to? It's a creepy little instrument."

"No, I don't want to play it, but I wouldn't sleep tonight if I thought I'd have to sit and listen to someone else hack away on what sounds like a floor model accordion. Any requests? Maybe a nice polka?"

"No, thanks, I'll leave that to you. Just be aware that they sing funeral hymns reeeeel sloooow around here."

"We'll see about that."

~

Choir practice was all about the music. The new section leads were bringing out the best in the rest of the choristers. A few singers spoke quietly to him—"Sorry for your loss, Tim"—but there were no great displays of sympathy, for which he was grateful.

At home afterwards, they searched the larder. Tim hadn't planned their snack, but there was always something if you knew where to look. A can of smoked oysters was the discovery.

"Any of that Sainte-Famille wine left, Tim? I'd be interested in tasting it."

Tim reached into the recycling bin and held the empty bottle upside down. "No can do, sorry, and I can't really tell you what it tasted like, though it must have been good, since it's gone and my head didn't hurt. My fish was good, too."

"Bravo! We'll go there again this summer and buy more. I enjoyed that drive."

"Oh, going for drives in the summer? Yes, please!"

"Okay now," Robert said, sitting back. "Let's hear your speech."

They spent the rest of the evening rehearsing the eulogy. Robert jotted down the salient points so Tim would have a written guide. Finally, Tim was confident of his presentation and his ability to give it without bursting into tears.

March 19: We have an anchor

Friday

They went to the funeral parlour early so Robert could have a look at the instrument he had insisted he wanted to play. It wasn't the very worst of electronic organs. The funeral director came into the salon a couple times to advise him that "we usually" or "we don't" do this or that. Robert politely nodded and carried on with his exploration.

The funeral director ushered Tim into the Family Room. He was alone, and that didn't suit him, so he wandered around for a while, chatting with the caterers who were setting up sandwiches and beverages in the reception area. He peeked into the salon, and was pleased to see a photo of GB, enlarged, enhanced, framed, and displayed on an easel next to the urn containing his ashes.

It seemed the entire staff of *The Times* was there. He saw Elaine Fong and walked over to whisper to her. She listened, nodded, and whispered to the others who were in her row. Soon, the staff of the newspaper filed out of the salon and into the Family Room, all except James, who stayed at the door to direct other staff to join them.

Then it was time. Accompanied by Robert's masterful deployment of the organ, the funeral home staff led the very large "family" to the front three rows, and proceedings began. Tim had left most of the details to the funeral director, who had engaged their usual minister to lead in whatever prayers and scripture readings he selected. No one at work could recall GB ever mentioning church. Perhaps those children's missions were his church. Perhaps Tim had rushed to judgment about that, though the state of GB's home did indicate he'd been over-contributing to something.

Tim rubbed the back of his bruised right hand to bring himself sharply back to the present.

He approached the lectern and set Robert's notes on it. He looked at the mourners assembled in the room, took a deep breath and exhaled slowly, as his massage therapist had taught him, then began to speak.

"Gregory Barss was known fondly and forever to us as GB. We all thought GB was exclusively ours. Speaking for myself, he was always just *there* at the office, quietly working away. We didn't always know what he did, but if we had a question for him, he would do his best to find an answer. I daresay the entire history of South River is filed alphabetically *and* chronologically in his ever-expanding banks of file cabinets. It will take some patience and a lot of effort to carry on GB's life's work, but we will do it. He left us with a valuable asset, and sad hearts."

He drew another deep breath.

"Just hours before he died, I realized how much GB meant to me personally, and I regret that I was too late to act on it. I thought we still had time. I indulged in feeling sorry for myself for a bit, I confess, but I'm moving on to gratitude for the steadfast caring that he showed me when I was a kid growing up, until now—still growing up.

"I invited everyone who's here from the office to join me in the Family seats. His wife is in the hospital, at death's door, barring some miracle, and to my knowledge, she is all the family he has—except for all of us. He taught us constancy and respect for our co-workers, and I for one am grateful for his great legacy.

"Now, I'd like to invite any who wish to do so to come up and speak briefly about GB, maybe share a personal memory."

Several said that he was a lovely man and he would be missed. One woman said he had loaned her money when her purse had been stolen, which was news to Tim. One man said he had arranged to plow the Barss' driveway this past winter when GB wasn't able to shovel it out, and Mrs Barss had made him the best biscuits he'd ever had.

After everyone had spoken, Robert beckoned to someone at the back of the room. Tim noticed Stella near the back, Behind her, the choir's new lead bass stood to sing three verses of "Abide With Me" as a solo. The funeral director had warned Robert it would cause more distress than it was worth if he left it out, so Robert had put it in, with feeling.

That hymn could pull tears from the hardest of hearts on a good day, and all hearts were soft today. Then Robert played the introduction to the final hymn, and everyone stood to sing "Will Your Anchor Hold?" He created more trumpet-sounds than that instrument had been designed for.

> We have an anchor that keeps the soul
> steadfast and sure while the billows roll,
> Fastened to the rock which cannot move,
> grounded firm and deep in the Saviour's love.

Stella made a quick appearance at the reception. All funeral-goers were impressed.

"Did you know GB?" they asked her.

"Oh, yes. I think he baby-sat me, back in the corner sometimes, in my day. Lovely man."

Tim thought that was actually his story, but he wasn't about to quibble with Stella in this setting. She honoured GB—and *The Times*—by attending this funeral. A little fiction when facts were in short supply seemed more than kind.

The funeral director spoke to Robert as he gathered up his scores. "Thank you for the lovely music," he said. "Not sad enough for the regular mourners, but our staff enjoyed it."

"You're welcome," Robert said. "But check the organ. I may have blown a fuse."

The staff had attended the funeral during office hours. It had been some weeks since Elaine had offered to trade time off for an all-nighter, but everyone who was able to work around personal and family requirements had signed up. The whole day was a team-building event.

Tim carefully placed the urn containing GB's ashes on the back seat and wrapped his car blanket around it to protect it. The wind was strong and decidedly colder now than when they had entered the funeral home in the morning, and the sky looked heavy. One of the mourners, holding on to her hat in the parking lot, called out, "It's Sheila's Brush coming!"

Inside the car, Robert said, "What was she saying? Who's Sheila?"

"Sheila's Brush is the last snowstorm of winter, between Saint Patrick's Day and the arrival of Spring. It's folklore, better known in Newfoundland than here. Sheila puts the run to the drunken Saint with her broom."

"And you know this because?"

"Because I run a delightful little community newspaper, and we get to report on such unwelcome storms every so often. Looks like this might be one of those. We'd better lay in some provisions to keep us from resorting to cannibalism!"

The wind was carrying sharp bits of ice now, and soon it would be slippery underfoot. No matter how nasty the weather became tonight, Tim knew of two places he was certain wouldn't close down. They stopped at their favourite pizza shop, and ordered three large with assorted toppings to be delivered to the Intensive Care Unit at the hospital at five o'clock, and three large with the works to go to *The Times* at seven. Both to be sent "With gratitude, from Tim".

For their own dinner, Robert found two rib eye steaks at the grocery, well marbled, just waiting for his touch. Tim picked out potatoes to bake and some nice-looking out-of-season asparagus. There would be suitable wine in the cellar at home.

They went home in swirling snow.

~

Tim lit a fire, glad of both the flames and the storm, as they seemed to go together so well. Snow was sticking to telephone wires and windshield wipers outside, but it was comfortable inside.

When he brought GB's urn in from the car, he had taken it to the den and placed it on the small table between the two recliner chairs. Once the fire was blazing, he brought the urn to the coffee-table in the parlour.

In response to Robert's raised eyebrows, he said, "It's too soon for him to be in the room by himself. Maybe he can hear us. I'm reading a story to his wife and I don't know if she can hear me either, so what's the difference? I'll find a permanent place for him later."

While the potatoes baked in the oven, they sat on the sofa to talk about the day and week. Tim got up and moved the urn to a side table, which relaxed Robert, and then to a bookshelf against the wall. GB could listen in from there if he wanted to.

Evelyn had left a message apologizing that she couldn't make it to the funeral, because they were short-staffed today.

"My goodness, I enjoyed meeting Evelyn," Robert said. "Let's bring her over again soon."

Tim mentioned how surprised he was that Stella had come to the funeral home. "And she called you to tell you, too. That surprised me."

"She's quite a caring person, you know."

"So it seems."

Robert looked at him, eyebrows raised.

"No, really, it's mostly hearsay to me. After my mother died, Stella set herself up as my—I dunno what, guardian, maybe, or governess—and she never hesitates to tell me what to say or how to behave. I was an adult then, still am, but it's only recently that she has recognized that, or shown glimpses of warmth toward me. She's really nice sometimes, if the claws don't come out. I wish they wouldn't."

Robert nodded without comment.

"Anyway, Rob, you pulled in a lot of the choir to the funeral, and Elaine brought staff. That was really nice. I've been to funerals where I was almost the only mourner."

"People were happy to come, either for Mr Barss or for Timothy Brown. You're pretty highly regarded, you know."

"Am I? That's nice of you to say."

A timer rang in the kitchen. "The potatoes will be ready soon."

Tim asked Robert to cut up his food as his right hand wasn't ready yet to wield a steak knife.

Dinner was over when the phone rang. Tim said hello, heard someone counting, then multiple voices: "One, two, three, thank-you, Mister Brown!"

"You're welcome! I guess the delivery guy's still on the roads. Drive home safely, everyone—whenever the boss lets you leave, ha-ha!"

Elaine took the phone off speaker. "It's almost raining down here at sea-level," she said. "But anyone who lives inland or up near you might run into some slippery going. We'll be careful. James has offered to drive everyone home in his Jeep. You okay to-night, Tim?"

"Yes, I am, Elaine. I'm very okay. Thanks again. Good night."

March 20: Sheila's Brush

Saturday

This year's Sheila's Brush was more legend than event. The sun rose in a clear sky, and while it wasn't a warm spring day, it was the final day of winter.

They slept in, a luxury. The Ghost of Whatever She Was hadn't visited again, though Tim did glance at the bolt on the attic door as he padded to the bathroom. If he ever saw that bolt pulled back, he thought he might just abandon the house and put it up for sale.

He didn't mention the apparition to Robert when he carried espressos upstairs.

"What would you like to do with this bonus day, Rob?"

"You won't like it."

"Try me."

"Well, first, can we go to the Daisy Café for breakfast? Will Evelyn be working? I like diner food."

"Sure, if you like. Yes, she works six days a week, most weeks, poor thing. Hey, I'll challenge you to the Battle of the South River Log-Jam Platters!"

"I'm not sure what that is, but it sounds fabulous. So, the other thing is...do you mind if I spend a couple hours at the church today? I have a lot of practising to catch up on, and it would make me very happy and mellow to do it on that organ."

"How can I object, then? You can practise while I run errands. I'll pick you up when you call me, how's that?"

"Oh, that's perfect. Thank you so much. Easter looms ever closer, and you know me, Mister Preparation."

"I do know you. Do you want me to invite a hundred guests to dinner so you can throw knives around in the kitchen to soothe your nerves?"

"Ha-ha, not at this time, but thanks. I think I'll keep them under control, if I can spend some time at the console."

Evelyn was surprised to see Tim come in on a Saturday, and excited to see Robert again. "Wow, my two favourite guys," she greeted them, then dropped her voice. "I'd better keep that to myself. They all think they're my favourites."

Then she erupted in laughter, and all was well with the world.

Evelyn brought coffee and menus, and then passed by carrying platters to another table.

"See that?" Tim pointed to the pile of food. "That's the Log-Jam."

"Thanks for the warning. Can I just have toast and jam?"

"I'll order for you. You'll need more than that if you're going to play for hours."

Robert took a sip from the cup and grimaced. "What's in this?"

"*Shhh.* They call it coffee here. It's been awful since 1967. It's okay if you've just had a big mouthful of something greasy, though. Stick with me, pal, I'll show you how South River lives, down here at sea-level, as Elaine says."

While they waited for their order, Tim produced the list he'd made after last weekend, a lifetime in the past now, it seemed to him. One special lifetime, anyway.

Robert pointed to one item:

Dopamine??? Evelyn.

"Good list, again. I agree that Evelyn is a natural source of dopamine."

"Who you callin' a dope?" Evelyn said, setting down their plates. She had cut Tim's food into bite-size pieces.

Tim grinned and held his injured hand over his heart.

Robert said, "Dopamine is a drug that the brain makes when it's happy, according to Tim here, and you bring out the dopamine in me." He grinned a made-for-TV grin, and Evelyn swatted his shoulder.

She was busy this morning with the local brunch crowd, but she bumped Tim sideways and sat down for a moment. "Everything go okay yesterday?"

"It did, thanks. I was gratified with the turnout and all the cards and messages. Thank you for yours. Thanks for cutting up my food, too."

~

Robert asked Tim to wait while he checked that the church wasn't in use. He returned to the side door in a few minutes and waved him away.

Tim drove to the hospital. It was not yet visiting hours, and the door to the ICU was locked, but he rang the bell and waved at the nurse who came to the door.

"I'm Tim Brown. Constance Barss is my friend, and I'm wondering—"

"You're Tim Brown? I've certainly heard of you! Thank you so much for the pizza!"

"You had the pizza? How long have you been on duty?"

"Oh, I just came on at seven this morning, but leftover pizza is a great treat at the start of a shift. Listen, we're not supposed to allow visitors yet, but—you're here to see Mrs Barss, right?"

Tim nodded.

"You follow me. Just for a minute."

"How—what's her status?"

"Same. She's low, but she's like an old cat. They just conserve energy and hang on for a long time."

"Is she conscious? Does she know I'm here?"

"I would never say never. I've seen some amazing recoveries, so it's best to assume she can."

"Hi, Mrs Barss, it's me, Tim. We held GB's funeral yesterday. I think you would've been proud. So many people were there, and a lot of them spoke about how much GB meant to them."

There wasn't a flicker from the patient.

"There's no expenses for you to worry about. Your home is locked, so things are safe. I brought GB's ashes home with me until, uh, until you decide what you'd like us to do with them. Plenty of time for that. You rest, now. I'll come back later."

Staff nodded and smiled at Tim as he left the unit. Pizza was never not appreciated. He smiled back.

He was over being sad. He wanted a little happiness.

~

Happiness began at noon when he picked up Robert.

"Good practice?"

"Oh, my goodness, yes. That is such a gorgeous instrument, I always get a lift when I have a chance to really play it. It shook off the leftover jangle from that he-haw thing at the funeral home."

"Be nice, now. If you practise, I bet you could be really good on that he-haw thing. You could be their back-up supply organist for funerals."

"Just kill me now. Oh, I'm sorry, I shouldn't joke about death, not after the week you've been through."

"What I want more than anything today is jokes, laughter, happiness in all its forms. I was very, very sad about GB, and I will miss him a lot. What I was grieving, I think, was that I could've been closer to him, and I missed it by a day. I realized, when I took him home and sent his wife to the hospital, that I could be family for him, for them, and they for me. He'd been my uncle-in-lieu, d'you see, always there, always a kind word for me. It struck me Monday evening that I wanted more time with him, and it wouldn't be a stretch at all. I could drop in, have tea, maybe help out with a few things around the house, take him for a drive—nothing big, you know, just the small change of life. Just sharing time. So when I went back on Tuesday to take him to the hospital, you know what I said when I went in the door?"

Robert waited.

"I said, 'Hi, uncle, it's me!' But he was gone."

He paused. His eyes stung sharply. He cleared his throat. "I guess I'm not entirely over it. That's okay. What hurts me right in the heart, to tell you the truth, is that I loved saying that. 'Hi, uncle!' I wanted that so much. I've never in my whole life gone in a door and called out 'It's me!' to anyone, certainly not my mother. Maybe my father, I don't remember. That's kind of tragic, don't you think?"

"I do. I made many an entrance through many doors in my childhood, hollering my presence. To mixed reactions, I might add."

"Sure, but mixed is good. I got only one reaction, and it was 'Hush!', from Mother, who was my entire family. I learned to let myself in quietly. Aunt Stella seems to have appointed herself Mother's successor in disapproval, though that's improving."

They drove along in silence for a few kilometres.

"Where are we going, if you don't mind sharing?"

"I don't know. Is that okay? We're driving and talking, something we haven't had time nor weather to do forever, it seems. I'm looking for somewhere to have lunch. Then we'll head back. I went to the hospital this morning so I still need to pick up a few things for supper. It's Italian night, and it's my turn to make it."

They were on the secondary highway past Mahone Bay and Chester to the village of Hubbards, where a roadside diner was advertising the special of the day.

"Oh, can we stop there? They have chowder."

Tim braked, turned the car around, and pulled into a parking space in front of the little place. They went in and ordered the special, which was delicious.

For the homeward leg of their voyage, Tim drove out around the Aspotogan Peninsula, which formed the eastern shore of St. Margaret's Bay on the outward side of the peninsula, and the western side of Mahone Bay heading in. It was a twisty road, offering many vistas of the Atlantic Ocean and those bays, though not to the driver. Robert hadn't been on that road before, so as the passenger, he admired and commented on every kilometre.

Once they were back on the straighter road back to South River, he was quiet. Glancing over, Tim saw that he had fallen asleep. He slept soundly until Tim returned to the car with grocery bags.

"What—what happened to the gorgeous scenery? Where's my ocean?"

"It's still there, but we had to leave it behind for the more mundane cares of the day, like getting ingredients for dinner.”

“Another meal? I hope it’s not a big one.”

“I concur. I can’t fit into anything but sweat pants. Even so, today’s dish is pasta. I can make the sauce, if you’ll open the cans and roll the meatballs. I think I can twirl the fork to eat spaghetti, but anything more complex still hurts my hand.”

Dinner was delicious. Tim was good with garlic, olive oil, tomato sauce and spices. He didn’t make his own pasta—though that challenge might be in his future—but fresh pasta from the store was acceptable. Sunset was around six-thirty, so they began their meal in welcome vestiges of natural light.

“I’m very sleepy,” said Tim as he was rinsing their dishes..

“I’m dead already, even though you say I slept this afternoon. Oh, damn, I’ve said it again. Sorry.”

“No sorry needed. Do you have any interest in watching a *feelm* tonight?”

“I couldn’t possibly. You go ahead if you like.”

“No for me, too. I may need help getting upstairs. Why are we so tired?”

“I think we’ve had the opposite of dopamine,” Robert said.

“What’s that?”

“It’s called life. We’ve had a lot of it. Maybe too much. Let’s lie down and let it pass.”

Preparing for bed, Tim said, “Did I tell you about my ghost?”

“No, you didn’t, and I forbid you to! Not ever! Ghosts? They are so possible in this house. Please, Tim, I care about you deeply and wish nothing but your happiness, but unless a ghost comes at you on wings of real fire, please do not tell me about it or I won’t sleep here tonight. I’m serious. Please. Promise?”

“I promise. It was just a dream, and there was no fire. No wings, either. Wings go with angels, like you.”

Tim gave him a bear hug.

“Today was great, Rob. Thanks for being here.”

March 21: Vernal equinox

Sunday

Their "raveled sleave of care" was knit up with a good night's sleep. There may not be such a thing as caring too much, but caring and looking out for loved ones can be exhausting.

They woke a bit dunderheaded, but as they showered, shaved, and coffeed, they began to feel restored.

"What's today, Tim?" Robert was at Gloria's controls this morning, extracting their first infusion of the day.

"Hmm, I dunno. March twenty-first, I think? Sunday?"

"Right on both counts, but two more correct answers are required before you win the grand prize. What else?"

"Must I? Oh, is today the first day of spring? Yay! We made it! Then let us, peasants all, dance around the Maypole—oh, I guess it's a couple months early for the Maypole. *Wolcum Yole?* No, that's Christmas. Do we gambol now?"

"One more."

"Oh, I can't think of what else would be significant today."

"On March twenty-first, forty years ago..."

"Oh, that's ancient history, Rob. Before my time. You can't possibly expect me to recall, or remember, or know, or confess, or admit..."

Robert reached into a cupboard behind the cups and glassware, and brought out a small box, wrapped in silver paper with a bow on top. "Forty years ago was the beginning of a life more dear to me than any other. I'm so glad you were born then, and are very much alive now. Happy birthday to the man I adore."

Tim knew it was his birthday, of course. It's a rare person who isn't aware of turning forty. He didn't mind birthdays, not even this one, but as the events of the previous week had unfolded, he'd hoped there wasn't any surprise birthday event planned.

"What's this, Rob? Should I say, 'You shouldn't have'?"

"Not yet. Open it."

Tim untied the bow, pulled off the wrapping, and lifted the lid of the little box. Inside, resting on a bed of jewellers' fluff, was a pewter pin of a bird in flight.

"It made me think of you," Robert said. "It's graceful, wings extended, flying onward."

"It's gorgeous, Rob. I love it. Thank you so much. I'll wear it today!"

~

In the choir room, Tim accepted more heavy hugs. He was grateful to receive expressions of sympathy on the passing of a cherished family member. His family had grown by one, whose loss he grieved. It felt like a blessing.

Since the main business of the choir's social secretary was to know every member's birth date, she announced that today was Tim's and they sang "Happy Birthday" in four-part harmony but quietly so they wouldn't disturb worshipful activities going on elsewhere in the building.

On the way home, Robert asked, "How would you like to celebrate your day, Tim? We already had breakfast out, lunch out, and a scenic drive. What's next?"

"I'd very much like to do nothing today. Is that possible? I was afraid that someone might have planned a party of some kind, but I'd rather not be in a gathering for a while."

"Perfect! I was hoping you'd say that. If you feel like going out for dinner later we certainly can. No party today, sorry. I didn't secretly invite anyone. We'll celebrate your birthday when we can stroll in the garden in balmy summer breezes."

"What a lovely thought. I'll take you up on it when that season rolls around. But today is spring on the calendar, and that's good enough. Let's take off our churchy clothes, put on our sweatpants, and pretend the fireplace is sunshine. I'm sure the earth will warm up soon, so we can burn the rest of the woodpile without a care now."

After lunch, Tim said, "You know what? Let's order Chinese food later. I think I have a take-out menu here somewhere. It's not great, but it's different. Yes, beef broccoli and chow mein is exactly what I want. And spring rolls."

"Your wish is my command," Robert said. "Do they deliver?"

"You can ask when you place the order."

Robert browsed through the huge menu and selected their dishes. He placed the order and was assured that they would deliver it at the specified time.

With the afternoon thus freed, Robert worked in his study while Tim dozed in front of the fire. Mid-afternoon, Tim reminded Robert that they should go for a walk.

While they were strolling, Tim said, "You know, GB remembered that today was my birthday."

"Is that unusual?"

"I don't know. I was at work every birthday since I was born, until this year. There would have been some mention of it. Nobody remembers those things until they see the card coming around for everybody to sign. But he did. He mentioned it earlier this month, when I asked him to confirm some birth and death dates."

"That's nice."

"Yeah. That is nice. My uncle remembered my birthday. That's who he was and that's what he did."

Later, Robert thinly chopped some vegetables to stir-fry, to improve whatever the restaurant sent for Tim's birthday dinner.

Stella called. The connection was poor, but Tim could make out that she was in the car, in an area where the signal was the best she had found driving cross-country. She was calling to wish him a "Hap— —day" and would see him on Tuesday. Then the signal dropped.

"Spencer's at the wheel and Stella's fuming in the back seat because there's no signal for her to make her calls," Tim reported. "I share her frustration. The cellular phone invention is ahead of itself: phones but no signal. They didn't invent cars and then start building roads. It's stupid."

"What did she call about?"

"To wish me a hap-*shhhhh*-day, as far as I could make out. And to confirm our meeting Tuesday."

"You two have a meeting?"

"Yup. I asked her to fill me in on my family background, especially about my late father. She bared her teeth at me, but she agreed. I'm learning to ignore her hissing and wait for the thing I want."

"Then you are learning something valuable."

"Yeah? Like what? Is that what you do? Now that I think about it, you almost never argue if someone crosses you."

"It's just not worthwhile to argue. If I have stated my case, there's no point repeating it."

"Not everyone is as content to rest their case as you are. Everyone says how nice Stella is, so I get the feeling that it's just me."

"What do you hope to learn? About your father, I mean."

"Anything, really. He died when I was only five, as you know. I recall so little about him. He liked me, I think, and I'm grateful for even that. But maybe she can tell me something about him, his interests, and what he was good at. Maybe why he died."

"She knew him?"

"I'm not sure she did. I think she was still overseas at some mission when he died. But she would've heard something from Mother, one would think. Stella said I wouldn't like it. Perhaps what I won't like is the way she'll tell whatever she knows, you know, being judgmental. I'm willing to risk it. My massage therapist said I am fearless, so I'm going in with her belief behind me."

"Mine too, Timo. You have all the strength you need, especially if you don't try to fight with her. You are also toweringly respectful. Stella might mistake that for weakness."

"Oh, that's interesting. Too respectful? What should I do about that?"

"Not a thing. You said you didn't engage when she started in on you the last time. If that worked, do it again. She'll catch on. She's a smart cookie. She loves you, and she'll not want to lose her connection with you. And I said 'toweringly', not 'too' respectful."

"Thanks, Rob. I'll try to be a good student."

"You'll be fine. And, for the record, your aunt remembered your birthday, too."

March 22: What else?

Monday

As soon as Robert left for the city, Tim filled a container with leftover Chinese food and drove downtown. He went directly to his room, picking up more cards from the mailbox on the way. Not all were messages of sympathy. His birthday had not gone unnoticed by his staff.

He reviewed his notes, still on the walls. The list of seemingly unrelated words, plus his attempt at listing his family's important dates, had led him to request vital stats from GB, whose own set of dates was now complete.

He had the dates from Harold, who would no doubt "do something" with GB's life's work of clipping and taping. That was a comfort.

GB had also pointed Tim to his family Bible, which revealed little new information other than his grandparents' names, and a surprise tucked in its thin pages. He would take that envelope to Stella tomorrow. Another good find, kindness of GB.

GB might have been a good Watson to his Sherlock, someone to listen to his hunches, maybe offer an incisive insight. He might even have enjoyed sitting quietly in this white room, listening while Tim thought out loud...or not. He had asked GB an open question back in the winter, but GB hadn't known how to respond. Perhaps he'd lacked confidence in his own opinions after decades of supplying very specific information. Tim would have encouraged him, trained him in the Watson role.

Maybe he'd needed more interesting questions. As a newspaperman, Tim knew that questions mattered, but did he need a different kind of question now, in this Year of Delving? What would it be, besides the famous five: who, what, where, when, and why? What else?

He wrote on a paper on the wall: *5W: What else?* He wandered around the room, looked out the window, and looked at the sheet again.

The question he needed was right there: *What else?* That's what he would ask Stella, whenever she released some tiny tid-bit of family history. He drew a red circle around that question.

"She'll tell me my father was funny and kind, and I'll say, 'What else?' And then she'll say he was tall and thin like me and I'll say, "What else?'"

He wrote down other phrases designed to encourage more in-formation:

> How interesting.
> Do tell.
> In relation to what?
> Compared to whom?
> Is that all?
> Tell me more.
> How do you know?
> Who said / who told you this?

These last two could sound argumentative. He'd try to come at them gently. Stella was better at the thrust and parry of interviews than he. Rather than a fencing match, he'd strive for a gentle Q&A.

He'd solved a puzzle right under her nose in January because he had made visual aids, which she believed to be authentic, and her reaction provided him with good clues. What aids did he have now?

"Every good question deserves a list," he said, taping another sheet to the wall. He entitled it *Visual Aids*, and listed items he could take along to support the questions:

Family Bible
Envelope
Vital Stats report

He wished he could show her the apparition that had appeared in his dream, pointing upward. What would Stella make of that? Since it was a dream from his imagination, she'd likely deride him for even mentioning it, so he wouldn't. The woman in the nightgown wasn't a visual aid, but she was still an invisible aid, so he'd keep her in mind.

He'd asked Stella to tell him what she knew, but he hadn't really identified his expectations. These questions would help.

He heated lunch in the staff room microwave. While the device was whirring, the clerk who took classified ads over the phone said, "Got a big meeting up there today, Mister Brown?"

"Me? No. Why?"

"I heard people talking. Just wondered."

"Oh, that was me, sorry. Just me. I talk out loud when I'm trying to work things out."

"Oh, well, then, I hope you won the argument."

"Did I sound argumentative?"

"Kinda."

"Then I'd better soften up. If I go in arguing I'll come out in a fight, and that's not what I want at all. Especially not with myself. Thanks for the feedback!"

As he nibbled the tasty leftovers, he searched the perimeter of his room, examining the floor. Behind the cabinet he'd dragged in for storage of his rolled papers, he discovered a goodish hole in the floor where something had been removed years ago. Directly below it was the dropped ceiling with acoustic tile, but evidently his voice carried through this hole if he was speaking near it. His privacy was an illusion, it seemed.

He balled up a sheet of manila paper, stuffed it into the opening, and shoved the heavy cabinet over it. He needed to hear himself talk, but the newspaper staff didn't. It was odd that he hadn't noticed office sounds coming up through the floor before, but now that the opening was closed, the ambient sound was much diminished. It was an old building. Nothing was tight.

~

It was springish, and he was over forty, two good reasons to go for a post-lunch walk. Also, he had the library's copy of *The Adventures of Sherlock Holmes* to return, finally.

Marlene Wentzell, the Chief Librarian, was on the phone when he entered the library. He waited. This wasn't just any book return. It was a chance to exchange words with Marlene, always a bright spot for Tim.

"Good afternoon, Tim. What brings you to our hallowed halls today?"

"Any excuse, Marlene. But today I am pleased to return Sherlock Holmes to you, more or less in good condition."

He swung the bag containing the heavy book up to the counter.

"My own copy finally arrived at the bookstore in Lunenburg. Oh, phooey—it just occurred to me that I should have brought you the new copy and kept this one. Darn! I'll do it right away, okay?"

"There's no need to do that, Tim," Marlene said with a laugh. "We expect a certain amount of wear and tear, and this looks fine."

"Yes, but this one is marked in, and the binding is broken in, too, where the new one is stiff and unyielding. In fact, it refuses to stay open without two hands on it, like this one did when I first borrowed it. I'd really prefer to keep this copy. Please may I?"

"Certainly, if you wish. Leave it here and I'll get the tags ready for the duplicate. By the way, Tim, my condolences on the loss of Mr Barss. He was a regular visitor here. We'll miss him."

"Thanks, Marlene. It was quite a shock in many ways. GB came in here often, did he?"

"Oh yes, every week."

"I didn't know he was a reader. May I ask what kind of books he borrowed?"

"All kinds of people are readers, thank goodness. They keep us busy. Mr Barss's tastes varied widely. From wild animals of the

Amazon to Gothic novels, he consumed them all."

"That is something I did not know about him, Marlene. Gosh. I'm surprised."

"Perhaps you also didn't know that he took them home to read aloud to Mrs Barss. That's how they spent their evenings. Not watching television. A superior life, in my opinion."

"Indeed." Tim tried to envision GB reading a vampire bodice-ripper to Constance. The image wouldn't come.

"Will there be anything else just now, Tim?"

"Hm? Um, yes. Could you look him up to see if he has any books out?"

"Surely." She clicked through screens on her computer.

"Yes, it looks like there are two. They're not priorities."

"His house is locked now, Marlene, and I don't have a key. The place could be unheated, so the books could be damp. May I pay for them, please? GB wouldn't want to leave a debt, not here. Mrs Barss either, though I fear her reading days are over, too. She's in the hospital."

"Leave it with me. I'll have the accounts ready when you return with your new acquisition. You're a good person, Tim."

Marlene's comment made his walk twice around the two bridges a pleasure. He stopped on the Old Bridge to take out his little notebook and a pencil stub to write down her words: *A good person.*

On the New Bridge, he stopped again to add: *Fearless. Toweringly respectful.*

These were good notes. Maybe he'd keep little notes of what people said about him, good or bad, and see what kind of profile emerged. He tucked the notebook back in his pocket and carried on for another lap, whistling as he went.

~

Tim spent a couple more hours in the room, refining his questions and identifying things to ask Stella about. He didn't expect to arrive at any conclusion, so logic or proofs weren't factors. His father was a mystery, but not the kind to solve. Heck, he had just written down "clues" describing himself, whom he had known for the better part of forty years, so he'd need to accept some uncertainties about a man who died thirty-five years ago, at age twenty-three.

Maybe there wasn't a lot to tell. He expected Stella to say that. She wasn't even living in South River at the time, so what stories she could tell would be only hearsay.

And who would be the source of that hearsay? Brownie, of course. She made no attempt to hide her bitterness toward her late husband, and Stella may have adopted her attitude. Rumour and gossip could still be helpful; they might add some context.

He wrote *Hearsay vs Rumour vs Gossip.* Did one contain more truth than the other? He thought that hearsay was the superior form of dubious information. Rumour and gossip were often tinged with carelessness or a desire to harm, whereas hearsay could well be truth, just unproven. He considered this to be a valuable insight.

He transferred these notes from the wall to the little notebook to help him stay on track tomorrow. He locked the door and drove to the grocery store. Stella was coming to his house tomorrow, so he searched for something to serve with coffee, to be hospitable. Everything in the bakery department looked unappealing, all icing on dough. He knew the bakery downriver would be sold out of their creations by this time of day, so he went home with nothing. He'd bake something himself.

Stella had left a message that she would arrive at half-past ten tomorrow, following an unavoidable meeting earlier.

He hoped he was ready.

March 23: Yearbook

Tuesday

"Fearless, are you? I don't believe it. You're as jumpy as a cat."

Tim spoke out loud to calm himself as he rolled out the pastry for cinnamon rolls, but it didn't help much. He'd had just one latté, anticipating that he'd be nervously drinking much more coffee this morning.

He tidied up in the den. The electric fireplace would be enough ambience, and the small room might work best for sensitive conversation.

Stella arrived at ten-thirty sharp. "Nice door," she said as Tim held open the new storm door.

"Thanks. Finally got it installed. I'm going to send the bill to *The Daily*."

"Good luck with that. They'll refuse. Aren't you friends with the publisher?"

"An editor, yes, somewhat, but I don't think I should escalate a damaged door claim all the way to the management."

"Don't you? That's where they say yes. The minions can only say no, and the execs won't override them, not for this. My advice? Expect, don't ask. Offer to write something for publication—maybe an essay on something you've learned this year—so when they cut your cheque they'll think they're paying you for that. And you'll get your piece published in a paper where it will live for twenty-four hours before someone lines their cat box with it."

"I was going to thank you for the advice, but now I don't know. I'll think about it, though. I ask them to reimburse me for the door, and to clinch the deal, I'll offer to write an essay? Seems cockeyed."

"Just a suggestion. Always look at it from the point of view of what *they* want, not what you want. And a little surprise never hurts. In Opposition, we wouldn't be effective at all if we didn't tie one thing to another. Not all my colleagues agree, but I get what I want from the Government because I give them something they want, a *quid pro quo.*"

"All the time?"

"I'll never tell. What's that delicious aroma? Have you been baking?"

"Guilty. Cinnamon rolls. Allow me to take your beverage order and we'll try them out."

When the coffee was ready, they took their cups to the den. Tim brought extra cushions so Stella could sit upright in the soft recliner chair, meant for a taller body.

"All right, Timothy, let's get to it. When we last met, we didn't anticipate that Gregory Barss would die suddenly. That must have been difficult for you. You spoke very well at his funeral, by the way. Now we're going to talk about the dead again, but by your choice. You asked me to tell you about Ford Brown. Is this still your wish?"

"Yes. You said I wouldn't like it, but I'm prepared for whatever it is."

"Good. I've had some time to think about it, and I heard what you said about rumours. I live with rumours every day, about me, my thoughts, my intentions, my party. I prefer not to acknowledge them, but this deals with someone about whom little is known, so perhaps we can consider rumours, if only to debunk them. All right?"

"Yes. Whatever you have."

Tim had his list of conversation-prompts ready.

"As you know, Ford was an athlete, captain of the football team."

"Wait—what? How do you know this? I mean, is this fact, or second-hand from Mother, or rumour or—or hearsay? Forgive me, but I know so little about him, and the first thing you tell me is a surprise, so—"

"Your mother didn't tell you even this much? My goodness. All right. Look here."

Stella reached into her large designer bag and lifted out a book with a blue embossed cover and gilt letters. It was the South River High School 1958 Yearbook.

"Where'd you get that?"

"From someone who graduated that year."

"Of course. I suppose you keep records of all your constituents, and you'd know when they graduated from high school. By the way, we're looking at how to make GB's records searchable and available to people in positions like yours. File that away."

"Interesting. Keep me informed." Stella pointed to the yearbook. "Open it at that tab."

He opened the yearbook. He saw two pages of teenagers from long ago, looking so mature in their out-of-fashion clothes and haircuts. *Brown, Ford* was among the first. Tim had never seen a photo of his father before, and he stared at it now, turning on the reading lamp between them to get a better look.

Ford looked like a serious boy, almost menacing, as a football quarterback might. Even in a shirt, tie, and gown, he looked like a guy who meant business. Physical business.

And there was the evidence, in the caption below his picture. "*If it's in the air, I'll catch it. If it's in front of me, I'll hit it. If it's in my hand, I'll throw it.*"

Tim read these words out loud.

"Charming," Stella said. "Not an academic, it seems."

"Easy now."

"Of course. He was unlikely to be a good journalist, is what I meant, but that attitude would be welcomed in politics, on the other side of the house, at least." She paused. "But I did question your mother's choice."

"About?"

"About whom she would marry. She knew she would inherit the family business; that was never in doubt. Being a Johnson is like being a member of the royal family, or so it seemed then. Only one descendant could inherit the throne—that was your mother—and everyone else was expected to pledge loyalty, or be banished. I didn't wait to be banished. I fled, instead, and was banished anyway. We can talk about me another time, though I'd rather not."

"I'd like to, sometime. So, you felt that Mother didn't choose wisely. Why?"

"It's not fair to judge her. Ford wasn't a good match for Lucia's position in the community, as a commoner, one might say. But you know, hindsight is not entirely twenty-twenty. We are living in the present which was the distant future of those youngsters, and we know how things turned out for them. But back then, they thought they had all the options in the world open to them, not just the one path we now know they chose. We can never really know how it was for them. For anyone."

"Very perceptive. So, did Mother have multiple, uh, options?"

"In what way?"

"Boyfriends, university, other jobs?"

"She was discouraged from having any of that, but your mother was headstrong, as you well know. I paid attention to my schooling, and I did her homework too, though I was a year behind her in school. While I was doing her algebra assignments, she was out the bedroom window, over to the Exhibition grounds or on a beach or riding in someone's hot-rod."

As Stella revealed this snippet of family history, she pointed upward to indicate where the window was that Brownie had escaped through, and Tim's pulse quickened. Fashionable Stella looked nothing like the spectre of his dream. *But still, that gesture.*

He looked at the yearbook page again. In addition to the quotations ascribed to the students, there was a "most likely to" rating that the yearbook committee had probably created. For Ford, it was *"Most likely to have a head injury."*

"That's kind of cruel, isn't it?"

"Maybe so, but perhaps not inaccurate. There's another tab; go to that page."

He turned to the group photos of clubs and teams. Stella leaned over and pointed to the football team. They were posed standing and kneeling in their uniforms. Every player wore a helmet except Ford Brown.

"Seems our boy Ford was a macho man. No helmet. Maybe what

you'd expect from an obsessed football player. Maybe too much bravado. There are rules about helmets now, but back then, per-haps people could make their own choice about them."

"I see. What did Mother say about him?"

Stella was silent for a moment. "Honestly, Timothy, I don't recall her describing him. I left home soon after, and not much news came to me at the convent or, later, at the mission. I'd been disin-herited, written out of the will and business, so our parents weren't about to send me snapshots. Lucia had risked being disin-herited too, because of her sudden marriage, but Father would have loathed leaving his newspaper empire to a non-Johnson."

"I didn't think Mother could be forced to do anything she didn't want."

"You'd be right, but something happened that wasn't in Father's or her plans."

"What was it?"

"She got pregnant."

"With me."

"As it turned out."

"Right, but, I mean...what do I mean? Were she and my father an item for long, do you think? Childhood sweethearts, that sort of thing?"

"I can't answer that. She was 'running around', as I mentioned. I knew that myself. I think Ford took her to the graduation prom, though. There's a picture of them in there. A handsome young couple. I'll leave this yearbook with you so you can browse."

"That's great, Aunt Stella, thanks."

"Your mother's in it, too, of course. She ran the school newspa-per, and probably was yearbook editor."

"You think she could have done better than him—this boy? Your personal opinion?"

"Had she waited until she was in her twenties, you mean, seen the world a bit? Possibly, who knows? She didn't always act in her own best interests, so who's to say she would have? But pregnancy is hard to argue with. It's like a narrow gate, and everything that doesn't fit through it gets discarded."

"Why did she go through with it? I know we're talking about me, but do you think she ever considered, you know, ending her pregnancy?"

"She did come to see me when she learned she was pregnant. She grieved bitterly. I think it was not for the loss of her innocence —she was never that—but for her loss of independence. She told me who the father was, told me her choices, and asked for my advice."

"What choices?"

"You're here, so..."

"Was there a real chance I mightn't have been?"

"She was a teenager, in trouble no matter which way she turned. She wanted to make the best choice for herself."

"That's fair. I guess I have you to thank that she kept me, then."

"Abortion wasn't what it is now. She might have died. I counselled her to keep herself safe and make the best of a hopeless situation. If she aborted the pregnancy—which wasn't you or anybody at that point—and chose someone else, or no one else, to marry, she would likely lose community standing and possibly her career. Marrying the football hero at least ensured that her social and financial standing would continue for her and the baby that grew up to be you. Win-win, more or less."

"Yeah, I guess there's no clear win there. She couldn't have been certain that anything would work out." Tim sighed. "Those poor kids. Can you fill in anything about my father after they married, like where he worked?"

"I know very little about that. Your grandfather was adamant that Ford would *not* work at *The Times.* He was unsuited for management, and Father would not permit his daughter's husband to work a non-management job at his newspaper. I think he arranged for Ford to work at the mill, which he must have hated."

"Why?"

"He'd had a full football scholarship to university, which he gave up that summer when they got married. Your mother wouldn't allow him to leave South River to be preyed upon by city girls. You can delay going to university, but you can't delay a football scholarship. It must have disappointed him very much."

"What's the source of this information?"

"Hearsay, as in I hear people say things, or I employ someone to do the listening for me."

"So, do you know if it's true hearsay?"

"The hearsay is consistent. It wasn't said to impress me or injure me."

"So, that's the short, unhappy career of Ford Brown, the best football quarterback to never play in the big leagues. He must've won awards in high school. When I was in school, the athletes always got trophies and plaques, while my debating team got certificates printed on a Gestetner and rolled up in red ribbon. I made some of them myself. Did you ever see any football trophies?"

"No. I think he destroyed them, poor fellow. I doubt that your mother kept any; but if so, they'd be in the attic." She pointed upward again.

"That attic again. I've been up there only rarely, and not for a long time. I don't recall any trophies. I must tell you something, Aunt Stella. I recently dreamed about a mystery woman who stood at the foot of my bed and pointed up, as you just did. Gave me the creeps. She had long dark hair. Ring a bell?"

"Seriously? No."

"Are you sure? People have told me that they've seen Bertha appearing at the attic windows."

"Who?"

"Bertha. Your mother."

"Oh, right. She was always Mother or Mrs Johnson in our time. How did you learn her name?"

"It's in here." He took the Bible from a shelf and pulled the red ribbon to open the Family Register page. "And Ebenezer, too."

Stella glanced at the page but didn't offer to hold the book. "Yes. His name is all over Saint John's Church. That's the only time we encountered it. I prefer not to speak about him, myself. Why were you reading the Bible? It doesn't seem like something you'd do."

"GB mentioned I should look there when I asked him for some vital statistics. I guess nobody was interested in keeping up family records after your parents and their baby daughters. No marriages, not even the happy birth of little Timothy Johnson Brown. Nobody died, either."

"You can update them."

"Perhaps I will. This whole quest began because something triggered a sudden, clear memory of my father, and that led me to want to know more about my origins. Thank goodness I have you, Aunt Stella, to connect me to my family, to *be* my family. I've unofficially adopted GB into my family, too. I always thought of him as my uncle, so uncle he shall be. And you know who else? Evelyn Whynott."

"I don't think I know her."

"You've been in the Daisy Café, I expect? Campaigning, maybe?"

"Yes, I have. Campaigning."

"She's the head waitress there. Lovely person. We went to school together. We've always liked each other, but our circles didn't intersect. My circle has rarely included anyone outside *The Times* or the church choir. I just never learned how to make friends. Anyway, I recently gathered up my courage and invited Evelyn to dinner here, which was easy and good. And fun. We're friends now. Maybe I'll adopt her as my sister."

"I likely met her. I've met everyone in the riding, or tried to. I don't make friends, but I do make eye contact, and people remember that. Good luck with your adoptions, Timothy. I never yearned for family. But we are quite different, you and I."

This is going well. Keep going.

The Bible was on the side table between them. He flipped the pages until they fell open where the thin envelope was sticking up.

"What's that?" Stella said.

"I thought you might tell me. I found it just as you see there."

She picked up the envelope and rubbed fingers and thumbs to feel its contents.

"I held it up to the light, and couldn't read anything inside. One folded sheet of note paper, but surely it wouldn't be blank."

Stella looked at the flap. "Not opened. You weren't curious?"

"*Au contraire.* I've been *very* curious, but I first wanted to see if I could determine—to the best of my delving ability—who put it there, what it contained, and why, and who was meant to find it—Sherlock Holmes style. It's not a lock of my baby hair. Not money, or not enough to create a shadow in the envelope. Given the pristine state of the Bible, few hands have held it since Bertha wrote those four names in it. Do you recall reading it ever, or putting this in it?"

Stella grimaced as though the suggestion was ludicrous, and shook her head.

"No, I didn't think so," he said. "That eliminates you. So, my considered conclusion is that my mother placed it there, where it is highly unlikely she'd ever expect *you* to find it. So I believe it is a message from her, meant for me. What do you think of that, Aunt Stella? What message would she have for me? Is there a vault somewhere and this is the combination? Not sure I want whatever's in it, if so."

Stella tapped her fingers to her lips. She placed the envelope back between the pages. She drew in a long breath. "There is no vault."

"I know, I was just—"

"I know what it is."

"Really? What is it, then? Let's open it."

Stella put a restraining hand on Tim's arm. "Wait. Let me think."

"All right. While you're thinking, let me get our lunch. Just sandwiches. Would you like more coffee, tea, or water?"

Stella chose tea, and Tim left the room to boil the kettle. He called her to come to the kitchen island for lunch.

"Here's what I suggest, Timothy," she said. "You study the yearbook, and think about what I said. Then, if you're still curious about the contents of that envelope, we'll open it together."

"Why not now?"

"Because...because you're not ready. I don't mean to be dramatic or insulting. Quite the contrary. I admire your dogged ability to think through things. So, think through things. What's in the envelope? My guess is it's the answer to a question you haven't asked yet, and until you ask it, it's meaningless."

"Oh boy. Are you sure they didn't baptize you Stella Enigma, instead of Stella Clara?"

Stella permitted herself a small smile. "Life is all enigma, Timothy. Nothing is as it seems. And you—you refuse to accept what you're told, which is your strength, much as I dislike running into it sometimes. You want to decide everything for yourself, but you leave a little door ajar, just in case. No harm. Nothing suffers because Timothy Brown doesn't buy into it one hundred percent. You might feel constantly unsure of yourself because of it, but at least you aren't living with false beliefs...or not many."

She took a leather book with coil binding from her bag and consulted a page. "We might as well finish this discussion while it's fresh. Will you be able to think about it between now and Friday? Otherwise, I have nothing until next month. I could be available Friday afternoon at four. At my house?"

"Sure! I have no idea where my delving will take me between now and then, but if you have the time to spare, I'll do my best to use it wisely."

"All right. Friday at four. If you'd like refreshments, you'll have to bring them. You know the state of my pantry, and I don't have a moment between now and then to shop. I could send Spencer to the store, but his selections are quite pedestrian. He might pick up turnip and cabbage for stew rather than *hors d'oeuvres*."

"Ew—though I do like a good stew, thanks for the reminder. I'll bring something for us. You didn't get Spencer to drive you here today?"

"No, he earned the morning off. Also, I don't want him knowing where I go all the time. Driving myself here puts a gap in his knowledge of my whereabouts. All right, are we good for now? Thank you for the lunch and those wonderful cinnamon rolls."

"I put some in a bag for you. If you're not going to eat them soon, pop them in the freezer, then warm them in the toaster oven."

"That sounds like a complicated recipe. They'll be eaten quickly."

"Aunt Stella, thanks so much—"

"Don't thank me yet, Timothy. This isn't over."

They hugged at the door. It may not have been for the very first time, but Tim thought it was the first time they both meant it.

He wanted to sit right down and scrutinize that high school yearbook, to study every picture and casual comment. But first, he had an important errand. He picked up the new copy of Sherlock Holmes stories and drove back down to the library with it.

"Here you are, Marlene, a brand new book with stiff binding and no underlinings."

"You needn't have hurried, Tim. I'm not ready for you."

"Take your time. I have another request, though. You mentioned that GB read Gothic novels to his wife. Could you suggest one for me to read?"

"Sure can. Your literary tastes include the previous century, just like the Barsses, from Arthur Conan Doyle to, umm, I'm checking, yes, I thought so: Robert Louis Stevenson. They borrowed this one three times. They really enjoyed it, he said."

She went to the stacks, and returned with a copy of *The Strange Case of Dr Jekyll and Mr Hyde*. "Perhaps you've read it?"

"In my teens, maybe, but I'm curious to read it now. Thanks, Marlene."

He drove to the hospital, hoping that visiting hours weren't over in the ICU. It might cost him a few more pizzas, but he really wanted to visit Constance Barss today.

They granted Tim a short visit. He sat as close to her as the wires and tubes would allow, told her he was there, and began to read aloud from the library book.

> Mr. Utterson the lawyer was a man of a rugged countenance, that was never lighted by a smile; cold, scanty, and embarrassed in discourse; backward in sentiment; lean, long, dusty, dreary, and yet somehow lovable.

He enjoyed the story, and hoped Constance did as well, though she gave no sign one way or the other. He read until a nurse came in and told him his time was up and he must leave.

"Okay, sure. Mrs Barss—Connie—I hope you're enjoying hearing this story again. I'll be back tomorrow to read more. See you then."

Since he'd adopted GB as his uncle, then Constance could be his aunt. As he'd read the nineteenth-century story to her, he felt he would've enjoyed spending this simple time with both of them. He was doing the best he could about it now.

That done, he could give unfettered attention to the yearbook.

March 24: Truth exists

Wednesday

The blind piano tuner knew his seasons. The distance from the car to the porch was only a few steps, but snow or ice could have turned any one of those steps into a disaster for a man who couldn't see.

"Bonjour. I am Alphonse Dufour, and this is my wife, Sophie."

Other than the dark glasses he wore, nothing in the man's bearing would indicate that he couldn't see. He extended his hand toward Tim, who shook it and then Sophie's as well.

"I'm Tim Brown. Thanks so much for coming. My old piano has been eager to have you fix her up. A friend did a little remedial tuning in February, but—"

"Uh-oh," Alphonse said. "The only thing worse than well-meaning friends with tools is friends with the wrong tools. I've seen it all. Vice-grips can do so much damage."

"Oh dear. I assure you no vice-grips were used here. I'd invited some friends for a madrigal dinner. I'd neglected the piano to the point where it was so out of tune I didn't want to play it, but one of the guests brought her leather tool bag, which didn't have any vice-grips in it. She brought the middle octaves into tune with each other, if not to concert pitch."

Tim pointed out the washroom and the kitchen to Sophie.

"Please make yourselves comfortable. Would you like a coffee now, or later? Lunch?"

"You are very kind," Sophie responded. "Please don't worry about us. We bring everything we need, as we are not your guests. This is our workplace."

"As you wish. I'll be in the den, just off the foyer, if you need me."

Alphonse sat on the bench. Sophie opened a folding table beside him and quickly laid out his tools, undoubtedly in a familiar pattern. He played scales from the lowest keys to the highest and down again, then chords all over.

"Tell your friend," he called out, "she did no harm."

"Great! I will!"

~

For the next two hours, Tim studied every page and photograph in the South River High School 1958 Yearbook, accompanied by the happy sound of his piano's tuning being restored. He loved hearing dissonances resolved, twang and jangle dissolved.

He read with a pack of sticky notes beside him, placing one in a page or beside a photo whenever he had a question to ask Stella later. Her own yearbook would be the 1960 edition, he supposed. He wondered if she had one, or had she run off to the convent without waiting for it? Hers seemed a story that belonged to the previous century with Dr Jekyll.

Perhaps he was reading too many old stories. He'd select something modern next, just for contrast. At least the print would be easier to read.

He tagged the page with the photo of Ford Enright Brown. He'd get that enlarged and framed. *Where did the name Enright come from?* Likely an ancestor on the Brown side, someone he'd never heard about and likely never would. He knew nothing about his paternal grandparents.

This must be what an orphan feels like when they see their birth family for the first time. But I'm not an orphan. I had more than enough mother, in many ways. She was probably just trying to make up for the deficiencies or absence of my father, teaching me to be self-sufficient.

That quotation beneath Ford's photo was interesting: "If it's in the air, I'll catch it. If it's in front of me, I'll hit it. If it's in my hand, I'll throw it." He loved football, that was evident. And a full scholarship to play at university? He'd have to be very good to get that.

But that "most likely to" statement was interesting, too: "Most likely to have a head injury." Tim copied that into his notebook. Something about that was trying to ring a bell. Maybe it would come to him later.

He paged past the Eisenhauers, Eisners, and Isners, and came to *Johnson, Lucia Linda*. She was a beautiful girl. Her dark hair was cut in a pixie style, evidently popular that year, as he saw the same cut on several other girls. She glowed. All these kids were poised to leap into the river of their future lives, and the innocence was lovely on them.

Young Lucia's quotation was puzzling: "Truth exists, only falsehood has to be invented. –Braque"

As an adult, Lucia-Brownie had never wasted any oxygen on high-minded quotations, to his recollection. Not even proverbs like "spare the rod" or "a fool and his money".

He scanned other photos and captions in the book. Some seemed to be something the students actually said, as Ford's did, while others quoted Shakespeare, the Bible, or other sources. It would be someone's task to find inspirational phrases to paste in if they couldn't think of something personal to say about the student. Their school years might have been mediocre, but at least the yearbook would make them appear full of potential at the end of that chapter in their lives.

Didn't Stella suggest that his mother had worked on the yearbook? That'd be a slam-dunk for her, given her family's business, in which she had likely been working since she turned twelve. It wasn't child labour if you didn't get paid for it.

Lucia Linda Johnson's rating was "Most likely to have fun and get paid for it."

Tim shook his head. The girl in the photo didn't look like the woman his mother had become. She got paid, all right, but she hadn't seemed to be having any fun at all. As editor of the local weekly, she acted like she was the boss of the town, scrapping with anyone who got in her way. Perhaps that became her idea of fun.

The girl in this photo had her fun, got pregnant, and married the football hero in a shotgun wedding, trapping him with her in a small town and an unsuitable job. He couldn't accept his lot, so he committed suicide, leaving Lucia Linda Johnson, aka Brownie Brown, to pay for his sins.

No wonder she had treated Tim like he'd committed a crime. He *was* the crime personified. If she hadn't gotten pregnant, so many things would have been different for her and for Ford.

Brownie had asked Stella for her counsel. Stella advised her sister to have the baby, which started a juggernaut of events, quickly rolling away from any other possibilities. Tim wondered if Stella felt some quasi-parental responsibility for him, given her advice.

It was a puzzle, but not one that he was meant to solve. Those lives had been lived. He was trying to fill in some of the "five Ws", but he'd be wary of "why". That could lead to speculation, and that could lead to fiction: a tidy little story, perhaps, but not truth.

Truth exists, only falsehood has to be invented.

"Wise words, Mother," he said aloud. "A bit enigmatic, though. I think I'll get them made into a plaque to go with Oliver Wendell Holmes' advice to sail and not drift. One or the other may prove useful, depending on the day."

He checked in on the work in progress in the parlour.

"Your instrument is in remarkably good shape, considering you have it in a room with a fireplace," Alphonse said. "It's not good to dry it out so much. I highly recommend that you put some humidifiers in there."

"Okay. Where do I get those?"

"I think we have some in the car," Alphonse said. "Sophie will bring them in. I can install them before we leave. I had to replace a couple of worn felts on the pedals, but I found no damage, nothing major. Just finishing up here, done in a half hour."

Tim tagged more pages in the yearbook with sticky notes, pages that mentioned his father or his mother, and class photos of the Grade Elevens, where he found a serious-looking Stella Johnson. Her light brown hair was in a French braid. She was looking into the camera lens with an intensity not matched by her classmates. He wondered what Stella's graduating photo quotation and caption might have been. *Per ardua ad astra? To thine own self be true?*

Most likely to survive and thrive and look great doing it? That would be prophetic.

The piano work was finished. Sophie was a fine pianist, and Tim was delighted to be invited to a five-minute recital of music that revealed all the colours of the instrument, from bass to treble. He thanked them both, and they politely praised his piano.

They showed him the humidifying system which he must remember to water regularly "just like a house plant."

"Do you see any houseplants in here? Oh, sorry, no offence, Alphonse. Take my word for it, there are no houseplants here because they all died of neglect. I have no affinity for them. But this piano, despite the state of neglect you found it in, I do have affinity for. I promise to do better."

"I think he needs the Advanced Piano Maintenance System, Sophie," Alphonse said.

"The APMS. I agree." Sophie reached into one of their tool cases and produced a roll of red dots, which she handed to Tim. "Pick a day of the week when you're most likely to be home, and put one of these dots on each of those days on your calendar. Weekly in winter, less often in summer."

"Advanced system, eh?" Tim laughed. "I hope I'm skilled enough to use these. I'll try hard."

After they left, he returned to the yearbook. Among the photo collages were some of the football team in action. Tim didn't know football, but he knew huddles and pile-ups were part of it. Ford's jersey number was rarely visible in them. He always seemed to be inside the huddle, or on the ground under a pile-up of bodies.

One photo showed an unidentified player being helped off the field by two large teammates. His face was covered in dirt or possibly blood, but that face was grinning. He wasn't wearing a helmet.

~

It was half-past one. ICU visiting hours were from one till three. He picked up Jekyll and Hyde from the hall table and drove to the hospital.

The physician happened to be on the floor when Tim checked in to see his Auntie Connie. "I hear you're reading a book to her," the doctor said. "Is this something you've done before?"

"No, not I, but I found out that her late husband read Gothic novels to her. This one was one of their favourites. I don't know if it makes any difference to her but it does to me."

The physician asked a nurse to record Mrs Barss' temperature and blood pressure before and after Tim read. "Just curious," he said.

"Hi, Auntie Connie, it's me, Tim. We're reading *The Strange Tale of Doctor Jekyll and Mr Hyde*, remember? I know you've read it already, so you already know what happens, but I don't, so don't tell me. Here we go, then. 'Chapter two: Search for Mr. Hyde.'"

He finished reading the chapter just as the nurse returned to the room. She recorded the still woman's vital signs again.

"Any difference? I don't imagine that she can hear me, can she?"

"A little rise in both. The thing is, her hearing is not impaired, as far as we know, so it's up to her brain to pay attention to sounds, if it can. We can check her next time you come in, if you like. If someone's available."

"Interesting. It'd be horrible to be able to hear and not to have anything to listen to while you're lying there all day. I'm enjoying the story myself, so I'll keep on. See you tomorrow, Aunt Connie."

Tim *was* enjoying the old story. The English language had changed considerably in a century, so reading it aloud was challenging. He frequently had to pause or repeat a word or phrase to give it the proper emphasis once he understood the meaning.

He found it interesting to learn that there was no light in houses or on the streets at night unless somebody lit something, a lamp or candles, or there was moonlight, or light from a fireplace. There was gentle humour in the writing, which he imagined had kept the Barss couple from getting too spooked as they read.

Tim had paused in his reading to bookmark one line: "If he be Mr. Hyde, I shall be Mr. Seek."

Brownie had tried to erase Ford, but he would be erased no

longer. His son, Mr Seek, was on the case.

~

"Mr Seek" scrutinized the yearbook again after supper. He looked at all the photos, and recognized some of the names, if not the faces, of his parents' contemporaries. After a while he didn't know what he was seeking, so he closed that book.

He refilled his glass with a modest *Mercredi chercher* and carried it into the parlour. The piano bench was bulging with books of best-loved music which he hadn't played in some time, due to the noise of the untuned instrument. Now it was all proper harmonics, and even the clunk had disappeared from the pedals with the new felts in place.

He began to play, then stopped. He brought a silver candlestick to the piano, found a fresh taper in the drawer of a side table, lit it, and turned out the lamp. Had they really read music by this feeble light a century ago? Perhaps the better homes—ones that could afford a musical instrument like a forte-piano—could also afford a candelabra with several tapers burning to illuminate the page. He let the candle continue to burn but returned to the late twentieth century by turning the electric lamp back on, and played through his favourite pieces until bedtime.

He didn't know how to play football, had never wanted to learn, but he could play a darn good piano.

March 25: Accidents

Thursday

Evelyn was in full flight, dishing out dishes and compliments to all. "Morning, sweetie," she called to Tim. "Make yourself comfortable. My lap's busy right now, so you'll have to sit in a booth."

She came over with the coffee. "Too much?"

"Maybe a little."

"Sorry. I'm just feelin' frisky today, y'know? It's spring, and soon the Easter Bunny'll be here."

"Don't ever change, Evelyn. Scrambled eggs and bacon today, please, one piece whole wheat toast."

"Newspaperman's regular," she called to the kitchen.

When she brought his order, Evelyn said, "I was hoping to see you more often than just Thursday mornings."

"Me, too. Let's work on that. I have a, uh, a project I'm working on right now, should be completed in a couple days. Then we'll get together, okay?"

He hoped that didn't sound like a brush-off.

Don't put off pleasant things just because they're not work-related. Remember GB. Tomorrow could be too late.

~

"On the other hand," he said to himself once he was settled in his upper room, "you can't do everything at once."

He checked his datebook, and wrote *Evelyn?* in next Wednesday's box. He'd have to check with her, of course. He hadn't a clue what she did or liked to do outside of work.

He took out the 1958 Yearbook with the colourful sticky notes bristling from its pages, and the notebook with *Things To Note* and *Questions*. All his preparation before Stella's visit had seemed unnecessary when it got underway, but for a good reason. With the yearbook, she had given him more information than he'd expected without his well-rehearsed prodding, though she might still need that later.

He taped more manila sheets on the walls and began to put his discoveries in some kind of order. He still didn't know what any of it meant. It didn't have to mean anything, if his goal was simply to know more about Ford Brown. But since Stella had shown him the yearbook, he'd had a hunch that there was another story behind the snippets of information.

A hunch? This was familiar territory. He'd explored hunches, red herrings, and all manner of clues true and false last month. *Why not use these tools now? Why didn't I think of that before?* He'd been jotting words on the sheets, but he wasn't making them work, wasn't demanding anything of them.

He had a great thought, and stood so quickly to write it down that his chair rolled backward and toppled over with a clatter. Within seconds, his cell-phone rang.

"You okay up there, Tim?"

"Oh, hi, Elaine, yes, I'm fine. Sorry, I just knocked my chair over."

"We heard. As long as you weren't in it. Wouldn't want you to hit your head."

"No, I wasn't. I hadn't realized the floor was so—how do you say —un-soundproof? Can you hear me talking to myself, too? Or on the phone?"

"Yes, and pacing. We can't hear the actual words you're saying, especially since you plugged that hole. Might I suggest we look at some floor covering, with a sound-deadening underlayment?"

"Oh my. Can it wait until I meet with my trusty panel of advisors to see how we're sitting, financially? It's in a couple weeks. Until then, I'll tiptoe, I promise. Thanks for checking on me, though."

Tim went down to the staff room for a broom and dustpan. He took them upstairs and swept up the surprising amount of dust that had accumulated in the weeks since the room had been cleaned and painted. Then he removed his shoes so he could pace in his sock feet without disturbing everyone below.

He was pacing now, his thoughts racing. Instead of making another list, he drew a circle in the centre of a sheet, and wrote *FORD* inside it. Then he drew lines radiating from the circle, leading to comments he had *HEARD* on the left side, and comments he had *READ* on the right.

He sat to review this handiwork, and that's when he remembered why he had jumped up when he knocked his chair over —confirming his theory that thoughts were things that occupied real space and time. He stood, carefully, and wrote across the top of the FORD sheet the quotation from his mother's yearbook page:

Truth exists. Only falsehood has to be invented.

Was this important? It seemed wise. At least, ascribing some quotable wisdom to his mother might add some honey to her acidic memory.

On the "Heard" side, he wrote the following:

Your father killed himself
Your father was crazy
That fool
That damn fool

On the "Read" side, he wrote:

Football hero
Football scholarship
If it's in the air, I'll catch it. If it's in front of me, I'll hit it.
If it's in my hand, I'll throw it.
Most likely to have a head injury.

Most everything else in the yearbook was simply Ford's name in a caption. No narrative. Where could he find more? There might be photos and even trophies in the school hallways, but they'd be about what Ford had done, not who he was, especially after he'd graduated.

Tim slapped his forehead. *Of course!* He was standing one floor above a huge repository of information on South River citizens. He descended the stairs quickly without the usual clattering: he'd forgotten to put his shoes back on, but he didn't bother to go back now.

The sign in GB's memory was still at the entrance, but it was now beside the door and the lights were on. Presumably Harold was getting to know his way around in there. Harold wasn't in just now, though, and Tim was relieved. He wanted to do his own research.

He rested his hand on top of a cabinet for a moment, quietly thanking GB for his fastidious attention to details. To his recollection, GB had filed everything that had ever appeared in *The Times* in at least two places. Individual and business names were filed alphabetically and by date. Every date contained clippings of people and events, filed alphabetically again. If there were more parameters, Tim wasn't aware of them.

He found Cabinet A-D and pulled out the B drawer. There were few Brown files. The first was *Brown, Brownie*, a surprisingly slim file. Tim opened it. Inside was a note in GB's handwriting: "The contents of this file were removed by Mrs. Brown, August 1990."

Why would Mother have cleared her own file? Whatever could have been in it that she wouldn't want known? Everything in here was clipped from the pages of her own newspaper, and she never permitted anything to be printed about her that wasn't complimentary. She must have been mad at the world that day, and GB would have been unable to interfere. And she knew she was dying by then.

He pulled the *Brown, Ford* file. He knew before he opened it that it was empty, too.

All right, Mother, did you erase him from the Dates files too?

This would be more challenging. Names appeared in only one of twenty-six categories, whereas events had three hundred and sixty-five possible dates on which to occur in a given year.

His father died on the first of August in 1963. He'd start looking for that. On top of the table which GB had used as his desk for decades was a binder labelled *Files Master*.

Tim was surprised at how simply it displayed the information. Under the tab DATES were calendars for each year, with an X marking the date of publication of the newspaper. In 1963, August the first fell on Thursday, so the issue following that date would be August seventh.

He found the cabinets containing Obituaries, found the drawer with deceased B people in the August seventh issue, and looked for Ford Brown. Disappointment. Ford had not received the special family obituary treatment, as they had just done for GB. Not even a paragraph. This was only the free listing under DEATHS:

> BROWN, Ford Enright – 23, South River, born January 25, 1940, died August 1, 1963 as the result of accidents. Funeral arrangements under the direction of South River Funeral Home.

Tim was stunned by what the death announcement said and didn't say. With GB's reedy voice in his ears reminding him not to remove the file from the area, he returned it to its place and rolled the drawer shut. He wouldn't forget what he'd just read.

Back upstairs, he drew a line with a red marker from the circle on the "Read" side, and wrote a new word: *Accidents*.

Brownie had been a stickler for spelling and grammar. Typos—inadvertent errors in spelling or punctuation—were not mistakes, but unforgivable sins in her newspaper. He had often heard her berate someone—himself included—for a misspelled word or other blunder in the pages of *The Times*.

"I suppose you'll claim this is just a mistake," she'd say. "Maybe paying you to do it is my mistake!"

Brownie would have personally seen that Ford's death notice was printed exactly as she wished.

"As the result of accidents" was deliberate. Not "an accident". "Accidents". Plural.

Tim sat in the chair and swivelled to look out the window to ponder the meaning of this. The absence of an account of the young man's brief career as the town's football hero, no mention of the grieving widow, heir to the Johnson family empire, no mention of the preschooler crying for his daddy—these were cold, cruel omissions, yet not out of character for the mother he knew. It seemed Ford was a non-entity in the family household at the time of his death

Had they been separated? He wrote this question at the bottom of the sheet, and returned to the window. If their marriage was on the rocks, that might explain his mother's enduring antipathy toward his father. If they had broken up, did her anger imply that Ford was the cause? Had he found another girl? Brownie herself found plenty of male company after she was widowed.

He didn't know what transpired before Ford's death. He didn't know about "accidents", but seeing that word written right below the comment about a head injury rang the first clear bell of his quest.

He pulled on his shoes and walked to the office of Doctor Muhammed. The receptionist was surprised to see him.

"An emergency, Tim? We don't have you down for today."

"No, I'm great, thanks. I was just wondering, do you have any brochures or pamphlets on head injuries or concussions?"

"I'll check. Did you hit your head? Have a fall? We had a spate of those this winter. Seniors, mostly."

"No, it's just something I'm researching. A list of symptoms and side effects would be very helpful."

She returned with a booklet and a pamphlet and handed them to Tim.

"These should help get you started in your research. If you want more, the contact information for a head injury clinic in the city is on the pamphlet. Have a nice day."

He thanked her, pocketed the reading material and resumed his walk, back down the street to the river and twice around the bridges. By the time he returned to his room, the eggs and bacon from breakfast had worn off entirely and he was glad he'd brought lunch.

The printed material didn't raise an alarm about concussions, but it did suggest that brain injuries weren't good. There were warnings about repeated concussions, especially if the first one had not fully healed.

> Never return to play or vigorous activity while signs or symptoms of a concussion are present. An athlete with a suspected concussion should not return to activities that are associated with the risk of another concussion while still showing concussion symptoms. Adult, child and adolescent athletes with concussions should not return to play on the same day as the injury.

In the yearbook, Tim had noticed references to the hero being carried off the field during a game, always returning to the field, always without a helmet.

"There's your damn fool, Mother," he said aloud. "He probably had a serious brain injury building up long before you married him. What a guy! Headstrong is an attribute in some lines of work, including football, but it's not meant to be taken literally, is it? No matter how thick the skull, there's a brain inside it floating in jelly. If the brain hits the skull from the inside once, that's dangerous. Repeated hits and—*boom*—lights out."

The booklet itemized symptoms.

> Weakness in the arms or legs; Changes in behaviour; Confusion or disorientation, such as difficulty recognizing people or places; Slurred speech or other changes in speech; Obvious difficulty with mental function or physical coordination; Changes in physical coordination, such as stumbling or clumsiness.

Even one of these would disqualify someone from playing on a varsity team, if they had known. They wouldn't permit their star player to charge into a solid wall of padded and helmeted muscle without his own armour on.

Tim let the pebbled window glass open his mind to this new world of "maybes".

Maybe the university scouts came around and saw what condition their potential new player was in, and withdrew his scholarship. So he married one of the town's most vivacious and well-connected daughters. Who happened to be pregnant.

Maybe he continued to participate in recreational activities that thumped his poor noggin, which he would have refused to protect. He was no sissy. "If it's in front of me, I'll hit it." A fella like that wouldn't tolerate a desk job in the newspaper office. He'd be more likely to charge at a tree just for fun if there was no other physical challenge.

Maybe his misfortunes hadn't depressed young Ford to the point of suicide. Maybe he wasn't depressed at all. Or, if he was, it was because he had taken "headstrong" too literally, and his brain was doing what a repeatedly-injured brain will do.

Maybe he didn't deliberately drive his truck over the riverbank. Maybe his damaged brain did. Any of those horrible symptoms could have caused him to have an accident of any kind, anywhere. He might not even have been conscious when the truck smashed into the rocks and water below.

This window overlooked the banks of the very river in which Ford had been found in his mangled pickup truck. Rumour was that he'd plunged in upriver, where the banks were higher, where Tim had been walking just a few days ago. *He could've had a seizure and lost control. Thank God he didn't harm anyone else.* Tim hoped he had been killed on impact.

Brownie was correct—based on this conjecture—to publish Ford's cause of death as "accidents". Multiple blows to the head over time, resulting in physical and mental changes, might have decked a weaker guy long before, but it took a *coup de grâce* in the river to finish the short, imagined life of Ford Brown.

The lists of hearsay and reports on the sheet surrounding Ford had grown. Tim had very few facts, and he was comfortable with that. What mattered was the telling of the story, and he believed that rumour, and logic, were bringing him closer to the truth of what had happened.

Truth exists. Only falsehood has to be invented.

"You're so wise, Mother, but we don't have the truth now. So, let's invent the best falsehood we can, shall we?"

He was getting somewhere—but he was out of time. He had to prepare supper before Robert arrived. Tonight's rehearsal would be tense, as it was the second-to-last rehearsal before Easter and all the special music that entailed. He would need to be on his chorister game tonight, delvers and dreamers not required.

On the short drive home, he wondered if the message in the little envelope was about his father's death. *Maybe Mother figured it out later on, and wanted me to know.*

"Well, why couldn't you just talk to me about it, Mother? If that's what you're telling me in the envelope, it's a cowardly way of doing it. Shame on you."

He turned into his driveway and parked.

"No. Mother was a lot of things, but she was no coward. That's not what's in it."

~

While onions sizzled in the fry pan to signal that something tasty was cooking, Tim pulled a dictionary from the shelf and looked up a common word.

> Accident: an unfortunate incident that happens unexpectedly and unintentionally, typically resulting in damage or injury; an event that happens by chance or that is without apparent or deliberate cause.

Accidental death—whether from one cause or many—made more sense to Tim than suicide, based on the few truths he had. Ford's football style had certainly been reckless, but the bull-headed teenager hadn't been protected by his parents, whoever they were, nor his coaches. Whatever the practice at the time, no one would have intended the awful injuries that he must have experienced, nor how it would change him.

"Unfortunate incident" was the first definition. It certainly applied. The truck in the river was the second: "without...deliberate cause".

The brain damage would have inflicted suffering, not only on Ford but also on his family. If he experienced symptoms as described in the brochure, like slurred speech and stumbling, his wife may not have given him a moment's sympathy if she suspected he was drunk.

Much had changed in medical knowledge since then. This brochure, Tim thought, might contain more facts about brain injuries than even medical schools knew in the early sixties.

He imagined these misunderstood symptoms might have caused some spectacular rows in his home.

Maybe he didn't have to imagine it.

Wasn't he there?

His first massage had triggered a memory that had set him on this quest. Melanie had held his hands firmly in hers to massage them, which suddenly took him back to when his father had come home from work, and there was some kind of argument, sharp words were thrown, voices were raised. Little Tim had run outside to the front porch to escape the noise. His father came out and sat beside him on the porch steps, put his arm around his little boy, held his hands in his, stroking them, trying to assuage the scene that had just taken place inside the house.

"I'm so sorry, Timmy."

Tim saw them now, man and boy, through the clear glass of the new storm door. Then he saw Robert coming in, and Robert saw him.

"My God, Tim, what's wrong?"

"Uh, nothing, I was...just..."

"Well, you look like you've seen a ghost, and you know how I feel about them. But really, is something wrong?"

These memories always seemed to come at inopportune times.

"I'm delving into my family history, Rob, and I just remembered something about my father. Nothing wrong, just, uh, unsettling. I'll just make a note and then resume burning these onions for supper."

"Excellent, my favourite."

~

On their way to the church, Robert said, "Only one more rehearsal after tonight, yikes! I need you to be fully present tonight, Tim. Please? No daydreaming?"

"You got it, maestro! I love the music we're singing. I even practised it a little bit. It'll be great. I will concentrate, I promise."

The rehearsal went well, with hills and valleys. Because he had worked them very hard all evening, Robert ended the rehearsal with a favourite evening hymn, unaccompanied so the singers could harmonize as they wished. He nodded to Tim, who knew this was his signal to turn off the overhead lights in the choir loft, leaving just the glow from the organ lamp. They all knew the words to the first verse.

> The day thou gavest, Lord, is ended, the darkness falls at thy
>   behest;
> To thee our morning hymns ascended, thy praise shall sanc
>   tify our rest.

They gently sang "oo-oo" as the second verse, then quietly hummed the third time through. As always, they sat in silence for a few moments after the music ended.

~

Tim prepared a dish of olives and cheese to go with a late evening glass of wine, and took it to the parlour.

"Why in there? The den's cozier."

"Come in and find out."

He ushered Robert to the piano bench. The sheet music to one of their favourite pieces was on the rack, and Tim switched on the lamp.

Robert sat, raised his eyebrows skeptically, and began to play. He stopped.

"Oh my. Did you buy a new piano?"

"No, but I half paid for one. Alphonse Dufour thought it was worth working on. It didn't need much repair, anyway. I bought a humidifying system, too, and he gave me these red dots to put on the calendar so I won't forget to water it. Oh, and he praised Helen's interim tuning."

Helen was Robert's organ student and minister of a church in the city, who said she carried her own tuning tools "in self defence".

"He did very well. It sounds terrific."

Robert drank a toast to the piano, popped a block of cheese in his mouth, and played the short piece again. Behind that was a book of music arranged for four hands, which Tim had happily discovered after the technician had left. He joined Robert on the bench and they played one piece for fun, laughing as they hit or missed their notes or page turns. They would have played through the book, but both men were tired. Another time.

If music was a sport, Tim thought as he prepared for bed, *I'd join that team. Maybe our motto would be something like "If it's in the air, I'll hear it. If it's in front of me, I'll sing it. If it's in my hand, I'll play it." Come to think of it, I am on a team. Choir is my team.*

In that thought, he felt a connection to his father. Tim loved music as Ford had loved football.

If only Ford had loved his helmet, too.

March 26: The big reveal

Friday

Tim's brain woke him in the wee hours. It wanted to review all the options, suppositions, and conclusions. He was meeting Stella tomorrow afternoon—no, *this* afternoon, as it was already a couple hours into tomorrow—and he wanted to be ready, to make good use of her while she was in the remarkably cooperative frame of mind she had been on Tuesday. He was eager to solve and settle his family history so he could see it all in a glance, know it, and believe it, and leave the rumours and unknowns behind.

Especially since he felt he had debunked the worst rumour.

He needed a pencil and paper. He needed more light than one of Doctor Jekyll's lighted tapers would provide. He needed to get up. Carefully, he slipped out of bed and quietly picked up his dressing-gown from the chair where he had tossed it a few hours before, grateful that he hadn't put it on a noisy hanger in the closet.

He crept down to the kitchen with the intention of heating some milk, to soothe himself back to sleep. But he wanted to be awake now, so he made a cup of orange pekoe tea instead. A little caffeine might be helpful. He added lots of milk anyway, to balance the effect. He closed the doors to the parlour so any noise he made wouldn't travel up the staircase to wake Robert.

He now believed that Ford had not killed himself. Progressively, perhaps, but inadvertently. That lifted so much darkness from the story.

He opened the notebook and wrote the words *belief, knowledge, story*.

Below them he added, *Truth exists.*

"I wonder about that," he said to the kitchen. "Does truth really exist? As one all-encompassing truth, singular? Say if the house burned down and we all perished—heaven forfend—what would be The Truth that could be told? Why was I down here in my robe? Why was Robert in bed? Had we quarrelled? Had I lit a candle that started the fire?"

That reminded him that he had not taken the time to read to his Aunt Connie yesterday. He'd do that later today, before going to see Stella. He mustn't neglect those visits. He'd had enough regret for one month.

He resumed his speculation. "The fire chief or whoever it is would sift through the ashes to determine the cause of the fire, look for signs that it was arson, the bodies would be autopsied to make sure one of us had not murdered the other, but the conclusions of all those investigations would be—what—facts? Not truths. They wouldn't know *why* I was here or what I was thinking—not even if these notes survived the flames."

He was pacing around the island.

"*Maybe* truth exists, but truth is not facts on the ground. Truth floats far above the fray, in the smoke, but nobody can see up there. What we have to do is invent the falsehood that we believe comes closest to the truth of the story."

He wrote "Falsehood has to be invented" on the page and stood up to consider this. He had first read it as a criticism of falsehood. Now he saw it as instruction.

"It means we must invent our preferred falsehood, as a cake must be baked. But how?"

He paced another lap.

"By using truths!" he exclaimed. "Bits of truths exist—they're our hunches, and hearsay, and rumours, and guesses, even gossip. We use these to invent our story in confidence, knowing that we will never, ever know for sure!"

The parlour door creaked behind him. The hair on the back of his neck rose immediately as last week's dream apparition came to mind.

Slowly, he turned.

"What're you doing up?" Robert squinted against the bright kitchen lights. He looked around. "Who're you talking to? What time is it? What's wrong?"

"Oh, Rob, you startled me! Welcome to my insomnia! Nothing's wrong, I'm just trying to sort something out, and I think better if I think out loud, so my brain can hear my thoughts through my ears instead of from itself...oh never mind, another time. I'm getting somewhere, though. Can I get you something? Hot milk? Cookie?"

Robert was squinting at Tim's notes on the island.

"Belief, knowledge, story? Truth exists? Are you trying to solve a crime?"

"Indeed, I am, my dear Watson. Not a crime, exactly, but I am trying to right a wrong. Not only trying, but succeeding. I'm not ready to reveal all to you at this moment, but I will."

"Sorry, didn't mean to pry."

"But I'll want to tell you, Rob, when we have the time. It's my personal mystery, and it means a lot to me."

"It's a quarter to four in the morning. You should be in bed."

"Yes, I'll be right there. You go now, keep it warm."

"Love you."

"Love you."

No, Tim continued in his inside voice, *there is no such thing as truth in a story. To know the truth of an event, one would have to know* all *the truths leading up to it. From all points of view.*

When investigating in January and February, he had found the best way to uncover what happened was to posit all the unconfirmed falsehoods he could think of, and then rule out the implausible and the unlikely.

"Posit, eh? Hmm." He brought a dictionary from the den and looked it up: *a statement which is made on the assumption that it will prove to be true.*

"There! It's in the dictionary! I didn't make it up! I'm *positing* the truth that my father did *not* commit suicide, and I'm sticking to it! It's legit!"

He paced around the island twice more.

"I can't prove it, though."

Around again.

"But it *is* my assumption. Future civilizations may accept the Timothy Brown Assumption as a major advancement in philosophy in the dying moments of the second millennium!"

He gathered up the papers and put them in his backpack. Morning coffee-time was a whirlwind when Robert was heading back to the city, so a clear path was best.

Until then, he was assured of a good sleep. His brain was satisfied for the moment.

~

The alarm rang and rang again before he slapped it to silence. Ninety minutes was a good nap, not a full night's rest. Robert was first in the shower. He could get up as early as called upon, but an interruption mid-sleep cost him. Tim's eyes were gritty, but interrupted sleep was a familiar bump in the road. Life would go on for both of them.

But maybe not cleanly. Tim sprayed milk foam over the counter while making their lattés, and Robert spilled his drink into the saucer.

"Look at us! Let's hope the coffee will jolt us back on track. Sorry I disturbed you last night, Rob. It was time well spent for me, though."

"Glad to hear it. Too bad you couldn't do your thinking in the daytime."

"But I do. I ask questions in the daytime, and seek answers in the night. Or vice versa. You know what it's like. When you have a concert looming, you get wound up too, if you don't mind me saying so. As it happens, you *do* have a concert coming up. How're the nerves? Do you want me to invite guests on Sunday for you to cook for? That usually helps."

"No, no, thanks. It's no biggie. I'll be fine. Let's just keep it on the down-low for now."

Down-low suited Tim just fine. He needed to resolve the ever-unfolding questions in his quest before he could put it away. GB's untimely departure had been distraction enough.

He drove to his quiet room, where the walls were adorned with many sheets of paper. He removed his shoes—and made a note to *Bring Slippers* so the soles of his stockings wouldn't be blackened from wandering around the building in them. Mrs A would never permit his socks or any other item of clothing to proceed to the dryer until all stains had been removed.

He began with the first sheet, taped up behind the door. *ACTION* was the title, followed by *Secret FROM ME*. Good. He was on it now.

Next were the *MOTHER* and *FATHER* sheets. The dates weren't of great importance, but it was a sign of neglect that he hadn't been familiar with them before. He had them now. And he'd learned his grandparents' names and dates from the family Bible.

What was the point of that little envelope he'd found in the Bible? He had posited—that handy word again—that it was placed there by his mother, meant for him to discover. But it wasn't about the cause of Ford's demise.

So, why?

He had resolved the important questions, hadn't he? If this envelope contained an answer, he had no question for it, as Stella said he should have before opening it.

He moved past the sheet with *FORD* in the centre, *HEARD* and *READ* radiating outward. He taped a fresh page to the wall next to the window, but had no title for it.

He stared at the blank paper.

If the envelope did contain news about Ford, Tim felt he had already uncovered it: he had not committed suicide, he'd died by accident. *Accidents.*

He hadn't been murdered, not even secretly. The envelope would not contain a confession nor an accusation. Brownie Brown would have found a way to avenge such a thing had it happened. That was a falsehood he didn't need to invent.

Tim wrote on the sheet: *Not suicide. Not murder. Multiple accidents. Brain injury. Football.*

He had thought about how his father's devotion to sport related to his own devotion to music. As far back as Tim could recall, he loved music, especially church music, the choir, soloists, hymns and anthems, the symphony of sounds from the organ. He sang in the Junior Choir, and occasionally sang solos in a pure boy-soprano voice, until his voice changed.

He was permitted piano lessons after school, and his teacher sometimes gave him singing lessons if he'd accomplished his keyboard assignment. He would practise whenever he was home alone, which was often. In his teacher's opinion, he was very good at both.

If his mother happened to be in the house to hear him, she would call out, "I don't know where you got that talent from. Not from me. Must be from your father."

Then she would laugh, a hard, nasty laugh. That was when she was in her cups, rarely when he was in elementary school, but more frequently as he took over responsibility at the newspaper and she devoted herself to making and writing about the perfect beef Stroganoff.

Ford probably couldn't carry a tune in his lunch bucket, or didn't try. His son hadn't inherited his artsy talents from him, and definitely no sports. Tim's memory of any athletic activity, at home or at school, was painful. He couldn't catch a ball of any size, nor hit one with a stick, bat or racquet. He wasn't even good at running, as his growth spurts made him clumsy, all arms and legs.

Given that both his parents were on the short and stocky side, his "beanstalk" body type was a mystery. It wasn't the expected asset on the basketball court. He'd heard more than one jeer that he'd been a foundling, that he didn't belong.

He agreed that he didn't belong anywhere on the school grounds, but he did like to be home. His mother was often absent, but when his father came home, he greeted little Timmy/TJ the same way every time: loudly, enthusiastically, with big hugs. Ford often had headaches, so it was okay with him if his son didn't want to build a snow fort on the front lawn. He was happy just to sit quietly with his little boy.

Those headaches. Tim had forgotten about them. Now he knew what had caused them. He had posited it, and in the absence of any other information, it was truth: concussions.

Time was up. He took down all the sheets and rolled them into a tube. He took a roll of masking tape and his markers. Tomorrow, he would give Stella a "show and tell" with these visual aids, including the Bible and its enigmatic envelope.

~

He drove to the hospital, rang the buzzer at the locked ICU door, and told the nurse that he was there to read to Constance Barss.

"I'm sorry, she's not here."

The nurse saw the look of dismay on his face, and quickly put her hand on Tim's arm.

"Sorry, sorry! I mean, she's been moved. Her condition is critical but stable, so she's been moved to a step-down unit."

"Oh, thank goodness. I thought—"

"She's not worse, not better, but the doc wanted to free up the ICU bed because of the DNR order."

Tim walked to the new unit and introduced himself at the desk. Yes, he was welcome to read to her. No, there was no order to check her pulse and blood pressure, and nobody was available to do it, but the nurse offered to show Tim how to read the machines at her bedside.

"Hi, Aunt Connie, it's me, Tim, back to read more of the *Strange Case of Doctor Jekyll and Mr. Hyde.* I'll pick up where we left off. You've heard it enough times that you should remember it."

He began to read, but didn't find the story as engaging as he had at first. He could see that Mr Hyde was just Dr Jekyll, who was increasingly addicted to a poisonous potion that turned him into an evil mirror-image of himself. This was a bit too transparent for Tim, compared to the exercise he'd been working on. There were plenty of clues like broken cudgels, corpses, witnesses, letters and documents, so the mystery would eventually be solved.

He came to the end of the chapter and chose to stop there for the visit. He heard a sound from the bed, and turned to see Constance Barss looking straight at him.

"Aunt Connie? You're awake? Hi, it's me, Tim."

She didn't speak, and her gaze drifted just a bit. What did this mean? Tim quickly went out to the nursing station to report this, and a nurse followed him back to the room. Constance's eyes were closed again. The nurse reported that her pulse and BP were both elevated.

"Perhaps she knows you're here."

"I'm happy if she does. I'll be more faithful in my visits, Aunt Connie. See you tomorrow."

~

He stopped at his house to pick up items he needed for his visit with Stella, including two bottles of a better-than-standard *Vendredi* vintage, and then went to his favourite outlet for fish and chips. He knew two things: Stella never ordered take-out, and she would enjoy this as much as he did.

While he waited for the order, he thought about the movie he and Robert had seen. *The Cider House Rules* was more interesting than Dr Jekyll and his potion. Tim recalled the title scene in the cider house, where safety rules had been posted for men who could not read them. They had kept themselves safe, regardless.

That's what he had been doing. He knew there might be rules, or truths, but they would never be available to him. He was inventing his own truths, or story, and they were working fine.

He doodled in his notebook: *Truth vs Falsehood vs Invention.*

He had learned a lot, bringing his father into focus from a forgotten blur. Yes, the story was tragic, but he expected that. He also understood what turmoil there must have been between his young mother and father. It had left Brownie forever bitter.

There was just one more thing to clear up and he'd be satisfied: the contents of the little envelope. He didn't have a big question for whatever answer it contained. Whatever he hadn't found or deduced would be pretty much beside the point.

The fish and chips were ready, and so was he.

~

On the scenic drive downriver Tim felt good, satisfied, settled. March had not been easy, but he'd achieved a better outcome so far than he expected. Some other man might have avoided the digging, fearing what kind of bones they might dig up. He hadn't. Maybe he *was* fearless.

The sharp turn in the Barss' story had affected him deeply. He had gone from shock, to despair, to acceptance, with his old friend GB becoming his late uncle. Even spending a half-hour reading to Aunt Connie felt good.

Somewhere in there, he had turned forty and spring had arrived, making one forget the chills of today and look forward to a warmer tomorrow.

He felt a thrill, an actual, physical thrill, as he remembered that when he had set out to know more about his father, the method he used was *delving*. He had mumbled about delving since this sabbatical year began, doubting himself many times. Now he'd done it. He had delved into a topic without prejudice, without pre-determining an outcome. He had found so much more than one thing. He had found a family.

And not everyone was dead. Besides Stella—very much alive— he had pulled aside the curtain between himself and Evelyn, and he was eager to share good times with her. His Aunt Connie was at death's door, but he would accompany her to that door and guide her through it, as family should do.

Finally, as he turned into Stella's paved driveway, he remembered driving past on another Friday afternoon, wishing he could drop in for some cheers and a chat. He wasn't dropping in today: the visit was planned, but she had readily agreed to it, and he was looking forward to spending time with his flesh-and-blood aunt.

With wine and deep-fried fish!

Stella looked skeptical at the two armloads of papers and bags of items for his presentation, but she smiled when one of the bags gave a familiar clink as he set it on the kitchen counter.

"Open one, please, Aunt Stella, and put the other in the fridge to keep cool. I'll just get set up here and be with you in a few minutes."

"What's all this, Timothy? I thought we were going to continue our conversation about your parents?"

"Indeedy-do, yes we are. But I want to show you my thought process." Tim leaned toward his aunt. "My *delving* process, to be precise, except that delving is deliberately not precise—oh never mind, just pour us some of that elixir and stand by."

Tim was just on the edge of giddy, but Stella tolerated him, even when he taped the sheets to her cupboard doors, and soon he was ready. He opened several drawers until he found the cooking utensils—all shiny—and selected a long-handled fork as his pointer.

He led Stella around the room, sheet by sheet, explaining his queries and quandaries, as well as several roadblocks and how he had breached them. He returned to the 1958 yearbook several times, pointing out the stocky, un-helmeted player at the bottom of a pile of players, and the prophetic mottoes. He showed her the astoundingly tiny newspaper Death Notice with the deliberate typo. He showed the brochures on concussions.

Stella asked questions, which he answered as fully as he could. More than once she said she hadn't known this or hadn't considered that. He told her of his re-awakened memories of Ford as an affectionate father, and surprised himself when tears came to his eyes. It was the first time he had said any of this to another person, and the emotion needed to come out. Stella smiled kindly as he wiped his eyes.

She stepped back to take in all the pages. She refilled their glasses and took a seat at the kitchen island. Tim turned the oven on low, put their dinners on a baking sheet to warm, and joined her.

"Thoughts?"

"I have many. You've done a remarkably thorough job. You know, Ford Brown was *persona non grata* to me. He was my sister's husband who brought only shame to her family. It wasn't my family, since I'd been disinherited, as you know. But still, Lucia and I were sisters, and I never stopped caring about her. I think I may have taken her harsh words about Ford as truth: she said he was a damn fool, and on what basis would I challenge her?"

She paused to sip.

"So when you announced that you were going to delve into Ford Brown, I imagined that you were aiming to dig up dirt, and if you found dirt on him, it would be dirt on her, too, and possibly me by association, so I reacted—the way I reacted. I apologize for that. I knew my own parents and I wish to know nothing more about them. You barely knew Ford, and I thought that was best. However, you've uncovered a valuable memory about him, and perhaps solved a puzzle. His death is still tragic, but I think he will rest more quietly now with your excellent diagnosis of brain damage. Such a waste."

"Yes. A waste. Thank you for the apology, Aunt Stella. Sometimes I don't know what's behind your, uh, sharp statements, whether it's about you or me, you know? I want us to be on the up and up. I find the world is hostile enough."

"I understand. I think I've been trying to steer us both away from the shoals. You're old enough now to take care of yourself."

"I'm glad turning forty is good for something. I can handle what comes my way. I was thinking about that on my way over here, about how much has transpired just in this month. It wasn't an easy month, but I stuck with it."

"And your quest is satisfied now? No further questions to delve into?"

"Maybe one. I've often wondered how, with my build, I could be related to my mother, who shared your dimensions, and Ford, who, I've learned, was built like an oil barrel. I know it happens, genetic throwback or whatever. Do you know if there were any tall, skinny Johnsons back in the day?"

Stella tapped her fingers on her pursed lips. She stood and turned toward the picture window as she had done when he first broached the topic. She evidently shared Tim's penchant for thinking while staring out of windows, though hers were far wider than his, and without blemish.

"Oh, and if you will," he said to her back, "could you tell me again about the conversation you and Mother had when she came to see you at the convent? She had just discovered she was pregnant then, and asked for your counsel, I think you said?"

Stella turned back to the kitchen.

"I said that you won't like it," she said. "This is what I meant."

"What is?"

"This: that your mother had another, uh, suitor."

"Oh, I'm sure. I think she had many. She sure did when I was growing up, and her yearbook indicated that she…"

Stella was gently shaking her head.

"Another suitor? Singular? Someone she jilted in favour of Ford? That could have happened, I suppose. What difference—"

Tim stared at Stella.

"She was pregnant by someone else? Not by my—by Ford?"

"Yes."

"She told you?"

"Yes."

"She was certain?"

"Yes."

"Do you know his name?"

"If I did, I've forgotten it. I'm not certain she told me. I was concerned for my sister, but not the least bit interested in the names of her lovers or their social impediments."

Tim sat down, his eyes searching the room, the view, anywhere that would help this news fit into his new story.

"Why didn't she marry that fellow, then?"

Stella raised her eyebrows and nodded her head enigmatically. "Good question."

"Can you prove this—this allegation?"

"She married Ford within weeks of graduation. The baby—you—came early, she said. You don't look like a preemie to me."

Tim took a marker from a bag and stood before the sheet that was titled *FATHER*. Below Ford's vital statistics, he wrote *ALTERNATIVE*, and below that he wrote:

Suitor
Intimate relations
Tall, thin?
Could not/would not marry Mother
Not in school photos – older?
Brown hair?
Artistic?

As Tim wrote, Stella appeared amazed. When he paused for some wine, she said, "That's uncanny. Why don't you just write down the name?"

"Yeah, why don't I? I don't know it, is why. Given time, I might. How does this list look to you?"

"Intriguing."

Tim bent down to add more words to the bottom of the sheet.

Alive? Dead?
Where living?
Rich? Poor? Famous?

He straightened up and looked at Stella. "Was she raped?"

"He was a few years older than she, I believe. It would be statutory rape. Their affair began while she was in grade eleven, when she was under seventeen. But she was...willing, even eager. Poor misguided child. She was in love."

Tim wrote *Already married?* Then he added *Love child*.

He put the cap on the marker.

"I'm done. I think I have the story now, Aunt Stella. Let's have our fish and chips before they dry up, while all that settles."

"You *are* fearless, Timothy, I'll give you that. You haven't even flinched."

"I may flinch later, though it's really about other people, not me. I'm a slow sleuth. Things have to marinate for a while, before I believe anything I write down."

Stella had been disappointed to see take-out food when he brought it in, given that she was a poor cook and Tim was good at it. However, the re-crisped batter on the flaky fresh fish convinced her that he had chosen wisely. The wine matched the food nicely, and they tipped up the bottle to finish it.

Tim steered the conversation away from matters of paternity toward his adventures with movies and books, especially the Jekyll and Hyde story he was reading to Missus Barss.

"It's unexpectedly funny, too. I especially related to the line, 'If he be Mr. Hyde, I shall be Mr. Seek!' I do enjoy detective stories. I've been dipping into Sherlock Holmes stories too. Holmes is cleverer than I am, but I think I could have solved the Jekyll-Hyde conundrum in half the time. What that story has going for it is all the gruesome details along the way."

"Hmm. Your powers of deduction and perception are impressive, as demonstrated by these sheets. So, what does Mr Seek think about this afternoon's alternate ending to your search?"

Tim took their dishes to the sink. He was tempted to open the second bottle of wine, but he was fifteen long minutes from home on a winding road. He was "old enough" to switch to tea.

"Mister Seek often knows a thing, but it often turns out to be a wrong thing. So I'll keep the seeking open. You know, Mother's yearbook slogan was 'Truth exists. Only falsehood has to be invented.' I thought about that a lot. I've turned it on its ear. Truth may well exist somewhere in the ether, the angels may know it, but we mortals must construct our truths from what we can find here on the cold ground. In my world, truth and falsehood are made from the same ingredients. Just the proportions differ."

"That is profound. I had no idea."

"I know you've thought of me as a light-weight, and maybe I have been, but I'm trying really hard now to wrap my head around some concepts. Until this year, all my thoughts were ones your late sister repeatedly pounded into my head. I'm forty years old. I should have a thought or two of my own now. I'm getting there. Got any cookies?"

Stella shrugged, but Tim searched in the empty cupboards anyway. In the freezer, he found a package of chocolate éclairs with cream filling.

"Woo-hoo! Jackpot! Where'd these come from?"

"Oh, Spencer must have brought them after the New Year. They would have been on sale. He insists on looking for the bargains. Are they any good?"

"One way to find out," Tim said, putting them out on plates and pouring their tea.

He began to take down the flip-chart sheets that adorned Stella's fancy kitchen.

"Aunt Stella, there is still the matter of the little envelope I found in the Bible. I believe it contains a significant clue about this topic, an answer that was lacking a question. I know a good question now, thanks to your hints, and I believe the answer is what's in there. But it's not just a simple matter of opening it."

"Because?"

"It'd be just like Mother to force information on me whether I wanted it or not. To trick me into opening and reading it before I knew whether I wanted to know it or not. That's why I hesitated. Mother never kept a secret if she could find a good way to tell it, especially other people's secrets, and she didn't hesitate to tell them to her little boy. I heard many things that might have upset me if I'd been old enough to understand. I just ignored her. But here, I believe, is the answer not only to my question, but to her secret. Leave it to her to seal it in a blank envelope like that."

"You don't have to open it."

"I agree, though the temptation is strong, as you can imagine. Where's the harm? No harm if the name is not familiar to me, but if it's somebody I know, well, that could be very complicated, couldn't it? It's a bit like Shrödinger's cat."

"Whose?"

"It's the only thing I remember from Physics class. The scientist presented a theory that a cat in a box could be both dead and alive at the same time because of blah-blah. But I liked the either/and principle, that it could really be science and not just dithering."

"And this applies how?"

"The name of my biological father is, and is not, in that envelope. If I open it, the cat might have been dead for a long time—too bad

—or very much alive—also bad, possibly."

Tim sighed. "Can I leave the envelope here with you, Aunt Stella? If I decide I want to read the contents, I'll ask for it. If not, I won't accidentally trigger the poison gas that kills the cat or whatever is in there."

"I can't say I followed that, but if you were asking me to hold the envelope for you, I will."

"Good. For the record, I think you know more than you're telling me. I think, if there's a name written inside that envelope, that it will not be a surprise to you, whether you have temporarily forgotten it or not. But now the truth and the falsehood are both in one place, and I'm relieved."

"No comment."

"I don't expect any. I'm good with where we are right now."

"This has been a conversation like no other, Timothy. I did have some trepidation, but it was interesting, both the subject matter, and learning about your methods, too. I could use someone like you in our strategy and planning sessions."

"But there is no 'someone like me'. Sherlock Holmes claimed to be the only investigating detective in the world, and I claim to be the only full-time Delver in South River, perhaps in all of Nova Scotia. And you can't have me. Thanks, though."

"Hah. Never say never. If the price was right?"

"The price will never be right. *Not* working for pay has been the greatest luxury I could have asked for this year, and I'm nowhere near ready to abandon it yet."

"How's your interim editor doing? That's quite an expense, isn't it? She must come at a premium."

"Of course she does, but I'll let you in on a story. Mother and I were both on the payroll. Following her death, I didn't take a raise, and her earnings were retained in the company. So we bankrolled this year long in advance. I set up a panel of experts to oversee things for me this year so I wouldn't have to get in the management weeds, and I'll meet with them a couple times. The first review is coming up in May. All good!"

"Excellent. I see that money is not your motivation, but something must be. I do need someone with your skills, so I'll try to find a way to—"

"Save yourself the stress. There are lots of people with high-falutin degrees who can thrill a room with political buzz-words, and they will take all the money you can offer. Use them."

"But they're not effective. They don't know that truth and false-hoods are made from the same elements."

"But now *you* do! Anyway, I must wrap up and go home to my haunted house on the hill. Oh, did I tell you about my ghost dream? She was thin and wispy, wore a nightie, and pointed upward, like this. Know who it might be?"

"No. Maybe my mother. That's what people used to say. I don't believe in ghosts."

"Grandmother Bertha? What was she pointing to, d'you think? Are there bones in the attic?"

"Unlikely. Maybe photos. Your mother wasn't one for sentiment, as you know, so either she destroyed the old portrait photographs, or they're up there. Go up and look."

"Maybe. Speaking of photos, I'll hang on to that yearbook a little longer, please. I think I'll get copies of some of the photos, and have them mounted and framed to display like real families do. My house shouldn't look like I'm in a witness protection program."

"Interesting. The yearbook is yours. I'd rather not re-visit the source, anyway."

"Hmm, skeletons in your huge designer closets? If you need Mister Seek—"

"No, I do not, thanks. Not for that."

"Here's my card, ma'am, just in case." With a flourish, he presented one of the cards with only his name and two phone numbers.

Stella smiled. "Shouldn't it say Mister Seek?"

"I had them printed before I read that story. But I keep a low profile. Less is more."

At the door, he said, "Aunt Stella, this has been a wonderful visit. I really, really love talking with you. We got through some touchy topics this evening without bloodshed. I'm not saying that there had to be, but family is a touchy topic, especially our little family.

Thank you."

Stella reached up to hug Tim, and kissed his cheek.

Hugs again, twice in one week.

He was hyper-vigilant as he drove home. Sharing a bottle of wine over four hours shouldn't make him impaired under the law, but he wasn't taking chances.

Except for a few restless hours, he hadn't slept since yesterday morning. He was mentally exhausted. He went directly to bed and was out like a taper.

March 27: Down-low

Tim awoke refreshed. The ephemeral presence had not visited him in the night. Perhaps he had put all family ghosts to rest, in his dreams at least. He sincerely hoped so.

He had simple plans for the day, no heavy questions, no more lists to create. The little envelope's secret message rested lightly in the back of his mind, more an option than a need. His subconscious would work on it, and he wouldn't interfere.

Moving lazily, he cooked breakfast, tidied the kitchen, and made a shopping list. Robert had said to keep Sunday dinner on the down-low, meaning no guests, meaning he must be feeling pretty confident in the Easter music coming up, despite the hiccups in the lead-up rehearsals. The choir's Palm Sunday anthem tomorrow was under control, thanks especially to the new section leads—what a joy to sing with them—and Easter Sunday was a whole week away.

Tim decided to tackle making Beef Wellington for Sunday dinner. He checked the recipe. There were a couple of steps, but all seemed do-able. He'd enjoy working on this after church tomorrow. This kind of project could be eaten, unlike his investigations, and would make delicious leftovers, too.

He tucked the grocery list in his jacket and started off on his rounds. First was to the Johnson Building. He carried the manila papers up to his room. He intended to store them in the cabinet along with similar rolls labelled *January* and *February*.

He was pretty sure he was finished with them, yet he hesitated. He hadn't received the all-clear from the back of his mind, so he laid them on top of the cabinet. There was no rush. It was just housekeeping.

He shopped for groceries, including the tenderest cut of beef, the butcher assured him, and took it all home and put things away.

Then he went for a walk, wandering through neighbourhoods between his house and the downtown, so that his return was up-hill and strenuous, but it was good exercise and he enjoyed the fresh air. His mind was relatively empty of thought puzzles, and he didn't try to start any. He mused a bit about the Gothic story he was reading, how people could believe that a man's whole physique could change just because he drank a potion—and change back again—but potions and snake oil were what they had back then, he supposed.

Next task, but not a chore, was to visit his new aunt. The hospital hadn't called with news of any kind, but Tim was apprehensive as he parked and entered the building. She'd been hanging by a thread for days now.

Aunt Connie's thread continued to hold. He observed her pulse and blood pressure readings on the bedside monitors.

"It's Tim, Aunt Connie. Ready for more gruesomeness? I think they think I'm weird for reading this story to you, but you're weird, too, for listening. Okay, here we go."

He paused in his reading periodically to see if she might open her eyes as she'd done the last time, but he could detect no sign of life other than the slight, raspy sound of her breathing. Just as well.

He stopped reading at a break in the story, and bade her good-bye.

~

Tim didn't expect Robert's arrival for at least another hour, so he tuned the radio to "Saturday Afternoon at the Opera", turned it up loud, and went upstairs. He stood in front of the door to the attic, still latched. This was a good time to unlatch it, with the late after-noon sun streaming in the windows, banishing all wraiths, and the aria "Pace, pace, mio Dio" from *La Forza Del Destino* wafting up from below.

He opened the door and climbed awkwardly to the attic. His feet didn't fit on the narrow stairs, which were remarkably similar to the stairs up to his room in the building downtown. His great-grandfather likely oversaw the construction of both buildings. Perhaps this style of steps would have fit his little feet just fine. *Proof that I didn't inherit your genes for shoe size, great-grandpa?*

"Hello? Anybody up here?" he called to the empty space.

Nobody answered—no surprise, but a relief nonetheless. What *was* a surprise was how little was up there. Brownie had evidently discarded the detritus of family history, and her only son found himself grateful. He had no interest in conducting a nostalgic search through trinkets or treasures, whether it was her schoolbooks or his baby shoes.

Tim stepped around the central chimney and there, leaning against the bricks, were half a dozen large pictures in ornate frames, and several boxes. The grimy glass on the photos obscured the subjects and reflected his own face. One by one, he dragged them to the top of the attic stairs. The opera was louder there, the voices at full volume. He heard another voice, too, but it wasn't singing.

"Hello? What's going on? Where are you?"

"Robert? I'm in the attic," Tim called. "Come on up."

Robert evidently found the volume knob on the stereo and turned it down. "What?"

"Sorry. I'm in the attic. Can you give me a hand with these? I'll just pass them down to you."

Tim lowered the heavy frames to Robert, who stacked them along the second-floor hallway.

They were studio-posed family portraits. Tim assumed one was of his mother and aunt, posed together on a wrought iron bench, both wearing white stockings, black buckled shoes, and ringlets. Their mother and father stood behind them, Ebenezer in a morning coat, Bertha in black lace from head to toe, presumably to appear Spanish. Not a smile on any face.

"Who are they?" Robert asked.

"My family. Ancestors."

"Really? I don't see the resemblance."

"That's fortunate. That's Aunt Stella in that one."

"Really? Don't let her see that. She'd hate it, and then she'd hate you. What do you intend to do with them?"

"I was thinking of hanging them in the parlour? One or two of these frames might need a little repair, and lots of cleaning, but they're cool, don't you think?"

"No. They're dark. Broody. Nobody's having a good time. Are you sure you want them glaring at you over the dinner table?"

"You may have a point. I'll think about it. Here, help me put them in the spare bedroom until I think it over."

They stood them against a wall and went downstairs.

"Let's call for pizza," Tim said. "What's your pleasure tonight?"

They spent a pleasant evening, each remarking on how relaxed the other seemed.

"I'm trying to be more like you," Robert said, though he excused himself several times throughout the evening to make phone calls upstairs. Later, he asked casually, "Any plans for tomorrow?"

"I'm looking forward to going for a walk after lunch and making beef Wellington."

"Oh, can I see?" Robert went to the fridge and admired the cut of meat. "Mmm, that'll do nicely,"

"I thought so. It's a little big for just us, but I went by the recipe. It'll make delish leftovers. You'll take a couple slices back with you on Monday, for sure."

March 28: Palm Sunday

Sunday

South River is nowhere near the Holy Land, but Palm Sunday at Saint John's provided a stark reminder of how far away it is. To commemorate the arrival of the Messiah at Jerusalem, hailed by throngs waving palm fronds, the Sunday School gave each child a strip of long-dried palm frond about the width of a large blade of grass.

"You'd think they'd give the kids something more realistic," Tim complained on their drive home later. "Where's plastic when you want it? It looks like they're waving a handful of hay. It's hardly celebratory."

"I thought the choir sang very well today, didn't you? I do like that last hymn, especially since it allows the organ to show off its colours. I thought my *faux bourdon* was especially snappy today."

"Yes! But I wanted to listen to it instead of concentrating on singing the melody with those unusual harmonies going on, even with the wonderful help from our new tenor. I'd like to be in the audience sometime, just to enjoy listening."

"Well, I hate to break it to you, but if you're in the audience, you won't enjoy listening because your lovely voice wouldn't be in it."

They changed out of ironed shirts and ties and into polo shirts and comfortable pants. Robert pointed at Tim's choice as they sat for lunch, and asked, "Where's the nice pair of pants I gave you for Christmas? It's spring. You could wear them now. What you have on looks wintry."

"I thought they might still be a little tight, but maybe that has corrected itself since I'm skipping the honey crullers. I'll change for our walk."

Robert asked, "Anything I can do to help with the Wellington?"

"Nope, thanks. I'd like to do it. I made it once, but a long time ago, to impress you when we first met, wasn't it? I don't want to lose my touch. You never know."

Robert disappeared from time to time to make calls, not unusual on a Sunday afternoon. He always had arrangements to make for events or classes.

He asked, "When do you think we'll go for our walk? When the beef goes in the fridge?"

"Sure, that works."

Tim called out as he was stirring the duxelles. "Doesn't that smell delish?"

"Sure does," Robert replied from the dining room.

"What're you doing in there?"

"Just getting the table ready. A fancy dish like that deserves a nice setting. I must check the wine glasses, too. Oh, these are dusty. I'll wash them."

"Well, okay, but don't get in my way here. I need counter space for rolling the prosciutto and pastry."

Robert frequently checked his watch, finally announcing it was time for their walk. Tim assumed he was having pre-performance jitters a week early, and tolerated his buzzing.

"It'll have to be a short walk today," he said. "The recipe says to let it rest in the fridge for thirty minutes. Then it must go in the oven."

They walked on a nearby street with little traffic because it was Sunday, and turned back after fifteen minutes. As they rounded the corner toward home, Tim stopped.

"What's wrong?"

"Well, *look*, look at all those cars in our driveway. What— what're they doing there?"

Robert broke into a wide smile. "Let's go see!"

The hardest thing about a surprise party is keeping it a surprise. A cat can wiggle out of the bag; someone may come a day early or send regrets.

Not this time. Tim *was* surprised, and totally delighted as he entered his own front door to see friendly people wishing him a happy birthday. A huge "40" balloon was bobbing in the foyer, and more banners and streamers decorated the dining room and parlour.

The Member of the Legislature for South River and the Harbours was the official greeter and coat check clerk, a role she apparently found hilarious.

"Welcome!" Stella said to all, and pointed to the den. "Put your coat in there."

Tim was gently pushed toward the parlour to make room for the guests still coming in. The house was filling up, happy chatter everywhere.

"Rob," he called, "Rob, the beef! Help!"

"Got it!" Robert said, waving a potholder. "Evelyn turned the oven on as soon as she got in. It's my kitchen now, Timo. Enjoy!"

Evelyn is here?

Indeed she was, smiling a big smile. She raised both arms and walked toward Tim with a stride that models practice for years to get right.

"C'mere, loverboy," she purred, enveloping him in an embrace. "I didn't know you had birthdays."

Tim was hugged, squeezed, kissed, back-patted, and handshaken all around the room. Choir members, newspaper staff, friends, and spouses or dates, all seemed happy as could be to greet him, and he was more than likewise.

Someone had barricaded the entrance to the dining room with a table of wines, beer, ice water, and sparkling glassware. Tim was amused to see Edward Garamond, the newspaper's design guru, in a snappy sommelier costume, tending the bar.

As Tim approached, Edward bowed and said, "Bonjour, monsieur. May I suggest...?" He extended a wine bottle, label side up, and Tim assured him that it would do nicely.

Glass in hand, Tim wove his way back to the kitchen. Robert's forehead was glistening as he tended to dishes warming in the oven and on the stove, while discussing the care and feeding of Beef Wellington with someone. He grinned and said to Tim, "I was hoping you'd plan a simple roast pork today, but nooo."

"Gotta impress the neighbours, it seems. My goodness, there's a lot of gorgeous food in the dining room. And people, everywhere!"

Elaine Fong had just arrived. "Happy Birthday, Tim." She extended her hand but Tim bent down to give her a hug. There's a first time for everything, and he was feeling very huggy today.

"Thanks so much, Elaine. Allow me to introduce you to some of these fine people."

James Olsen was there with his digital camera. "Shoot lots, James, please. And before you go, please make sure we get a few poses of my aunt and me, and maybe a couple others in twos and threes."

"Sure will, Mister Brown. Oh, and I'd like you to meet my girlfriend. Stacy, this is Mister Brown I've told you so much about."

James' girlfriend was wearing too-tall heels and a too-small dress, and braces on her teeth, and she almost curtseyed to Tim. He shook her limp hand. "So pleased to meet you, Stacy. Help yourselves to the beverages."

Spencer from the choir was there with his wife. Spencer leaned in for a bear hug.

"Oof! Good to see you, Spence," Tim said. "Are you here as yourself? Not on the job, are you?"

"Not now, but she requested that I come back for her later with the limo." *Clever Stella.*

Guests volunteered to serve the hors d'oeuvres. It was not unexpected that people discovered and played the piano, given that many choristers were there, and singing and playing are not disassociated skills. Each wave of new arrivals launched another chorus of "Happy Birthday". There was a call for Tim to play, and he was pulled toward the bench.

"Rob! Rob, come here! Help!" he called over the din.

"You're on your own, buddy!"

Tim saw Evelyn, and said, "Please get him in here, Ev. It'll be worth it."

It was. They played not one, but two of the four-hand pieces, and the guests cheered.

Garland Greene, South River's gregarious mayor, made his entrance, his frumpy wife Patty on his arm. With his rumbling voice, Garland was well-equipped to make himself heard over the hubbub, and he did so now.

"Voters—I mean—friends ha-ha, we're here today to celebrate the birthday of our dear friend Tim Brown, a week late, but there were circumstances. First, our heartfelt condolences to Tim and all the newspaper family at *The Times* for their loss."

Several in the room said "Amen."

"Yes, amen. Now, we're here to celebrate a wonderful man—but enough about me! No, seriously now, this isn't a political event, so I won't mention that I'm the mayor of South River and hope to remain so with your support, nor will I mention that the MLA for everything *outside* of town is here also. It's usually dangerous for me to speak for her but it's safe to say that we're both grateful to be included in Tim and Robert's social circle, even though"—he paused dramatically—"even though Tim has not yet purchased a vehicle from Greene Motors, and we have great deals on the ninety-nine models right now! No, friends, none of that matters today. What matters is that Patty and I and everyone here wish you a very happy fortieth birthday, Tim. Cheers!"

Hands shifted the bar table aside and a lineup formed to and around the dining table buffet. Tim took the moment to lay and light a fire. The room had warmed up with all the bodies in it, but a fire was festive. He dispatched people to open the front and back doors to allow some fresh air to cool the edges of the crowd.

He was pleased to see his Beef Wellington at the centre of the table, paper-thin slices fanned on a platter by some talented hands in the kitchen. Robert was presiding over the table, serving what needed to be served, keeping an eye on the items people served themselves. He had put out every chair he could find. When they were all occupied, and the parlour seats too, guests arranged themselves on the stairs or stood, leaning against the walls.

Evelyn slipped her arm around Tim's waist. "Happy?"

He slowly nodded his head in amazement and smiled. "Beyond. Beyond. Who are you people, anyway?"

Evelyn bumped him with her hip and laid her head on his shoulder. "Ah, you. Never ever think you don't have friends, Timmy. Now, please excuse me." She disengaged. "I must go to my other lover." And she headed toward Robert.

Tim found Stella in the den amongst the heaps of coats, deep in conversation with Brittany Zwicker, her office intern and Gar Greene's daughter.

"You two look serious. Gar said no talking shop. Hello, Brittany. Nice to see you again."

Brittany looked up and valiantly tried a smile. Stella spoke for her.

"Not politics, Timothy, it's personal, but I agree, now is not the time. Brittany was running my meetings in the city while I was, uh, detained elsewhere."

Tim realized that Stella was referring to the time she had spent with him this week.

"I'll see you Tuesday, Brittany," Stella said. "Anything I can do, just ask. Anything."

"I know. Thank you. Happy birthday, Tim."

Outside the den, Tim asked Stella, "Brittany got troubles?"

Stella nodded. "Husband."

So many conversations. So many people. Tim was overwhelmed, and overjoyed. His cup was running over, and his plate was heaped high with food, as the makers of one dish after another urged him to try their famous whatevers. He looked longingly at his own contribution, disappearing quickly, but he didn't want to deprive his guests of even one thin slice, which he heard was exquisite.

Robert finally made his way to Tim's side. "Where's your food?"

Tim pointed to his plate, sitting on a shelf. "I've been too busy talking to eat. Food looks great, though. A shame to waste that."

Robert picked up the loaded plate and took it to the kitchen. He returned in a moment, bearing a saucer with one translucent slice of the Wellington on it.

"I knew you wouldn't get to it. You absolutely have to taste it."

Tim put the morsel in his mouth and rolled his eyes. "I made this? My God, I'm good!"

"You are. I'm going to enter you in the Big Exhibition this summer if they have a Beef Wellington category. Do they?"

"Just beef on the hoof, I think. We'll make this again, though, when there aren't forty guests. How did you get it cut so thin?"

"Turns out Cheryl Hawryluk's husband used to be a meat-cutter, put himself through uni doing that. So, she came to see what we were doing, natch, and then she called him over, and he sharpened your carving knife to a fare-thee-well. Nice guy. I wouldn't want to be on his bad side."

Cakes and pies appeared, and several coffee-pots were plugged in to brew.

Soon guests were pulling their coats from the pile in the den, making room for those remaining to sit in the parlour, and the hubbub of voices talking over voices subsided.

The fire crackled. Jasmine, a young choir member, began to sing, Elaine joined her, and soon the room was singing the hymn they had sung to end their last choir rehearsal.

> The day thou gavest, Lord, is ended,
> The darkness falls at thy behest.

"Wait," Tim said, and pulled three hymnaries from a nearby shelf. He handed them around so they could sing the verses instead of humming, and they continued on. When they came to the final verse, Jasmine sat up straight and sang the descant, high, powerful, floating, beautiful.

> So be it, Lord! Thy throne shall never,
> Like earth's proud empires, pass away;
> Thy kingdom stands and grows forever,
> Till all thy creatures own thy sway.

Instead of sitting in silence when it was over, the wine-fuelled singers erupted in applause and shouts of "Brava!"

"Why didn't you do that Thursday night?" someone asked Jasmine.

"I wasn't sure I should," she said, shyly.

Robert smiled and shook his head. So many times he came across such lights hidden under bushels.

A group of guests formed the clean-up detail, and they would not tolerate any nay-sayers. They closed the door between kitchen and parlour, "not so we can't hear you, but so you can't hear us talking about you!"

Nobody else sang or played. They were happy to just sit and talk. Tim turned out the overhead lights, and was amused to see how pleasant it was in the room with just the flames in the fireplace for light. Dr. Jekyll would be right at home.

He was at home, too. The guests couldn't have known how much he appreciated their kindness today. It was hard for him to describe it himself. Perhaps that wasn't necessary. It was just good to absorb it and be grateful.

~

Partying takes energy, no matter how happy one is. Robert had achieved his desired level of distraction, the one he had denied wanting, so he was happily exhausted.

"Keep it on the down-low, hey? You trickster. You really did surprise me, and right under my nose! I'll have a thousand questions later. Thank you, Rob. You gave me a great birthday gift today."

"Happy to do it, and so were Stella and Evelyn. When your uncle died, we had to blow the whistle on our plans, but everyone was great about postponing. It was a group effort. You're worth it—but don't expect a repeat until you turn fifty!"

After they turned out the bedside lamps, Robert said, "Did you hear what your mayor said? He said he and his wife were grateful to be included in *Tim and Robert's* circle, just as normal as anything."

"Yes, I sure did. Gar never ceases to amaze. Comments like that from someone like him help people to re-frame what is normal. It's so simple."

Robert said, "If you die, I'm going to marry Evelyn. Just for the wedding, though, not the other stuff."

Tim said, "Yes, of course. If *you* die, I'll buy one of Gar's giant trucks. Then Evelyn will marry me. For the truck, not the other stuff."

March 29: Image

Monday

Tim and Robert discussed the interruption to schedules imposed by the coming Easter weekend. All stores and restaurants would be closed on Good Friday. Where would they go if they didn't stay home? Robert said he'd be happy to use the time to practise again for Sunday.

They left it undecided, and Robert departed for the city with a slab of birthday cake wrapped in tinfoil.

Tim flipped through the newspapers, but nothing caught his attention. It wasn't the papers' fault. His head was still whirling. So many people! Just for him!

When he could focus, he'd try to make a list of everyone who had been there. He had a basket of birthday cards, which would help. He'd opened them all after dessert, because people like to see their cards being appreciated. The "40" balloon had survived, and was now bouncing against the ceiling over the stairway.

A few people had popped in to say hello on their way to something else. Raquel from the office had come with her twin boys, walking now, and harnessed. No, her name was Rachael. Nice of her to come. Who brought the dog? He'd been startled when the little thing ran around a corner amongst all the feet. It should have been harnessed, too.

Spencer and his wife hadn't stayed long, but he reappeared when Stella was ready to leave, dressed in chauffeur's livery. It seemed to suit him and Stella both, this charade.

Such wonderful people he had in his life. At the beginning of the month, he'd reached out to Evelyn, and what a good move that had been. He reached out to GB too, just a few hours and a lifetime too late. However, his heart was full with friends and family, dead and alive.

He looked around the house. It still needed some tidying up: chairs and side tables to return to their places, a final load to run through the dishwasher and dishes to put away, tea towels and tablecloths to launder, though he'd leave the ironing for Mrs Aquino, and the inevitable casserole dishes left behind, waiting to be re-homed.

Mrs A would glare at food dropped or spilled on the floors, if any remained by Thursday, but she'd deal with it.

He went upstairs to shower, and detoured into the spare room to have a look at the old photos in their old frames. Robert was right: they were gloomy. They weren't the happy crowd of yesterday. He hoped James had gotten some good shots. He had posed with this and that one, arms around those, groups of others. He made certain that James took one of him with Stella seated beside the fire, him and Robert on the piano bench, laughing at the demands of playing four-hands, him with Robert and Evelyn flanking him, and him and Robert on the love seat, with Stella and Evelyn on the arms, trying to look serious, and failing happily. It had been a challenge to get the photos taken in the midst of the party pandemonium, but he knew their faces would be party-happy, better than any stilted studio poses.

Tim knew he preferred the new photos to these old ones. He started to take them back to the attic, but set them down again. Why go to that effort? If he didn't want them, who would? He'd think about that.

A small card dropped from the back of one of the big frames. He bent to pick it up.

It was a wallet-sized black and white photo. He switched on the overhead light to examine it, and was momentarily confused.

He was looking at himself, in his early twenties—if he'd graduated from university and posed in an academic gown, that is.

He turned the photo over, but there was no name on the back. No inscription of any kind.

Tim sank down on the corner of the guest bed and stared at the photo with growing awareness.

There was no "To Lucia, with all my love".

No "I'll stand by you, darling."

No "I'll care for you and our baby."

No "I'll get a divorce and marry you and we'll raise our family together."

No "Come what may."

Nothing at all was written there, where something definitely should have been.

"Couldn't you at least have written something nice to Mother on this," he asked the image. "Like your name, f'rinstance? What's the big secret? She cared enough to keep your photo. Why didn't you marry her? Were you married already? That'd be complicated. If you were, you shouldn't have been screwing around with a teenager. There's no telling if pregnant young Lucia would have married you anyway, right after she graduated from high school, for God's sake."

He turned to look at the glum family in the ornate frame. None of them could have foreseen how their family story would play out.

"Mother had the courage to go to her estranged sister for advice. That must've been hell for both girls. They had to overcome whatever awfulness their parents had led them to believe about each other. But Stella had always supported her older sister, and she stepped up."

He turned back to the little photo. "Who were you, buddy? A visiting dignitary? A local leader? A priest? Imagine the scandal that would've erupted if Lucia had revealed your identity—the somehow-compromised father of her unborn child. Scandal for her, yes, but for you, too. I bet she saved your bacon."

He thought about this for a moment.

"If Stella counselled Mother to forget you and choose another father for her baby, it was wise counsel. Y'know, I asked Stella if Mother had considered an abortion, but now that I'm sitting here and we're having this talk, I know she'd never have done it. Mother was all about plowing ahead. She was not a quitter. She wasn't great with me, but she didn't quit on me. You did. Fortunately for you, buddy, she had Mister Plan B available, likely Plan C and D, too. She was a cutie, and she played the field aggressively, just like the captain of the football team played his game."

He turned to the stiff family in the frame again. "Ebenezer, you approved her marriage to Ford rather than have the family name sullied with an unwed mother, or a scandal with whoever's in this photo, if you knew about it. So you, Grandfather, and you, Stella, separately endorsed Ford Brown. Poor little rich girl, Lucia. Six years later, she was a widow, so young, with an inconvenient baby and eventually a busy community newspaper to run."

He poked the little pocket photo. "And you, Mister Handsome College Graduate, you got away Scot-free. No wonder she was bitter. She had suitors again after Ford died—were you one? She didn't marry to have another little brother or sister for Timmy, that long-legged kid who must have reminded her every day of you, her first love. He grew up to be the spitting image of you. Look at me! Look at you!"

The man in the small photo looked like a nice fellow, not the least bit devious. He really did look like Tim, or vice versa. Friendly. Not a jock. Perhaps he was a musician or a writer or a doctor or a judge or a teacher. Perhaps he still lived in South River.

Tim owned the community newspaper now. It would be easy enough for him to place a small advert in the Classifieds to flush him out. It had happened only forty years ago. People had long memories.

~

He finally stood up and took the photo down to the kitchen. He picked up the phone and made a call.

"Hi, Aunt Stella. It's me, thanking you again for all you've done for me recently, listening to my questions and quandaries. *And* for yesterday's blow-out! What a party, eh? My guests were impressed that the hat-check girl was their MLA—so was I! You were a hoot! In other news, I have made a decision about my quest which involves you, so please call back whenever you have a chance."

He left more thank-you messages on answering machines, grateful for that technology, otherwise he'd never get through the list. He called Evelyn's home, promising to talk about getting together later this week.

He looked in the fridge, full of Tupperware containers. *Pick one, Tim, they're all good.*

He heated somebody's Stroganoff for lunch, then went to the hospital.

"She's fading, Tim," the nurse said. "Not steeply, but there'll be a tipping point. Just so you know."

He thanked her and entered the room. Constance seemed about the same to him, just a little less alive. He announced himself to her, then read more of the story, but not for long.

"I'll be back tomorrow, Aunt Connie. I'm going to pick up another book at the library so we'll have something to read next."

He went to the library right away. He didn't see Marlene Wentzell, but a clerk was there. He asked for *Dracula* and *Frankenstein*.

~

Leaving messages on answering machines only delays conversations. His phone rang through the evening as people returned his call to review all the fun they'd had at a party like none before.

One call was from Stella. "I'm just in. It's been a busy day. You called?"

"I did. I recall that you sent me leftover food from the caterers after your birthday in February. Would you like me to reciprocate? There's tons here."

"Thank you, but no. I'm going to the city early tomorrow for a couple of days and it would go to waste. You have something to tell me?"

Stella was back in business mode, but not cut-off rude.

"I do. I found something mighty interesting today. I'll show and tell later, but I wanted you to know that I've made my decision."

He paused to draw a deep breath. "Please destroy that envelope."

"Destroy it?"

"Yes."

"Unopened?"

"Yes, unopened. Please burn it to ashes. That'll be a very good thing. If it contains what we think it contains, I don't want to know it. I found something better. Okay?"

"It's your issue, and your decision. I will comply."

"Thank you. And please give my best to Brittany. She looked very unhappy yesterday, poor thing. Young people have tough decisions to make. Sometimes, it's hard to know what's best until decades later."

March 30: Family proofs

Tuesday

Tim went downtown. The manila sheets he had marked notes on through the month were on the cabinet where he had left them. On Saturday, he hadn't been certain if they should be put away now, or whether there was more to do.

Now, he was sure. He wound tape around them, labelled them *March 1999*, and put them in the bottom of the cabinet with the other rolls.

He tacked another sheet to the wall and began to sketch a design on it. It took several tries before he was satisfied. He folded the final sketch and took it downstairs.

"Hi Ed, great to see you Sunday, thanks so much for coming. You look great in a cummerbund. How's deadlines?"

"I'll be finished in about half an hour, boss, if those ad sales hotshots don't run in with a last-minute full-page advert we can't afford to ignore."

Tim picked up Ed's desk phone and put his folded paper under it. "Okay. I'll leave this here. See you later."

He stood in the entrance of the Daisy Café and waved to catch Evelyn's eye. He mimed *I, phone, you*, and for *tonight* he pointed upwards. She burst into laughter and came to see him.

"What the heck is that?" she said. "You'll call me, I got that, but what's this mean?" She pointed to the ceiling. "From Heaven?"

"Yes, I certainly will, when I get there, the first call I'll make. But 'till then, can I call you tonight?"

"Oh, that means *tonight*? Sure you can. Anytime between six and six-oh-five. I turn into a pumpkin very early on weeknights."

He went for a walk, looping around the bridges. These walks

were doing some kind of good, he was sure, whether it was the better fit of his jeans, or the dopamine, or simply the fresh air. He was walking in downtown South River. It was a homely-looking downtown, but it was home, and it was springtime, and he was feeling a lightness of spirit.

He chuckled at Evelyn's interpretation of his gesture. The ghost in his dream could have been trying to tell him that she'd see him in Heaven, or that she would call him tonight, or he should go upstairs and have a look. He'd done the last, and that had been fortuitous. He knew it was just intuition, or his subconscious, directing him to the only place in the house where family records might be stored, but he hoped intuition wouldn't visit in the night like that again.

~

He returned to Ed Garamond's corner. "I see what you want," Ed said. "Interesting. I'll copy these photos and arrange them like you have there, with these inscriptions. Right?"

"Right. And make it sort of faded around the edges, like old photos, and sepia-toned? I'll bring in the frame tomorrow and you'll see. Bright white wouldn't look right."

"Got it. Should be ready tomorrow at noon."

"You don't have to rush, Ed. Your work comes first."

"It's not a rush if I find it interesting. A week of assembling two-page spreads of chocolate bunnies for the pharmacy has been a design wasteland. This is a welcome change."

~

"Hi James. Got any proofs for me from Sunday?"

"Sure do, Mister Brown. Here's two sheets of 'em to look at. I picked out about twenty for you, but I can show you more. Just let me know. Printing's on your tab anyway, right? You can have as many as you like."

"Right. It was nice to see you at my party, and to meet your girlfriend, uh, don't tell me, Stacy, right?"

James beamed. "Yeah, Stacy. She was pretty shy with all the big shots and all, but I told her that famous people are just people, right, Mister Brown?"

"Famous people? Uh, yes, they're just people, just like you and me and Stacy. I'll look over these images and mark which ones I want printed. I'll leave it on your desk."

Having no other reason to hang around downtown, and no errand anywhere in the region, Tim drove home. He felt a little at loose ends. Perhaps it was due to the cosmic position of the final Tuesday of March. Maybe it was the letdown after a great party, though he had been, and still felt, buoyed and supported.

Or maybe it was that he had completed the work on his family history to his satisfaction. He had invented falsehoods where he needed them, and discarded truths he didn't need. The result felt right.

At the beginning of the month, he had entitled the first of the big sheets *ACTION*. He didn't have any immediate action planned, and he knew that made him feel uneasy.

The next word on that sheet was *Enjoyed*.

"Go back to the top, Tim," he said aloud. "Write it down in your notebook and keep it handy. It's important."

It wasn't just for dopamine that he needed action, and it wasn't only enjoyment that he got from it. Working on a project such as he had done—actual delving—was just so darn *interesting*, and personally validating. It felt great to have a worthy puzzle to work out. His brain felt slightly more muscular. Instead of pushing his mind to do his regular tasks, he had felt pulled, and that was exhilarating.

He wanted more of that. He'd stumbled onto interesting explorations so far this year, but maybe there was a way that he could go after more of them. Being proactive was all the rage. He would be proactive, just as soon as he knew how.

He ate lunch, then went to the hospital to read the last of Mr Hyde, and a teaser page from *Frankenstein*. He hoped Aunt Connie was getting something from his readings, or his presence, at some level. He certainly was benefiting himself, and he wasn't going to delve into why.

Returning home, he saw that the action before him right now was to clean the sticky floors before spilled food from the party got tracked everywhere. He swept the kitchen floor, found a dried turd from that free-range dog, filled a bucket with hot, soapy water, and mopped the black and white tiles.

The floor gleamed, and Tim felt great.

~

He poured a second glass of wine from one of Sunday's leftover bottles, still wondering who had sponsored the generous bar, and phoned Evelyn at six o'clock sharp.

"Good boy," she answered. "I appreciate your promptness."

"And good evening to you, my friend. Do you really turn in this early?"

"No, but early enough. I'm out of here at six every morning, and standing on my size nines all day, so I soak my tired body after supper, and then I watch something mindless on the teevee. Slow evenings are my luxury. You suck at charades, by the way."

Tim laughed. "Oh my, I do enjoy you, Evelyn. I was so happy you were at my party—heck, you likely managed the whole thing—but you were working every time I saw you. A busman's holiday for you, I think?"

"A little, but it was a great bus ride. Poor Robert was having a fit because he had to hang with you and pretend nothing was happening. My goodness, those people love you, Tim. Nobody turned me down when I called the list Rob gave me. I had to refuse some offerings of food, can you believe it? When's the last time you had a party? There seemed to be pent-up demand for that one."

"It's beyond me, Ev. I'm still gob-smacked. What do the movie stars say—humble and proud? My only regret is that I didn't have time to sit and talk with each person, y'know? It all goes by in a blur. Very nice, though. I'll invite some of them back to quieter Sunday dinners."

"You go right ahead and do that," Evelyn said with a laugh. "But skip the bedsheets and the crap movie? I'm not sure it would go over well with everyone."

"Please forgive me. It was a thought, just not a good one. But you came, and now we're friends, so I win. You could have bonked me on the head and told me to get lost."

"I'll never do that. Look, I got my foot in the door with you, finally, and I got to meet Robert, whom I adore, so it was only gain, no loss."

"Robert loves you, too. We're going to schedule a duel to see who wins you."

"Don't you dare! You can both have me, no need to hurt each other. So, have you finished your project or whatever was making you frown and run around the bridges today?"

"Ah, you saw me? Yes, I've finished. Everything's done but the photographs. You'll see what I mean when you come up next time. Will you have some time to get together this weekend? I don't want to interfere with your resting and soaking and Easter observances. My schedule's open, but also up in the air."

"I need to check on a couple things. Can I get back to you Thursday? You'll be in for breakfast then anyway, won't you?"

"For sure. Can't wait. Lovely to chat with you, Ev."

"Me, too, Timmy. G'nite."

Timmy. It seemed a little juvenile, not a name for an adult businessman, now over forty years of age, with a little gray at his temples.

"Says who?" he asked the air. "Tim is my business name, short, quick and efficient. Rob calls me Timo sometimes. I like that. It's creative. Mother called me Timothy without fail. Aunt Stella does, too. My father called me TJ and Timmy. It feels affectionate and caring to me, and I like it when Evelyn calls me that. It sounds intimate from her, inner-circle-ish. Like family."

He considered what he had just heard himself say through his ears, not just in his thoughts.

"My father. My *real* father, I mean—Ford Brown, not that other guy. He might've been entangled with my mother for only one hot hour before he deserted the scene. He liked her enough to give her his picture, and she liked him well enough to keep it, I'll acknowledge that. But Ford showed up and stood up and gave up his dream scholarship and stayed until he died of his injuries. He was the best father he knew how to be, for over five years, poor battered fella."

He pored over the party photos that James had printed. He loved every one of them. They were all about the present. There was nothing complex in them, no sadness, nothing enigmatic about who was whom. Faces were party-happy. Everyone was exactly as represented.

He marked the quantities and dimensions next to each for James to get printed. He'd put them all in a photo album to commemorate the party and his "coming of age", as he thought of it now. Some would also go in frames with stands so they could smile from various shelves or side tables. He would display one on the mantel above the fireplace. He'd take them to a professional framer and ensure the frames and mats conveyed no gloom. The collage he left with Ed would hang on the wall at the head of the dining table.

Which reminded him, he needed to take the oval antique frame in the spare room to Ed. He brought it downstairs and prepared it with a box-cutter knife and some glass cleaner. When this job was done, he went to bed.

March 31: Full moon

Wednesday

The Times was in its box on the porch, and it was fat with advertisements for the essentials for a Happy Easter, if that happiness involved chocolate or those garish but cute yellow marshmallow inventions called "Peeps".

In the pages of his newspaper, Easter observations were totally impious, except for the churches' ads, but they kept his newspaper in business so it could serve the merchants who employed the believers, so that closed the circle, didn't it? He'd leave that to the clerics to decide. He was not uncomfortable with his role in it.

Today's calendar box had a bright red dot in it: the Advanced Piano Maintenance System reminder to add water to the humidifiers inside the piano. Alphonse Dufour knew his clients would need this reminder and Tim was grateful for the prompt. He took a pitcher of water to the parlour and carefully filled the tubes.

He packed a lunch and drove downtown. It had been three days since the party, and the current paper was out on newsstands and porches, so he could visit the office without interrupting.

The staff smiled and waved with more ease than previously, he thought. They'd been in his house. They'd seen his things, net his friends. They'd had access. He'd never meant to keep people out in the first place, so this was good.

He handed the pages of photo prints over the cubicle wall to James, who was on the phone. He gave Tim a thumbs-up.

Ed Garamond arrived. Tim went out to his car and brought in the large oval frame, dark mahogany with a gold rim on the inner and outer edges, and a gold escutcheon at the top.

"What do you think of using this, Ed?"

"Wow, that's an oldie, boss. It's a beaut. Yeah, it'll work perfectly. I have your mock-up here now: look."

He opened a drawer in his wide artwork cabinet and withdrew a rectangular cardboard poster. He laid it on his drafting table and placed the ornate frame over it.

"Oh my," Tim said.

"Pretty good, eh? Now that I have the frame, I see I need to adjust a few elements, wider margin for one thing. Can you leave it with me? I'd like to play with this. I'll take it to the production shop myself, if you don't mind. We might as well do a good job on this."

"You're a prince among men, Ed. I'm happy to entrust you with this. Can I ask one more favour, though? Can I take this draft printout with me now?"

Ed put the artwork between two discarded posters of past events and taped them together. Tim took it directly to his car, and then returned to see how James Olsen was doing.

"I can print all of these," James said. "You can get frames for most of them at Zeller's."

"Good to know. This is work above and beyond. Can I please pay you for your time?"

"Gosh, no, Mister Brown. Happy to do it. Oh, well, maybe you can."

Tim reached for his wallet.

"No no, I don't want money."

"What, then?"

James leaned close and said in a low voice, "Got any leads? You know, like you did in February? That abandoned-well story really paid off, and I liked working with you. I need another good mystery like that, or a good crime we can get our teeth into."

"A good crime? Hmm. Those are elusive. We sure don't want a bad crime, do we, ha-ha. Funny you should mention it, James, because I was thinking the very same thing yesterday. *I need a good crime*, I said to myself. One that James can help me with."

James smiled so wide that dimples appeared in his cheeks. "Count me in, Mister Brown!"

~

Tim tried not to be too eager for his massage, but now that it was time to go, he could hardly contain his joy. Yes, that was true: his joy. Joy because he would see that sweet Lisa. Joy because he would receive comfort and wisdom from perceptive Melanie with hands that could reach inside him and sort it all out. Joy because he had come to the NuYu Spa so wounded in body and spirit, and had healed so well.

"Good afternoon, Tim," Melanie greeted him in the therapy room. He was wrapped in the sheet, sitting on the edge of the massage table, swinging his legs and grinning.

"I was going to ask how you are, but all signs point to the answer. What word would you use?"

"Joy," he said. "I'm joyful. Happy and more. With so much gratitude to you."

"Your back tenderness is resolved?"

"Oh, yes, though you can give it a good going-over. But as you know, you triggered some memories on that first visit, and I pursued them, because you said I was fearless. Then my dear old friend died, and that knocked me sideways, but it was all good, turned out well. And a whole lot of friends surprised me with a birthday party. And much more. So, yes, joy."

"I'm so happy for you. Happy birthday, too! You've worked hard for your joy, Tim. Hang on to it. Not everyone gets there. Some people stop seeking too soon and then they're left with chronic issues as mental scar tissue builds up."

She kneaded his lower back. "I think this is healed, too. This massage will be all reward for achieving a feeling of well-being, and acknowledging it."

When the session ended, Melanie said, "I've enjoyed meeting you, Tim. I don't see anything, mind or body, that requires further treatment. Some of my clients come periodically simply because they enjoy it, and I'll welcome you for that anytime. Meanwhile, be careful of heavy lifting, whether it's physical or emotional. Take good care."

~

That evening, fortified with a celebratory glass of *Fin de Mars*, he lit a late-season fire. While the kindling ignited the logs, he took Ed's graphic design work into the dining room and had a good look at it. Curved at the top were the words *Truth, like Falsehood, must be discovered.* Below that were the enlarged yearbook photos of Lucia and Ford, hers flipped so they were facing each other. Below those, slightly smaller and centred, was a photo of another graduate in an academic gown, who appeared to be Timothy. There were no names or dates.

Tim's revised slogan curved from one side of the lower half to the other:

> *If it's in the air, I'll sing it. If it's in front of me, I'll face it.*
> *If it's in my hand, I'll use it for good.*

He tacked the poster to the wall behind the ornate chair at the head of the table, where he would hang the finished product when Ed had it mounted in its ornate frame.

He turned off the dining room light and went back to the parlour to sit in the firelight. He could see the collage from across the hall, illuminated by tonight's full moon shining through the window.

Tim felt as though he had just graduated from university, having successfully defended a dissertation. Not only had he inherited his looks from the man in the little photograph, but he felt he'd earned the academic gown as well.

He fully accepted the enigma in the oval. It was his story.

Acknowledgements

- My Dear Readers: Judi McDonald, Cynthia French, and Margaret MacDonald Trites: it's remarkable that you stayed with me to be thanked again, and I now welcome Janet Barkhouse to this honourable circle. Each of you expressed consternation about "the envelope"; I hope you now agree with Tim's decision.
- Moose House Publications for this amazing project: three down[1] already out of twelve!
- MHP Editor Andrew Wetmore: CBC's Stuart McLean always referred to his editor as "long-suffering"; now I know what he meant.
- The sudden and too-early death of one of my grandmothers was a whispered topic when I was a child; her name is hidden in the text of this book.

---

1   *I would say "up" - editor*

Jan Fancy Hull

About the author

Jan Fancy Hull lives in a log chalet beside a quiet lake in Lunenburg County, Nova Scotia, where she has written non-fiction, award-winning poetry, short stories, and novels.

In former lives, she worked as a radio broadcaster, arts administrator, sailing tours skipper, and employee benefits broker.

During the winter, Jan watches snowflakes fall as she writes. In warm months, she carves Nova Scotia sandstone into sculptures. She enjoys the occasional round of golf, and drifting on the lake in her little boat, which she claims is a great place to edit.

In 2022, Jan received the Rita Joe Poetry Prize for her poem, "Moss Meditations."

Website: janfancyhull.ca
Facebook: Jan Fancy Hull

Sneak peek into *April: Sweetland*

Here is a chapter from *April: Sweetland*, the fourth Tim Brown mystery. It will be available in early 2023.

April 3: Budino

Saturday

While Robert worked in his upstairs study, Tim continued to rehearse the Tuesday presentation. He usually spoke out loud when doing this, but today he mumbled, in case Robert should wander in and ask questions. He knew that if one idly asks, "What're you doing?", and the response is, "Nothing," that can ruffle feathers. If the responder tries to explain, but the inquirer says, "Never mind," hours of uncomfortable silence may follow. It was a mundane exchange often subject to malfunction.

Best to avoid the situation from the start.

That's what Tim was hoping to do on Tuesday: to avoid any misunderstanding with Evan. He realised that strategizing interviews in advance was not a sign of weakness, as he had accused himself yesterday. It was, in fact, a clever tool in his toolbox. He was learning to be a delver—actually, a capital-D Delver—for which open-ended questioning was best. But when the issue was specific—reimbursement for his storm door—he did need to steer the conversation toward his desired conclusion.

"Would you do it?"

Who said that? No one else was in the room, and it was not an echo of his late mother, whose voice he had taken steps to silence last month. She wasn't apt to ask a question, anyway. Declarations were her signature speaking style.

Perhaps the question had come from his own mind. This would be an exciting development.

He went to the study to retrieve a new notebook from the supply on the desk, along with a fresh mechanical pencil from the substantial collection he had recently discovered there. On the first page, he wrote *TESTS*, and below that, *Would I do it?*

Where was this leading? What were these words indicating? He tapped the pink eraser against his chin. In his earlier explorations, following the Delver's "deep and wide" principle, he'd considered every option—the hunches, the rumours, hearsay, purported falsehoods, truths, and posits. *Is posit a noun or a verb? Never mind.* Once he had everything laid out for consideration, the trues and falses seemed easier to see, though sometimes an enigma remained.

Well, such is life. The mature thing is to accept inconclusions. Maybe. When they fit.

He shook his head. His mind was drifting.

He turned back to the list, if a single entry could be called a list.

"Would I do it?" he mumbled. "Would I hand over close to a grand just because somebody complained, even if supported by pictures and a story about some night-time maverick?"

He tapped the eraser again.

"No, I would not."

There it was, then. His first test question had already produced results. If he wouldn't do it, why would Evan, or whoever he might pass it off to?

What would the next test question be?

What would I *do?*

"Yes!" he exclaimed.

"What?" Robert's tiny study was right above him and the sound carried through the floor.

"Nothing—I mean, I just discovered something. Carry on."

He hastened to add *What would* I *do?* to the list, making two items.

He had taken to pretending to be the actual persons of interest, to test-run his interviews, especially if the person of interest was unavailable. Using a modicum of awareness about human nature, he could explore how a conversation might go, without stepping on anybody's toes. Interviewing himself as *himself* was a new twist. He went back to the den to try it out.

"So," he said quietly to the empty recliner beside him, "if I have your story straight, one of *The Daily's* delivery persons threw their newspaper onto your porch, as you requested, and you say it dented your door, and you want them to pay for the replacement door, including installation charges. Do I have the facts of the matter?"

The gold brocade cushion in the chair, as Tim the Claimant, meekly replied, "Yes, please."

"Well, well," said Tim the Prosecutor, "what's to say your door wasn't dented previous to the incident you describe, huh? They can't be paying claims like this every time somebody complains or they'd be out of business!"

"What?" Tim stage-whispered. "How many claims "like this" do you get? Dozens—maybe hundreds—from unknown subscribers? Plus this one from Mister Timothy Brown, who is well-known and well-liked. Whatcha gonna do with that?"

He heard Robert coming down the stairs.

He cleared his throat and pointed an accusatory finger at the cushion, "This isn't over, fella. To be continued."

They met in the kitchen and rummaged for lunch bits.

"What're you working on, Tim?"

"I was going to ask you the same question. Tell me all about your exciting musical life."

~

After lunch, Robert had a snooze and Tim visited his inert Aunt Connie at the hospital. He told her he was trying to practice putting himself in other people's shoes, but he was unable to imagine what it would be like to be in hers right now.

He had been holding her hand—the one without the IV needle in it—while he talked. He kissed it and left.

In the hospital lobby, a woman he knew slightly was one of the gift shop volunteers.

"Happy Easter," he greeted her as he passed.

"Spring forward!" she replied.

"It sure is!" Then he was out the sliding doors and on to the next thought.

If someone told him his head was often in the clouds, Tim wouldn't argue. He was making a practice of it, and had accomplished a lot by letting his mind wander. As he drove the short way home, he wandered back to that forgettable exchange in the lobby. It came into sharp focus now.

"Spring forward" wasn't about spring or Easter. It was about changing to Daylight Saving Time.

Tonight!

It was a clear indication of what was important to the overlords who had decreed the "spring forward" and "fall back" time changes, that they applied them overnight between Saturdays and

Sundays. Tim thought they must have said, *If the populace is going to be an hour late for anything, let it be for church, not for work. Give them Sunday to figure it out, for they must keep the Monday trains running on time.*

How many parishioners had pulled into the church parking lot on the first Sunday morning of Daylight Saving Time, only to see their more aware friends just coming out the church door?

Tim was in a near-panic. Robert had not reminded the choir to set their clocks ahead, and nobody—*nobody*—else had mentioned it. That meant that nobody had remembered. And that meant that some of the choir—it didn't matter how many—would be late for church, and Robert would have a fit.

What to do? He could call the choir president and ask him to get the word out. What about the trumpeter? Who would have his phone number, or would he have to ask Robert anyway?

What would Robert want me to do? Come on, Tim, you're treating him with kid gloves. That's sort of disrespectful. Don't do that. He can handle it.

"You're right," he told himself. "Of course I will tell him."

~

Robert was just coming downstairs from his nap.

"Sorry to disturb your restful mood, Rob, but I was reminded that tomorrow is Daylight Saving Time and—"

"Yes, I know. I forgot to remind the choir Thursday night, silly me. Silly everybody. You'd think someone would have said something. Anyway, the minister popped in while I was practising on the organ yesterday and reminded me. So did the music librarian. She saw my car in the parking lot. She said someone had remembered and thought they'd better activate the 'telephone tree' to get the word to everyone, which they did. And I called the trumpeter. No worries. Isn't that great?"

Tim settled his ruffled nerves by adding another question to the TESTS list: *What would they want me to do?*

~

"Evelyn wants to come early today, to help us prepare supper, and just hang out rather than officially visit. You don't have to sit up and wear a tie, or a toga. Is that okay?"

"Hanging out with Evelyn—my fav'rite thing to do on a Saturday afternoon! Besides hanging with you, of course."

"Of course. Now, where shall we do our hanging? The den, we know, is a bicycle built for two. But the parlour is so formal…"

"I've been meaning to mention that to you. Let's have a little look there, shall we?"

They began rearranging the furniture into a less formal, more social configuration. They were just finished when they heard knocking at the back door.

Nobody used that door except Mrs A, to shake mats and take out garbage bags. Curious, Tim went to see.

"Evelyn! What—why are you at the back door?"

"I'm not company, right? Company uses the front door, but neighbours and friends and family come in the back door, or side door in this house. So, can I come in?"

"Sorry, yes, of course! Here, let me take your jacket. Leave your shoes on."

"Tim, don't fuss. I know how to enter a house."

Evelyn found a hook for her jacket, pulled a pair of slippers from her bag and put them on, and carried a basket to the kitchen. She opened the refrigerator door, made room on a shelf, and put a container on it. Then she turned to Tim and Rob who were watching her with big smiles.

"There. Now, where's my hugs? Hi, Timmy. Hi, Robby. I'm so glad to see you both!"

She wore tight blue jeans and a large, shapeless sweater. She looked perfectly at home in a big armchair, with her pink slippers tucked under her.

"What did you sneak into the fridge, Ev? Something delicious?"

"Aren't you the curious one. Yes, it's dessert, but it needs a little final assembly, if whipping cream and toasting some hazelnuts isn't too stressful for somebody."

"Pick me! Tim's making supper, so I'm glad you brought something for me to do. I get fidgety before a concert, and there's one tomorrow."

"So I heard. Tim said he might have to put you in a corner and let you play with sharp knives."

"I deny saying *anything* about putting him in the corner!"

"My bad. Anyway, I brought something that might help."

She unwound herself from the chair and went to the back entry, returning with a large, thin box, from which she drew a dart board.

"Darts, anyone? They're as sharp as knives, but at least you don't risk cutting your precious fingers."

"No, but you could put somebody's eye out," Tim said. "Or I could, anyway. I'm not very, um, athletic. Or sporty."

"Me, neither," Robert said.

"Have you not played? No? Neither of you? Well, let's fix that right now. Where's your cellar door?"

They followed Evelyn to the kitchen. Tim opened the basement door all the way, and hung the dartboard on the back of the door, on the nail that usually held the kitchen broom.

"Now, listen carefully," she said. "Let's put a stool here, and here. Stay out of that area, okay? Never walk in front of the board unless you're retrieving your own darts, got it? And don't throw if somebody looks like they're going to cross your path, hear me? That's about it. Throw and learn, that's my method. Robby, you're up first."

"Why don't you show me first?"

"Because you can't learn by watching me. You have to do it and feel it and then do it again, just like—well, you know. Stand here, and have a go."

Robert's first dart hit the board sideways and fell to the floor. Tim and Evelyn applauded politely. He held the second dart in his fingertips, balanced it, and threw again. It stuck to the board, but outside the scoring area. The third one was very near the centre. Robert raised his arms in victory while his spectators cheered and whistled.

"Okay, now it's Timmy's turn. Go get 'em, tiger!"

Tim was actually nervous. This didn't require him to be athletic, maybe it wasn't even a sport, but he had so often proven his ineptitude at games that he would have preferred not to try one more, especially with such a discerning audience watching.

"Feel the balance, be the dart," Evelyn murmured as she placed one in his hand.

Tim threw, and his dart stuck in the scoring area, as did the next two. He, too, raised his arms, and bent for a kiss on each cheek from his fans.

"All right, Ev, now show us your stuff."

"Aw, you guys don't need to see me do it. I brought it for you to play with. You both work so hard, I thought you could use a little loosening up."

They insisted, with unison clapping and shouts of "Ev-Ev-Ev" until she took her stance. In an instant, her expression changed, her posture changed, and the game changed. Evelyn flew three darts near or in the bullseye in quick succession, and quickly pulled them out.

When the men's cheering subsided, Tim said, "Explain that,

please. You're a pro at this!"

"No, not a pro. But I do have trophies."

"Trophies! I don't doubt it. How? When?"

"Oh, well, sometimes I go out in the evenings, after my bath. If the pub has a dart board, I stay. Sometimes I stay longer than I should, and take home a little trophy. Or worse."

"There's a story there," Robert said.

"Maybe, but not for today."

"Tim, I think we should get ourselves a dart board."

"This one's yours, guys. It's a bit worn at the centre, but it'll do to get you started. If you like it, then you can get whatever you want."

"Amazing. I didn't know when I got up this morning that I'd be throwing darts this afternoon. May I?"

Tim and Evelyn returned to the parlour while Robert continued to throw and throw at the cellar door. From time to time he let out a victory yell, and they cheered back.

Tim announced that it was time to start making supper.

"Game over, then," Evelyn announced. "It's too dangerous."

Robert had hoped to keep playing, but the trajectory did cross very close to one end of the kitchen island. "And even though you don't feel it now, your arm will get sore if you throw too much at first."

That did it. Robert would need his arm for playing and conducting tomorrow, and nothing was allowed to impede his ability.

All three stayed in the kitchen and chatted. Wine appeared and disappeared. Tim put out a plate and set aside bits for tasting while he rolled pastry and stirred the sauce. Evelyn asked about tomorrow's concert, and said she had a ticket, which caused quite a stir.

Tim had wondered whether he should offer her a ticket, but he didn't know if she'd feel she had to go if he did. He began to regret not making the offer, but then he realised that attending was *her* offer to them. *If I were Ev, how would I show interest in me or Rob?*

The concert was Robert's stage. He launched into a description of the composers of the music he and the choir would perform, why he'd chosen them, and how they fit together. Evelyn and Tim felt they were hearing insider info.

"Oh, and do you know about standing for the Hallelujah Chorus?"

"Um, nope. Everybody stands?"

"Yes, many do. It's not obligatory, but it can be disconcerting if you don't expect it. Tradition has it that King George the Second stood up the first time he heard it, and people have been standing for it ever since. The facts don't back up the story, but audiences like to do it, two hundred and fifty years later. So now, oddly, the rumour is true, and the origin is in doubt."

"Weird. Thanks for the warning," Evelyn said. "Oh, Robby, can I interrupt you with that chore? The cream whipped, and the nuts roasted."

"Glad to. What is the dessert, may I inquire?"

"It's budino. Chocolate-hazelnut budino. I think it's Italian for pudding. It's to die for. I don't dare make it unless I'm taking it out somewhere, or else I'd eat it all and there'd go my girlish figure."

The evening passed with light conversation, great food, nice wine—not too much for Robert because of tomorrow's responsibilities—and a few more after-dinner throws at the dart board, which weren't great. They blamed the wine.

Tim took a moment to add another item to his list of *TESTS*: *What would I do if I wanted to show interest*? He'd examine that more on Monday.

Evelyn could not be persuaded to depart via the front door. She said it was bad luck to go out a different door from the one you came in. Tim insisted on escorting her to her car with a flashlight, as there was a spot where the back and front lights didn't overlap.

Must get that looked after. She'll be back.

263

Subscribe to **moosehousepress.com**
to get the latest news about the Tim Brown series,
and about all our other books.

www.ingramcontent.com/pod-product-compliance
Lightning Source LLC
Chambersburg PA
CBHW070446200726
48293CB00007B/2129